BREAKING
POINT

a novel

JENNIE HANSEN

Covenant Communications, Inc.

Cover image © Nick Koudis, PhotoDisc/GettyImages

Cover design copyrighted 2003 by Covenant Communications, Inc.

Published by Covenant Communications, Inc.
American Fork, Utah

Printed in the United States of America
First Printing: May 2003

10 09 08 07 06 05 04 03   10 9 8 7 6 5 4 3 2 1

ISBN 1-59156-213-9

BREAKING
POINT

OTHER BOOKS AND BOOKS ON CASSETTE
BY JENNIE HANSEN:

All I Hold Dear

Chance Encounter

Coming Home

Journey Home

Macady

The River Path   check amazon

Run Away Home

Some Sweet Day

When Tommorow Comes

Beyond Summer Dreams

Abandoned

High Stakes

Code Red

The Bracelet

"For where your treasure is, there will your heart be also."
—Matthew 6:21

This book is dedicated with love and gratitude to all my family.

PROLOGUE

The hairs on the back of his neck stood straight out. Something wasn't right. Dropping to his knees, he touched the damp ground, then glanced at the towering concrete-and-earth structure rising more than 300 feet above him. Instinct clamored a warning bell in his mind, telling him this wasn't the normal seepage found near rivers or dams. It probably wasn't even connected to the crack two-thirds of the way up the old dam. The crack was invisible to the naked eye at this distance, but he knew it was there. There could even be a new crack, far below the waterline and completely out of sight. The university forty miles away had recorded several seismic jolts in recent months. The episodes had passed unnoticed by most people, but they had been strong enough to increase the pressure on the aging dam.

Twenty minutes later he stood before a series of gauges. Sweat rolled down his neck and trickled down his back. The water behind the dam wasn't low enough. Ever since the crack had been discovered last spring when the water was at its highest, he had made a concentrated effort to lower the water level to allow repairs, but a wetter-than-normal summer had thwarted his efforts. Now water slopped over the sides of the spillways, and it wasn't just imagination that told him more than the normal amount of water was rushing into the river. He'd ordered more water to be released just yesterday, but even with the floodgates open far wider than usual for late summer, there was water where there shouldn't be any.

He didn't curse either fate or the politics that had kept the aging dam from being replaced years ago. As dams went, this one wasn't particularly large. It had provided necessary water, recreation, and power to the people below for close to a century. Now it was threatening to destroy the very people it had faithfully served for so many years. His mind focused on the more than two thousand acre-feet of water poised behind the dam, ready to fill the canyon and spread into the valley beyond—carrying with it death and destruction.

Four inches! That was all he needed. Just another four inches, and the repairs could begin. But even if the repairs started today, it wouldn't be enough. It was already too late. He snatched up the phone with trembling fingers.

"Open the gates. All the way." He didn't shout, but no one at the other end doubted the urgency. In an almost emotionless voice he added, "Then get out of there."

He had one more call to make. "The dam is going," he warned when he reached Sheriff Howard. "We've got a couple of hours at the most." He didn't add that this was Labor Day weekend and the canyon was full of campers—Howard was already aware of that frightening reality.

CHAPTER 1

"Watch your elbow. Okay, now flick your wrist like I showed you as you let it go." Web watched his line sail out in a graceful arc, then slowly settle behind the beaver dam.

"Better, much better," Bill murmured in approval while his own line flirted with a rivulet near the willows along the opposite shore.

"I don't know. I think I was doing better drowning worms." Web reeled in his empty hook and gave it a disgusted look before attaching a different fly.

Bill laughed. "Your cast is looking much better. It's the fish—they just aren't biting. I wish we could stay until evening; just before dusk is the best time for catching trout. But I'm supposed to meet with the Scout committee at seven."

"I appreciate the lesson. As busy as you are, I'm just glad you found time to sneak away for a couple of hours." A slow day had prompted Web to ask for a few hours off to go fishing when his friend had dropped by the office. Web began moving at a leisurely pace toward the creek bank, making short casts and playing his line as he walked. "Where I grew up there wasn't much fishing, and I never took the time to learn while I was at the academy." He'd grown to love the sport, mostly because of the opportunity it afforded him to explore the mountains and streams of his adopted state. Rural Utah was a far cry from Detroit, Michigan. He also enjoyed the friendship of the man almost everyone in Orchard Springs, except him, called "Bishop." He'd had few friends in his life, and this man's friendship meant a great deal to him. They'd met shortly after Web accepted a position with the county sheriff's office and he'd been assigned to search for an elderly Alzheimer's patient who had wandered away from his daughter's home and was lost in the mountainous terrain east of town. The local search and rescue unit, headed by a rancher by the name of Bill Haslam, had joined the search. Bill recognized how green the new deputy was to the conditions and took Web under his wing. Out of that experience a friendship had grown between the Mormon bishop and him. Of course he hadn't known anything about Mormons at the time, or that Bill was a bishop.

"I've always thought a man did his best thinking standing in a cold mountain stream trying to outsmart the fish and skeeters, but it's time to admit the skeeters got the most bites today." Bill signaled he was returning to the shore. Web watched him step from the water and begin breaking down his rod for storage in its lightweight carrier.

"Is it just my imagination or is this stream deeper than it was last month when we came up here?" Web asked. He sloshed through water that nearly reached the top of his waders.

"It's high, but we've had a lot of rain this year." Bill finished stowing his gear in his backpack.

"What's this?" Web bent to scoop up a handful of sand and gravel where a trickle of water from a tiny spring flowed into the larger creek. "Is this the real thing or the fool's gold I've heard so much about?"

"Neither," Bill said after a quick examination of the bits of yellow stone in Web's hand. "They're just rocks." He hesitated then asked, "Are you interested in treasure hunting?"

"I never thought about it." Web finished breaking down his pole and indicated he was ready to head back to the road where he'd left his patrol car parked beside Bill's Jeep.

"It's been my observation," Bill commented as they hiked along a narrow trail that followed the meandering stream, "that most people seek some kind of treasure. The whole key to happiness is in the kind of treasures we seek and what we do with them when we get them. Jesus warned us against what He called laying up treasures for ourselves where thieves can break through and steal them. According to Matthew, who recorded many of our Savior's teachings, Jesus also warned that where a man's treasure is, there will his heart be also."

"I take it we're not talking about money here," Web observed. He was quite used to Bill taking any opportunity to teach him more than fishing and mountain lore—things that made him think. At first he'd wondered if he should take offense at the mini-sermons, but he'd discovered he enjoyed these bits of his friend's philosophy, and he now looked forward to both the discussions and the quiet hours of contemplation that always seemed to follow.

"So is He saying we should keep our valuables where no one can steal them? I'm not sure there is such a place." Web attempted to answer his own question. He snapped off a twig from an overhanging branch and slowly stripped away the bark as he walked. "If someone wants to steal something badly enough, he generally finds a way. That's why people like me stay employed."

Bill chuckled before explaining. "Treasure can be many things. It can be money or jewels. It can be land or political power. It can be our thoughts, talents, or our families. It can even be our faith in God. It's whatever we value most. I think Jesus was warning us that if we set our hearts on earthly riches we stand a good chance of losing what we value, but if we seek the treasures of His kingdom we won't be disappointed. It's all a matter of setting our hearts on the treasure that won't wear out and that no one can steal."

Web reached for the top strand of the barbed wire fence that separated them from the road. He held it down and swung one leg over, then the other. His lanky rancher friend did the same. They shook hands before heading to their separate vehicles. Web took a moment to check his uniform—a few damp spots, but no mud. No need to change before returning to work.

"Think about it," Bill said in parting. "What is most important to you? And what would you do to hang on to it? Answer those questions and you'll have a pretty good idea of where your heart is."

As Web turned the key in the ignition, his radio squawked an urgent call. He pressed a button and instead of the dispatcher's, Sheriff Howard's voice boomed into his car. He acknowledged the call, then keyed back to listen to his boss's message.

"Bentley, I know you're off duty, but Dora said you'd gone fishing with Bishop Haslam along Orchard Creek. I just got an urgent call from the engineer up at the dam. He thinks the dam could go within the next few hours. You're already halfway to the reservoir. Get on up the canyon and clear out the campers. Warn Haslam to have a search team on standby."

"On my way." He signed off and flipped the switch to the light bar on the top of his vehicle.

Pulling even with Bill's car, he lowered his window to shout the warning, then pressed down on the accelerator. This was Labor Day weekend. The canyon would be full of campers and fishermen.

* * *

"Looks like we have company." Gage lowered the binoculars he held and pointed to a plume of dust moving up the canyon road.

Trent shrugged. "It's Friday. We figured we'd only have the canyon to ourselves until the weekend anyway." He stretched his arms over his head, leaned back more comfortably, then picked up his book again.

Gage settled himself against a fallen log and continued his slow perusal of the canyon with the field glasses. The sun was warm, causing him to shift a few feet farther along the log into the shade. After a few minutes he decided it was time to start dinner. He brought out the two large trout from the almost empty cooler and wrapped them in foil with butter and slices of lemon. He and his brother had each caught one of the trout earlier that morning at the reservoir, the biggest either one had caught all week. One fish would be all the two of them could eat, but what they didn't eat tonight they could put back in the cooler to reheat with eggs for breakfast. Adding the last of the potatoes, also foil wrapped, to the bed of coals in the fire pit, he leaned back on his heels in lazy satisfaction.

It had been a great week, one he and his brother had looked forward to for a long time. They'd started planning a week alone, just the two of them, before Gage left on his mission and they'd realized Trent's mission would overlap his by two months, creating a four-year stretch where they wouldn't see each other. They'd expected to miss one another, and they had. Between living on an isolated ranch with their closest neighbor ten miles away and being sandwiched in the middle of four sisters, the brothers had depended on each other for help and friendship.

Trent had only been back a month before they'd put their plan into action, packing Gage's small Nissan truck and heading for their favorite camping spot in an almost hidden canyon near a small reservoir across the Wyoming border into Utah.

Tonight would be their last dinner cooked over a campfire. In the morning they'd prepare a hasty breakfast before breaking camp, using whatever supplies they had left. They wanted to be on their way to Provo before noon and have Trent checked into his dorm by midafternoon. That way Gage would still have a few daylight hours for his drive back to Wyoming.

Gage couldn't help feeling a measure of sadness as he looked around the small canyon and their camp. It was as though he and Trent were leaving one life behind and heading into another. Their week here in this place was like the canyon itself, just a small spur off to the side of the larger canyon. Trent was on his way to school at BYU, while Gage had some serious decisions to make concerning the rest of his life back home.

"If you're thinking about Jena," Trent's voice cut into his thoughts, "I can tell you you've got it all wrong. You don't love her. I had enough companions who were in love with girls back home to know 'the look'—this sappy, silly expression on their faces when they were just thinking about their girlfriends. They never looked as miserable as you do until they got their 'Dear Johns.'"

"You know I've always cared about Jena." Gage didn't mind his brother's teasing.

"How can you even consider marrying outside the temple?" Trent was no longer teasing.

"Jena's willing to be baptized and wait a year so we can get married in the temple."

"And there's her father's ranch, which I know you love, and Jena is his only heir." Trent tossed a can of soda pop to Gage with a little more force than needed.

"Hey, that's not fair!" Gage caught the can and set it on the small camp table without opening it. "You know I wouldn't marry Jena just to get my hands on the Bar C." Trent's words brought Gage a stab of pain because he feared there was an element of truth in them. He'd spent many long hours examining his conscience, wondering if his love for the rolling hills and cool springs that dotted their neighbor's land played a part in his feelings for Jena. If so, that was unfair to her. Jena was a beautiful, intelligent young woman who was fun to be with, and he couldn't remember a time when the three of them—Jena, Trent, and Gage—hadn't been friends. Jena was closer in age to the two boys than she was to any of their sisters, and being an only child and their closest neighbor, she and the boys had formed a formidable threesome until Gage left on his mission.

After he returned, Trent was already gone, and Gage and Jena had grown even closer. Jena's father, Pat, had been diagnosed with lung cancer about the same time Trent left for the MTC. Because of their long-time friendship with Jena, and also because Gage felt at loose ends without his brother, he began spending more time helping Jena run the Bar C. Each fall he'd returned to school, but rushed home on weekends and holidays to help on both ranches. This summer, after his graduation from Utah State, they started talking about marriage.

Pat's health was deteriorating rapidly, and he'd begun hinting in Gage's presence that he could die happy if his daughter were settled with a man who could help her run the Bar C. Gage wondered if those hints may have helped along his and Jena's talk of marriage. This would benefit Trent as well since their own father's ranch could support two families, but not three. If Gage went into partnership with their father, as he and Dad had always planned, where would that leave Trent who loved ranching as much as they did? But if Gage and Jena worked the Bar C, then Trent could partner with their father.

"Sorry," Trent apologized. "I know you care about Jena. And even though you've always loved the Bar C, I know you wouldn't marry Jena just to get your hands on it. Jena is my friend too, and I've always considered her another sister. Most of the time I've considered her better than a real sister—not as much of a pest as our little sisters or as bossy as our older sisters. I just don't think you should marry someone who would join the Church only to please you, instead of having her own testimony of its truthfulness."

"How do you know she doesn't have a testimony?"

Trent just looked at him, and Gage felt an urge to squirm. He didn't need an answer from Trent. He'd known from the moment Jena offered to join the Church that she was doing it simply because he'd always claimed he'd never marry outside the temple. She'd tried to talk him out of having the missionaries teach her and then endured their visits in silent boredom. He also knew she hadn't even cracked open the leather-bound Book of Mormon he'd given her. She was a good person, and his whole family cared about her. He liked and admired her father too, but he had to admit it had puzzled him all of his life how such fine people could see no need for God in their lives. He'd hoped that this week in the mountains with Trent would help him know what he should do, but he didn't feel any closer to a decision now than he had a week ago. Though they'd talked about Gage's plans, Trent had almost seemed to take offense when Gage reminded him that if he went to live with Jena on the Bar C, that would leave the foreman's house and a partnership with their father open for him—as if this were all one big favor for his little brother.

"Wow! Look who's setting up camp across the road!" Trent held the field glasses to his eyes now.

"Ever heard of invasion of privacy?" Gage reached for the glasses. Trent laughed and surrendered them to him.

Even without the glasses Gage could see two slender blonde women and a taller, darker-haired one moving around the campsite farther down the slope on the opposite side of the road.

"Seems to me the neighborly thing to do would be to go help the ladies set up their tent." Trent arched an eyebrow toward his brother as though asking if he'd care to join him, then began moving with bouncing steps down the path toward the road.

"Might as well," Gage mumbled to his brother's back, then followed at a slower pace.

* * *

Hearing Emily giggle, Cassie looked up from the tangle of canvas and poles she was trying to organize to see a man crossing the road. He seemed to be headed for their camping spot—the one her sister had selected over both her and Diane's objections. She and Diane were avid fans of babbling brooks, but they'd learned the hard way over many camping trips that the sound of a fast-moving Rocky

Mountain creek was way too noisy when trying to sleep. Raccoons had raided their camp once several years ago when they'd started their meandering camping trips on their way to school in Provo each fall. The little bandits had destroyed their entire food supply while they lay in their tent, hearing nothing but the roar of water rushing over rocks.

Since then Cassie and Diane had made it a point to secure their food in coolers and lock them in the car, and they no longer pitched their tent next to rushing water. This campsite, however, was right on the edge of a small, but loud, stream. They'd given in to Emily's pleas because this was her first, and possibly her last, camping experience—at least as a precursor to beginning each year's fall semester at the Y. None of Emily's friends headed West to school; however, Cassie and Diane had been friends since high school, and they were in their fourth and final year of college.

A second man stepped from the trees behind the first one, and suddenly Cassie felt a shiver of some kind of premonition. The men didn't look threatening. Still, she moved closer to her younger sister and from the corner of her eye, she noticed that Diane, still holding the small hatchet she used to pound tent spikes into the ground, moved closer too.

"Hi! Need some help?" the first man called out.

Cassie relaxed slightly. The slender, young man hailing them appeared to be around her own age and about as dangerous as a puppy. His short, curly, blond hair and smooth cheeks gave him an almost cherubic appearance. The eager light in his eyes and the welcoming smile on his face brought an answering smile to her own lips. Her eyes moved to the other man, and she felt the muscles in her stomach clench. He was an older, more filled-out version of the first man, and he didn't appear particularly dangerous either in his flannel shirt, faded jeans, and hiking boots. But he certainly made her toes curl in a way the younger one didn't. His hair was a little darker and his smile more reserved. His leanness didn't appear to be so much a sign of youth (though he was probably only a few years older than the man she assumed was his younger brother), as it did of spectacular fitness. Cassie suspected from his build as well as his tanned skin that he spent a lot of time working outdoors.

"Trent," the younger man said pointing to himself, then he swept a hand toward the other man, "and Gage Edwards, experts in tent pitching, specializing in rescuing damsels in distress."

"We're not exactly damsels in distress; and besides, we've put this tent up enough times to know how to do it." Diane's voice sounded a bit barbed.

"Great!" Trent rubbed his hands together. "We're all set then. You give the orders, and we'll provide the muscle."

Emily giggled again, and with a flirtatious grin handed Trent the tangled rope she'd been holding, then stood closer to him than necessary as he untangled it. He then shifted the tent peg a few feet farther away from the stream before anchoring the canvas to the ground. Diane might not have been impressed with the friendly young man, but Emily was making no secret of her interest. Cassie would have to speak to her sister later, though she couldn't blame Emily for being drawn to their visitors; they were certainly attractive, and Emily had made no attempt to hide her disappointment in their trip thus far. She'd made it clear that she considered accompanying the two older girls on their trek west to visit their grandparents in Salt Lake and on to school in Provo to be boring at best. She'd expected the trip to provide more opportunities to meet guys and to have more exciting adventures than her parents had permitted back in Kansas. Cassie interpreted this complaint to mean that her seventeen-year-old, boy-crazy sister had thought she and Diane would gravitate to places where men their age hung out, giving Emily an opportunity to practice her charms on them. Now Cassie wondered if she were inviting trouble by setting up camp so close to where these men were camping. Perhaps they should load everything back in her used SUV and drive farther up the canyon. One glance at her sister's face told her it was too late for that.

The brothers really were a help setting up their tent, and soon even Diane was laughing at Trent's corny jokes. Learning that the brothers were both returned missionaries eased Cassie's concern, but she decided to still keep an eye on her sister.

"All right, ladies, gather around." Trent stood on a large rock and clapped his hands for attention. "Inasmuch as this project has been finished ahead of schedule, bonuses will be awarded. Report to that white spot there on the hill." He pointed toward his and Gage's camp, which could barely be seen through the thick foliage. "Dinner in fifteen minutes."

"You're inviting us to dinner?" Emily verified the invitation.

"You bet!" Trent jumped down from the rock to take her arm. "This way, please." He gestured for the others to follow.

Cassie's eyes met Gage's. He shrugged in an almost helpless gesture, then repeated his brother's grand gesture toward the path leading to the other camp. Something sparkled deep in his eyes, and she felt herself smiling in response. Then they both began laughing as though they were indulgent parents sharing delight in their children's precocious antics.

"Come on, Diane." She turned to her friend. "Grab the graham crackers. I'll get the marshmallows and chocolate bars. The least we can do is provide dessert." She hoped she wasn't making a fool of herself. She felt almost as lighthearted and giddy as her sister.

Cassie saw Diane look at her strangely, then, without saying anything, reach back to pull the zipper closed on their tent. At the far side of the dirt road, she waited for Diane to catch up. Her friend paused to let an old pickup truck with a battered camper shell go past before joining her and Gage on the steep trail to the young men's camp. From the cab of the passing truck a young boy waved, and Cassie waved back.

At the top of the trail leading to the Edwards brothers' camp, Cassie turned back to study the view. "So beautiful." Her voice reflected the awe she felt. "We almost stopped farther down, in the main canyon, but none of the campgrounds we drove through had openings. I'm glad we came on up this side canyon."

"I'm glad we found this canyon too," Diane added. "Even if we do have to listen to rushing water drowning out every other sound all night."

"I take it the campsite was your sister's choice." Gage grinned as though he understood perfectly. "It won't be as bad as it might have been," he added. "Trent and I shifted your tent a few feet farther from the water, and the stream is also lower than usual." Mentally he added that he and Trent had both found it odd that the small stream in the high canyon was so low when the larger creek it fed into down in the main canyon was washing over its banks, as though it were early spring when the snowmelt was high.

"Come and get it!" Trent called. Cassie could see he and Emily already held plates in their hands. Gage ushered Cassie and Diane ahead of him, and soon all five sat around a low camp table.

"Mm-mmm, delicious." Cassie savored the freshly caught trout. She noticed her sister was doing more flirting than eating, but she had to admit that she, too, was enjoying the conversation. She couldn't help but wonder at the odds of three girls from Kansas who were members of the Church meeting two returned missionaries from Wyoming in a remote Utah canyon.

Amid much laughter they finished their dinner, and Cassie reached for the marshmallows. Gage produced a couple more toasting forks, and they got down to the serious business of making their s'mores for dessert.

"Nice camping gear." Diane turned to speak to Gage while rolling a long, slender metal fork in her hand above the glowing coals.

"While I was on my mission, Trent replaced some of our older things. Then when I came home, I updated a few more items. We like to camp and we wanted the best for this trip. Besides, we plan to use it every summer for a long time." Gage pulled his fork from the fire pit to slide his marshmallows between two graham crackers.

"Your marshmallows are on fire!" Trent lunged to pull Emily's fork from the coals.

"I like them that way," Emily said with a mock pout as Trent blew out the flames.

"Sure you do. You just love to eat charcoal. Let an expert show you how it's done." He reached for another handful of marshmallows.

While Cassie, Diane, and Gage leaned back enjoying their s'mores, Trent and Emily toasted more marshmallows. Cassie smiled more than once at their teasing antics, but said little as she rested against the lawn chair the brothers had produced for their guests. The first star twinkled on the horizon. It had been a good meal, and the Edwards brothers were good company. A cloak of lazy comfort settled over her, and she was glad they'd decided to stop one more night instead of pushing on to Salt Lake. They'd spend Saturday and Sunday nights with their grandparents in Salt Lake and attend their ward on Sunday, then drive on to Provo on Monday, leaving them two days to get settled in their apartment before classes began.

"Make a wish?" Gage's voice was soft as though he were caught up in the beauty of the night too.

"What?"

"You know. First star."

"Oh." She laughed. "I wasn't thinking of wishes."

"Then what were—"

"I know what I'd wish for," Emily broke in. "I'd wish this night could last forever."

"Speaking of which," Diane's voice was filled with reluctance. "We need to get an early start tomorrow. We'd better return to our own camp."

Though Emily protested, she joined the others as they got to their feet and started toward the path.

"It's dark." Emily gave herself an excuse to move closer to Trent, who took her hand.

"I didn't think we would stay so long." Cassie felt a twinge of guilt for not bringing a light. She should have considered it might be dark by the time they finished dinner.

"Just a minute." Gage disappeared inside his and Trent's tent and returned with two flashlights, one of which he handed to his brother. "We'll walk you to your tent." He shined the light on the ground in front of Cassie and Diane. Diane walked a step ahead on the narrow trail, and Cassie found herself falling into step beside Gage.

In spite of a mental reminder that she'd probably never see him again, she felt herself drawn to the man beside her. She liked the way he moved, confidently and easily, and she liked the lazy smile that quirked one corner of his mouth when he was amused. Though she sensed he was mostly a serious man, he also had a sense of humor that seemed to match her own. Too bad it was the younger brother who was continuing on to BYU. Catching her thoughts before they could go any further, she reminded herself this was her last year at the Y, then she would move on to fieldwork with the Denver-based company she'd interned for last semester. Even so, after the brothers said goodnight and disappeared into the darkness, and she changed into sweats and settled into her sleeping bag, Gage's face kept drifting into her dreams.

* * *

Shalise Richards continued to sit on a short log in front of the small fire long after her son, Kobie, was settled in his sleeping bag inside the camper shell. She'd struggled to keep her anger from showing as she'd cooked dinner, but Kobie had been subdued. She supposed she'd hoped for too much. When Daniel's parents called to say Daniel had called and that he and his new wife were planning to stay in Las Vegas until Monday, so he wouldn't be needing the truck, she'd wanted to scream. Why hadn't he called Kobie? Why did he always leave his parents and her to break the news to their son that his father was standing him up again? Kobie's grandfather had offered to take Kobie camping in his son's place, but she insisted on taking him herself, though she had agreed to drive her former father-in-law's truck, which was already packed for the trip. She knew how much Kobie had been counting on going camping, and she hadn't wanted to disappoint him. Perhaps even more, she'd wanted to show her son they could get along just fine without Daniel.

Kobie had been quiet and withdrawn ever since Daniel had walked out on them last December. But when his father had called asking if he'd like to go camping for his birthday, Kobie had shown the first enthusiasm she'd seen in months. *Why couldn't Daniel have kept his promise to his son just this once?*

It was a rhetorical question. She knew why Daniel had stood Kobie up. He and that woman he'd been living with since before he'd asked for a divorce from Shalise had celebrated the finalization of the divorce by running off to Las Vegas to get married this weekend. Daniel wasn't the sort to let a little thing like his son's ninth birthday and a promised camping trip stand in the way of a glamorous Las Vegas vacation. He'd stood Kobie up last year, too, and missed his son's baptism to be with his singer girlfriend for her debut on a Las Vegas stage. Both she and Kobie had believed Daniel when he'd told them he had an out-of-town business appointment that weekend—until the credit card bills arrived. She wondered if he were dazzling his new wife with the money he'd selfishly emptied out of their joint account before requesting a divorce.

At least she had her son and the old farmhouse. The fire crackled as flames hit a pocket of sap, and sparks flew into the air. She hadn't been camping since before she'd married Daniel, but her grandfather used to bring her up here when she was a young girl, which was why she'd picked Hidden Canyon for this trip. Sometimes her grand-mother had come along, but most of the time it had been just her and Grandpa. Sitting beside a campfire, built just the way Grandpa had taught her, her thoughts turned to the grandparents who had raised her. Missing them still brought an ache to her heart.

She'd never been camping before with her son. Daniel hadn't been interested, and she'd never considered taking Kobie by herself until now. But camping wasn't an entirely new experience for Kobie. Daniel's father sometimes took his grandson in the old truck she'd borrowed for this excursion, and sometimes her father-in-law set up a tent in the orchard for the two of them. Last January, right after Daniel left them, the older man had shown up at her house with camping gear and talked Shalise into allowing him to take Kobie on a winter camping trip. She'd almost refused to let him go, but later she'd been glad she'd agreed. Something about the trip, whether it was the novelty of camping in the winter or just the old man's love for his grandson, helped Kobie turn a corner and begin the slow process of healing.

She looked up at the star-filled canopy overhead and wondered when she would begin to heal. Daniel had seemed so strong and dependable during those awful months after her grandparents died. He'd been there for her, helping and advising and offering comfort. When he'd asked her to marry him, she hadn't hesitated. Even after she learned he wasn't all those things she'd believed him to be, she hadn't stopped loving him. Just thinking about the day she'd stood holding the pages a deputy sheriff brought to her door—pages that told her Daniel had filed for a divorce—still brought a stab of pain to her heart. She'd still been numb with shock weeks later when she'd learned about Lena and the plans Daniel had to marry her.

All right, this isn't the time or place for a pity party. She rose to her feet and headed toward the camper. Minutes later, warm in thick fleece sweats, she crawled into the sleeping bag she'd spread out earlier beside her son's inside the camper shell. She woke once a short time later from dreaming she'd heard the wail of a siren. Deciding she'd imagined the sound, she drifted back to sleep.

* * *

Wade Timmerman swore under his breath. *Had everyone in the whole country decided to camp in this one canyon this weekend?* Slowly he backed up, then pulled forward, backed up again, then turned the wheel sharply. After several more attempts, he managed to turn the cumbersome vehicle and was on the road again, this time headed down the canyon. There wasn't a parking spot left, at least not one that would accommodate an RV the size of his. At least the kids had stopped whining and gone to bed.

Chelsea sat beside him, but she didn't say anything. She'd given up making suggestions a long time ago. He was glad they were finally on their way back to Chicago. He couldn't take much more of her silent treatment or the kids' fighting. He'd been out of his mind to let his parents talk him into this trip. It would have been far better to make the break quick and clean, so he could get on with his life. He had a great future ahead of him without dumpy Chelsea and two mannerless children holding him back.

Something caught his eye. It looked like a flashing red light. *Probably some other poor fool turning around so he can head back down the canyon too.* As the light came closer, his ears filled with the shriek of a siren. A short distance ahead his headlights picked up a turnout where he could pull over to let the emergency vehicle pass.

Chelsea sat up straighter and looked around as he left the pavement. "Did you find a place where we can stop for the night?" she asked.

"No. There's an ambulance or a cop coming up the canyon. I'm just pulling over to give him plenty of room to get by."

"Oh." She sounded sleepy. *Well, isn't that too bad? I'm tired too, and I've been driving since ten o'clock this morning with just two short meal breaks. If she had done her job and read the map right, we wouldn't be stuck in this canyon now. We'd be in Rock Springs. And if she had ever learned to drive anything but an automatic, she could take a turn driving, and we'd be back in Chicago by tomorrow night!*

"Look, there's a road!" Chelsea pointed, but he didn't need her to tell him what he could see for himself. What he'd thought was a turnout was actually a narrow, unpaved road.

"It probably doesn't go anywhere, but we might as well check it out." He aimed the nose of the RV up the narrow dirt lane. Tree branches scraped the sides of the long, sleek motor home and he cursed again. He'd have to have the scratches repaired or his mother would never stop lecturing him. She'd already made it her business to tell him he'd spent too much money on the luxury model. He'd almost told her that if he had to suffer through this trip, he'd at least do it in style.

At the top of the incline he could see the road dipped, then rose again quite sharply. His headlights revealed a picnic table in the small hollow. As he drew closer it became clear the parking spot was designed for a single small vehicle.

"Could we . . . ?" Chelsea began.

"Don't be stupid!" He cut her off. "There's no way this beast will fit in that little spot."

"I know that! I was wondering if there's enough room to turn around."

"Why turn around? This spot is empty. There are probably other, larger camping spots farther along the road that are empty too. This road is so well hidden, there probably aren't many campers who even know it's here." He pressed on the accelerator, causing the RV to jolt as he started up the winding hill ahead of him. Chelsea didn't say anything more, but he knew how she would purse her lips together, making her chin pucker. Once he'd thought that was cute, but now he thought it just made her look old and peevish.

The sound of the engine changed to a whine before it reached the top of the steep incline, and he wondered if he'd pushed it too hard. He just wanted to get back to Chicago and put this nightmare behind him. The only thing that had kept him going through fourteen straight hours of Chelsea's complaining and the kids fighting was the possibility of reaching the city in time to take Mandy to dinner at a quiet restaurant Sunday evening—free of kids quarreling and Chelsea whining—rather than wait until they both got to work Tuesday morning to see each other. He'd prefer their reunion to be private, away from the office where they both worked.

"Wade!" Chelsea's scream jerked him back to the present. Instinctively he slammed on the brakes, fishtailing to a stop. A large animal, an elk or an awfully large deer, stood as though mesmerized in the center of the road, staring back at him. After a frozen moment it bounded past them to disappear in the trees.

"Was that a moose?" a voice came from behind him. *Great! Chelsea's screech woke up Rachel.*

"No, dummy. That was an elk. Don't you know anything?" *So Bryan is up too.*

"Daddy, he called me a dummy!"

Wade sighed. This was all he needed, more bickering.

His hand tightened on the gear shift and he gave it a shove, at the same time slamming his foot against the gas pedal. The engine howled, then died. In the sudden silence, the distant sound of sirens drifted on the air.

Chelsea glanced over her shoulder toward the window as though she expected to see the source of the eerie sound.

"Are you going to get a ticket?" Rachel asked.

"You're so stupid," Bryan belittled his sister. "There aren't any speed cops out here in the boonies."

"But I can hear . . ."

"There's probably been a boating accident at the reservoir. Remember the sign we saw that pointed to Canyon Crest Reservoir and Recreation Area?" Chelsea attempted to give her daughter an explanation for the sound they could hear.

Bryan slid a window open and cocked his head, listening. "Must be some accident. That sounds like half a dozen or more cops."

"Sound is distorted in the mountains. Lots of echoes. Close that window and get back to bed!" Wade bent forward trying to coax the engine to start again. He noticed that Bryan closed the window, but he didn't make a move toward his bunk in the back of the RV. Chelsea had spoiled the boy to the point that he did as he pleased most of the time. His kids were obnoxious brats—one more thing Chelsea had messed up.

The engine sputtered, then roared. Easing his foot off the gas pedal, he adjusted the gears, then felt the shudder as the vehicle began to move.

"Are you going to drive all night?" Rachel was whining again. He gritted his teeth and stared straight ahead.

"Hush," Chelsea whispered as though there were some great secret. "Daddy's looking for a place to park the RV. As soon as he finds one, we can all sleep."

"Are we going boating at the reservoir tomorrow?" she asked.

"You're so stupid! I told you Dad just wants to hurry back to Chicago so he can see his girlfriend." Bryan's voice rose in a sneering falsetto.

"You're lying!" Rachel attacked her brother with both fists.

"Quiet!" Wade shouted to make himself heard. He might have known Chelsea would tell Bryan about Mandy in spite of their agreement to wait to tell the children until they got back home from this stupid trip. He didn't know how he'd been so dumb as to tie himself to a girl who had never quite grown up. They'd gotten married right after Chelsea's high school graduation, and she'd never gone on to school, held a job, or done a single thing to better herself or their finances. She wasn't even competent at handling the kids. Like right now, she wasn't doing anything to keep them from practically killing each other. He turned his head enough to glare at her and found her hunched in her seat crying.

"Go to bed! Both of you!" *Why is it I can negotiate the stickiest contract and stay unruffled, but my kids have had me yelling and out of control almost every day of this trip?*

Making a deliberate effort, he dropped his voice to a more reasonable level to add, "We'll talk about this in the morning."

"What's to talk about? I don't care if you get divorced. You're gone all the time anyway. We won't even miss you." Bryan stomped toward the back of the motor home.

"Janie's parents got a divorce. Now her daddy comes to see her every Sunday and he brings her presents. Are you going to bring me presents?" Rachel asked. He felt a twinge of sadness. Where had his little princess gone, and how had this whining, greedy child taken her place? He gave her a scathing glance and noticed the grubby cartoon character nightshirt she wore. It had been cute when he'd bought it for her at Disneyland, but now it looked disgusting. He gritted his teeth. With the money he gave Chelsea to buy clothes for the kids, his daughter should be dressed like the princess he'd once called her.

"C–come on, Rachel. It's time you were back in bed." From the corner of his eye, he saw Chelsea reach for their daughter's hand and begin to lead her away.

"Look, Daddy, there's a big parking place!" Rachel pulled away from her mother to point to a wide, graveled spot he'd almost driven past. Throwing the gear into reverse, he backed up. It wasn't really a camping spot. From the sign spotlighted by his headlights this appeared to be the starting point for some kind of trail, leading over the mountain to the reservoir. It would have to do, he decided. He pulled forward a few more feet, then cut the engine. It wasn't really a camping spot, more of a staging area for hikers and horseback riders, but he didn't care. He was so tired, he couldn't drive another mile.

Minutes later he was stretched out on his own bunk, fully dressed. He was too tired to even contemplate getting undressed. Besides, he only intended to catch a few winks, then keep going. But for now, this day was finally over. *In the morning, I'll backtrack to I-15, then find the exit I missed earlier. I can still make it to Chicago by Sunday night.* The light from across the short hall shone in his eyes. *I should tell Bryan to turn off his light and go to sleep.* But his thoughts soon trailed off, and he was asleep.

* * *

"All units! All units! Get out of the canyon! Now!" Sheriff Howard's voice was practically a scream coming over the radio. *This is it!* Web gripped the wheel tighter and pressed a little harder on the gas. He was almost to the Hidden Canyon Fork trailhead, and he hadn't seen any sign of the RV he'd caught just a glimpse of twenty minutes earlier when he'd raced up the canyon to alert the upper canyon campers of the pending disaster. It had probably just pulled over to let him by, then continued on down the canyon. But he kept his siren wailing, just in case there were any campers still needing warning of the emergency. Spotting the turnoff he whipped the wheel and left the pavement for the dirt road.

There weren't any spaces for RVs like the rig he'd glimpsed in this offshoot box canyon, and the road was nothing but a beat-up trail, so it wasn't likely the big outfit was in here, but something drove him to check. The entrance to the canyon wasn't marked, and it was pretty well concealed, but a few seasoned campers knew of its existence or stumbled onto it, so it needed to be checked anyway.

"Out! Everyone out!"

The sheriff's voice coming over the radio was now a full-fledged scream. Web could turn around just ahead. A cloud of dirt nearly choked him even through the closed windows as his car shot toward the trailhead, and gravel flew as he spun the car around in the small parking area. His headlights caught the bulky shape of a big RV.

His car swerved back and forth on the gravel as he slammed on the brakes and threw open his door. He cut the siren, but the cruiser's lights continued to flash. A deep booming sound hung in the air as he sprinted toward the vehicle.

"Emergency! Open up!" he shouted. His fists slammed against the door. "Police! Open the door!"

A teenage boy flung open the door just as Sheriff Howard's voice came from the radio shouting, *"She's going! Get out! Get out!"*

CHAPTER 2

"Do you hear that?" Trent sat up in his sleeping bag.

"Yes. What do you suppose it is? Whatever it is, I can still hear it." Gage was sitting up now.

"You're right. I can too. It sounds like a herd of stampeding cattle off in the distance."

"More like buffalo. Get your pants on. I think we'd better check this out." He was already standing, pulling on his jeans. Once his shoes were on, he picked up his flashlight, opened the tent flap, and stepped outside. Trent was right on his heels.

A quarter moon hung over the mountains, and a million stars added their light. The brothers stood together, listening. The sound seemed to be growing louder.

"Remember earlier we thought we heard sirens?" Trent paused as if fearful of continuing.

"You don't suppose . . ." Gage grasped his brother's arm, swinging him around to face him. "What if that's a couple million gallons of water tearing down the canyon?"

"No way!" Trent shook his head.

"Then what?"

"I don't know . . . You think the dam . . . ?" He paused, and Gage knew he was listening to the ominous roar coming from the main canyon. "Just in case, maybe we ought to wake the girls."

"You're right. They're a lot lower than we are and right next to the stream. They won't hear a thing." Gage was running before he finished speaking. He found himself stumbling over roots in the darkness, but he didn't slow down. A prompting deep in his soul kept telling him to hurry. He could hear Trent thrashing through the brush behind him and knew without asking that he felt the urgency too.

They hit the road yelling.

"Emily!"

"Cassie! Diane! Wake up!" Gage tore across the clearing and ripped up the zipper of the tent flap.

An ear-splitting scream erupted from the dark interior of the tent. Gage felt a pang of regret, knowing they'd frightened the young women. Turning his flashlight beam up to reveal his face, he forced himself to remain calm.

"We think the dam has ruptured. You're in danger here."

"Grab your boots and jackets, and follow us up the hill," Trent ordered.

"The dam?" He saw Cassie's eyes widen, then a look of suspicion cross her face, but it was Diane who spoke. "We're only a couple of miles from the dam, and it's at the top of the canyon. If it broke, you wouldn't just think it broke, you'd know. We'd be washed away by now."

"Nooo." Cassie drew the word out, and for a moment Gage thought she was refusing to leave. Then she was on her feet, shouting at her sister. Emily was coyly giggling back at Trent, who was trying to hand her the pair of hiking boots he'd found at the foot of her sleeping bag.

Cassie flipped on an electric lantern and turned to her sister who was sitting up with her sleeping bag pulled to her chin. "I don't think they're bluffing. Get a move on."

"Are you sure?" Diane took her cue from Cassie and leaped from her sleeping bag. She had her hiking boots on almost as fast as Cassie did.

"This canyon runs at almost a forty-five degree angle to the main canyon and the angle heads back up toward the reservoir behind the dam," Gage explained.

"The pie-shaped piece of mountain between us and the main canyon is at least a mile of solid rock," Cassie picked up the explanation, her civil engineering study becoming all too evident. She thrust her fleece-covered sleeve into a jacket. "It climbs at a steep pitch too, placing us considerably higher than the main canyon."

She took quick steps toward her sister, continuing her lecture as she grabbed Emily's shoes from Trent's hand. "If the dam has ruptured, the water is hurling down the main canyon at tremendous speed. When it reaches the valley it will spread out and move more slowly, but the debris it picks up in the canyon will wipe out roads, ranches, fences, and everything in its path until it reaches the Bear River. It will also back up the water in the canyon, raising the water level."

Taking his lead from Cassie, Trent jerked the sleeping bag from Emily's hands and shoved the girl's arms into the jacket Diane handed him. Cassie kept talking. "The first thrust of water would hurl past side canyons, but as the rising water behind the first crest fills the main canyon, it would continue more slowly to fill the side canyons."

"Cassie, you said this is a box canyon," Emily whispered, frightened now. "If the main canyon is flooded, how are we going to get out?"

"We'll get out. I promise." Trent attempted to reassure her, but he didn't slow down as he pushed her toward the tent flap.

Gage ushered the other two young women ahead of him. Cassie paused only long enough to snatch up a small nylon backpack and a flashlight. Once outside the tent, Gage reached for her hand and ran, pulling her beside him toward the trail on the opposite side of the road. A dark shape, perhaps a deer, darted past them, also heading for higher ground.

"Hurry!" Trent's voice floated back to them.

"Wait!" Cassie suddenly stopped, dragging Gage to a halt in the middle of the road. Diane, a few steps ahead, paused and turned to look back at them. Unidentifiable sounds carried on the night air, and rustling could be heard in the bushes and trees. The faint wail of a siren abruptly stopped.

"There was a truck with a woman and a little boy that passed by here a couple of hours ago. They must be camping at the top of the canyon. We've got to warn them." Cassie pulled free and began to run up the road toward the closed end of the canyon.

"Diane, catch up to Trent," Gage shouted. "Tell him we've gone to alert some other campers. Climb as high as you can, then angle toward the trailhead. We'll catch up to you there." Gage took off running, but Cassie had already disappeared into the darkness.

* * *

"A flood! You're telling me the dam broke?" Wade stared at the big uniformed man, not quite comprehending what the deputy was saying. He'd barely fallen asleep when he was awakened by a siren followed by pounding on his door. He and Bryan had reached the door at almost the same moment.

"Get your family! A wall of floodwater is headed this way!"

He remembered the sign he'd seen pointing to some reservoir. The deputy's face told him this was no gag or elaborate con game.

"Wade, what's the matter? Can't we camp here?" Chelsea approached him, tying the belt of a knee-length plush robe over matching pink pajamas.

"He says there's a flood headed this way." Wade jerked his head, indicating the officer who had brought the warning.

"Is there anyone else in there?" the deputy asked.

"Rachel!" Chelsea turned around to go after her daughter, but Rachel was already stumbling into the room in her thin nightshirt, rubbing her eyes.

"Why's everyone yelling? You woke me up." Wade ignored his daughter's petulant tone and reached for the compartment over the driver's seat for his wallet.

"There's no time to collect valuables!" the deputy shouted, picking up Rachel and swinging her into his brawny arms as he backed away from the door.

"The dam broke!" Bryan yelled, answering his sister's question as he shot out the door after them.

Several sharp cracks that sounded like trees breaking and a thundering roar galvanized the deputy. He paused only to shout, "There's a trail about twenty feet behind your RV. Run for it!" Rachel let out a squeak of alarm as the deputy began to run. Bryan bolted past the deputy and ran toward the trail opening in the trees.

"I'll just get my . . ."

"There's no time!" the deputy shouted while sprinting in the direction the boy had taken.

Wade grabbed Chelsea's arm, jerking her after the others. Gravel flew beneath his feet, but he kept running, dragging Chelsea with him. With the roar coming closer, he barely registered the difference as his feet found the trail, exchanging dirt and pine needles for the rough pea gravel. He only ran faster.

The trail was steep, and he knew they were climbing rapidly. His breath was coming in deep gasps, and Chelsea was a deadweight dragging on his arm.

"Got to stop." Her voice was a sob, and she suddenly collapsed, dragging him with her to the ground.

Struggling to regain his feet, he looked back down the trail in time to see a carpet of inky blackness spill over the parking lot they'd just left. A cloud of dust rose before it, clearly visible in the moonlight. The deputy's car with its red lights still flashing lifted in the air. Headlights spotlighted the brightly lit RV, then went dark as the patrol car smashed against the larger vehicle.

Shock gripped him like icy tentacles around his chest. For half a second he wondered if he were having a heart attack. "Get up! We're going to die if we don't get farther up this mountain!" He tugged Chelsea's arm, dragging her limp body several feet before he stopped, cursing as he stood over her prostrate form.

"I can't walk . . . or breathe!" Her breath was coming in wheezing gasps.

"Move, or I'll leave you here to die alone! I'm not drowning because of you." He gave her arm another jerk, forcing her to her feet. She stumbled and he cursed again.

"My feet," Chelsea whimpered.

"Catch up to your son." A calm, tight-lipped voice came from behind him. "He's with your little girl. I'll help your wife." Panic clutched at his gut, and he turned to do as the deputy instructed. From the corner of his eye, Wade saw the other man toss Chelsea over his shoulder. She squealed, then was still.

It was all he could do to stay ahead of the big man's ground-eating strides. Some warning of self-preservation told him that if he didn't stay ahead, the deputy wouldn't come back for him. It would be the floodwater that would come for him. Thinking of that creeping black water provided the needed adrenaline to keep him running, though his chest ached and his lungs were screaming for him to stop.

* * *

Shalise rose to her feet, then climbed out of the truck. She stood still and listened, then paced to the edge of the clearing. Something seemed to hang in the air, something ominous and threatening. She'd never been nervous camping with her grandfather when she'd been a child, but something was causing a prickling feeling at the back of her neck. Something beyond the circle of light from her campfire was making an eerie sound that hovered like a whisper in the air and didn't belong to the mountain setting. Or was she letting her anger at Daniel for rejecting them and her fear of a future alone frighten her into imagining something threatening was creeping up on their camp?

"Mom, are we having an earthquake?" She hadn't heard Kobie climb out of the truck and join her at the edge of the clearing.

"Earthquake? What makes you think . . .?" Then she felt it beneath her feet—a faint vibration. "I don't know what it is, but I think we should leave." She couldn't explain the feeling that gripped her, telling her to run, to get her child to safety.

She remembered how close to the towering cliff at the end of the canyon she'd parked the truck. It was a beautiful camping spot, a place her grandfather had introduced her to when she'd been a child. A trickle of water splashed down the rock face nearby to form a small clear pool. Pine trees surrounded the pool, which sat next to a small meadow where an occasional camper pitched a tent. Years ago the forest service had created a spot wide enough for a vehicle to turn around before beginning its journey back down the canyon and where one vehicle could park for the night. Shalise glanced at the solid silhouette of the mountain rising behind them and shuddered. *What if my son is right? What if an earthquake shook that mountain?*

"Get in the truck! We're leaving." To her surprise, Kobie didn't argue, and as he turned to sprint toward the truck she realized he was completely dressed. He paused to tip a bucket of water they'd hauled from the stream earlier onto the smoldering coals of their campfire. Fortunately, they hadn't unpacked much, since it was late when they'd arrived and they had planned to sleep in the truck anyway.

The engine caught on the first try, which was amazing as badly as her hands were shaking, but she ground the gears before managing to start the vehicle moving. Lurching onto the road she squinted into the darkness, then remembered to switch on the headlights. Her foot pressed harder on the gas pedal, and the truck picked up speed. Seconds later, she slammed on the brakes. Two figures emerged from the dark, running straight toward them.

"Lock your door!" But she was too late. One of the figures wrenched open Kobie's door and reached for him while the other pounded on her window.

"No!" she screamed and grabbed for her son.

"Follow me!" the man holding Kobie yelled as he ran toward the trees bordering the road. The other figure was now at the open passenger door. Vaguely she noticed this one was a woman. Shalise brushed past her, intent on pursuing the man who had taken her son. The stranger made no attempt to stop her headlong dash, but seemed to be encouraging her to run faster.

"Mo-o-o-m." Kobie's voice floated back to her, spurring her to greater speed. Her foot tangled with a root, and she felt herself falling. A hand grasped her arm, steadying her. Shaking it off, she plunged on.

Help me, Father, please help me, she found herself praying. *Help me save Kobie!*

"Hurry, Mom!" Kobie's voice reached her again, and she thought she could detect panic in his voice.

"I'm coming," she called back, panting from her exertions, then wondered if she'd made a mistake to warn his captor that she was following.

"Don't try to talk," she heard behind her. She'd forgotten about the woman. "And don't worry about your son. Gage will get him high enough to be safe."

To be safe? What is this woman talking about? She would have asked her, but it took all of her strength to keep running. Her mind whirled as she ran. Why had the man taken Kobie? Did he have a car hidden somewhere? No, he couldn't have a car up here. No car, not even a four-wheel-drive truck, could make its way up this steep mountainside. If the kidnapper thought he could escape her by running uphill, he was in for a surprise. She and her friend Dallas had been running for an hour every morning for almost six months. They'd even been talking about registering for the St. George Marathon.

We're almost to the trail that goes over the mountain to the reservoir. Could these people have a small ATV waiting on the trail? If they reach any kind of transportation before I catch up to them, they could take my son beyond my reach in minutes. She put on a burst of speed.

Her foot came down in water. *Water? There is no water this high up.* She hesitated and the woman behind her screamed, "Keep going! We can make it."

"Cassie! Where are you?" A man's voice came from almost over Shalise's head.

"Right here!" The woman who had been trailing her splashed ahead. "We're standing in water."

Water splashed in front of Shalise, and suddenly a man stood in front of her, startling a scream from her throat.

"Here, up you go." The man placed his hands at the other woman's waist and swung her to a ledge above them. Turning back to Shalise, he reached for her, and she stepped back, feeling the water close around her ankles.

"Where's Kobie? What have you done with my son?" She couldn't help the way her voice cracked, and the questions ended in a sharp screech.

"He's fine. I left him on the trail and told him to keep climbing." He reached for her again, and once more she stepped back, only to bump her back against a tree trunk. His hands grasped her waist and in seconds she felt herself leave the ground.

"Grab whatever you can to pull yourself up!" Obviously she was larger than the woman he had tossed to the ledge seconds earlier, because she landed several feet short of the ledge and found herself scrabbling for a root, rocks, anything to hold onto. Her hand closed around the thick, woody stem of some kind of shrub. Drawing on her desperate need to find her son, she kicked her feet, searching for a toehold. When she found one, she pulled and scrambled her way up to the ledge.

Gasping for breath, she lay facedown on the path for several seconds before she found the strength to pull herself upright. When she stood, she found the man standing beside her. He, too, was breathing deeply, the sound harsh and labored.

"Kobie?" Her son's name didn't come out the way she meant it to. She hadn't wanted to reveal how close she was to crying.

"He's fine. Cassie has probably caught up to him by now, but we've got to hurry. The trail dips down a short distance from here. We've got to get across that low spot before it's covered with water."

"I don't understand. Where did the water come from?" The man turned her toward the trail and gave her a small nudge. Before he could explain anything, she knew. The dam had given way, and the canyon where she and her son had come to camp was filling up with water. Suddenly she wanted to cry. It was as though she'd fallen through Alice's rabbit hole and nothing was the way it seemed. The man she'd thought would love and care for her all her life had abandoned her and stolen from her, while the strangers who appeared out of the darkness to steal her child had saved both of their lives. Tentatively she took a step, then another. Soon she was running for her life.

CHAPTER 3

Gage peered ahead, anxious to catch a glimpse of Cassie and the boy. He knew the woman who ran ahead of him was frightened and confused. He wanted to stop to reassure her, but there wasn't time. The explanations, along with an exchange of names, would have to come later. He knew one thing about the woman—she knew how to run. If neither of them tripped in the dark, they had a chance of making it.

He worried about the stretch of trail that crossed a meadow a short distance ahead. If it was underwater before they reached it, it would take longer to skirt it, climb higher, and cross a dangerous old rock slide. Crossing the slide in the dark would be chancy enough, but if the water covered the meadow, they might not be able to climb high enough on their side of the meadow to even reach the slide. The canyon walls were steep at this end and would require ropes to scale. At least Trent, along with Cassie's sister and friend, would be well past the low spot and onto the higher trail by now.

The woman gave a cry and began to run faster. Gage was hard-pressed to keep up with her. Then he saw what she saw. A smaller shape detached itself from the dark shadows ahead and flung itself toward her. She caught her son in her arms, and Gage felt a lump form in his throat as mother and son were reunited.

"Gage, look!" Cassie was beside him, tugging at his arm. He followed her to the edge of the meadow. Water glinted across one end of the meadow, and it wasn't his imagination that told him it was creeping closer to the path. There, without trees or rocks to slow its course, it assumed a rolling motion that carried it deeper into the meadow. It would completely cover the meadow in minutes with each succeeding wave of water deepening the lake forming behind it.

"We've got to run for it!" His voice was a shout. Turning to the woman and her child, he instructed, "We've got to get across that meadow before the floodwater cuts us off. Cassie will go first, then the two of you. I'll bring up the rear." He reached across the woman to pull a backpack from the boy's shoulder. In his rush to get the child to higher ground, he'd ignored the heavy pack the boy clutched as he was dragged from the truck.

"I'll carry this for you," he said, swinging the pack to his own shoulders. He couldn't allow anything to slow the kid. From the corner of his eye he saw Cassie begin running.

"The truck . . ." the woman started to protest, then her shoulders sagged, and he knew she understood.

"Come on, Mom!" The boy darted after Cassie, and to Gage's relief, the woman followed. He saw her turn her head toward the ripple of water that rose in a small, silvery crest and rolled toward them. She doubled her speed, her long legs quickly closing the gap between her and her son.

Cassie was already a silhouette on the path when he followed the others onto the trail. She'd turned her flashlight on, and the beam of light bounced and swayed with her movements. He felt more comfortable not switching on his light. His eyes, long since accustomed to the light provided by the glowing stars and slender slice of moon, moved from the dark shapes fleeing ahead of him to the water that approached closer with each sluggish ripple. How thankful he was that they weren't in the path of the flood's first onslaught, nor low enough to be in the way of the steady surge that was now pouring into the smaller canyon. He shuddered, thinking of the powerful force that was undoubtedly carrying boulders along like pebbles and ripping century-old trees from the ground.

He wasn't sure how high the water in the canyon would rise, but he knew they had to reach the point where the trail began its sharp zigzag up the one place where the canyon walls weren't sheer rock cliffs. The trail they now ran on was a scant twenty feet above the canyon floor, but once past the meadow it rose steeply until it joined the path he and

Trent had taken that morning to fish at the reservoir. They had a good chance if they didn't get cut off by the rising water here.

Cassie saw the dark shadow move closer to the path. She guessed that at this point the water was only a few inches deep and that the darker edge at the front was a layer of dust and debris being pushed ahead of the water. Lifting her flashlight beam she saw she was almost to the point where the meadow ended and the path began a steep ascent. A quick turn of her head didn't show her how close the others were, but she thought she could hear the pounding of footsteps behind her.

Her foot came down on something that crunched beneath her boot. The water had reached the path, pushing twigs and bits of dry plants ahead of it. Her next step brought a splash of water. Turning her head, she yelled a warning to those behind her, then she focused on the point where her light revealed the path rising above the water, and she lunged ahead. In less than a minute, the water was sloshing over her boot tops.

Reaching the tumble of boulders that marked the end of the meadow, she found dry ground and looked back, searching for the others. Shining her light back on the meadow she'd just crossed, she shuddered. The meadow had disappeared and a lake had taken its place.

"Hold your light steady!" Gage's voice reached her, and she shifted the beam until it picked out two shapes. *Three! There should be three!* Steadying the beam as much as her shaking hands would allow, she saw the second figure was actually two. The boy was riding astride Gage's shoulders!

"This way!" she shouted back. "Come straight toward my light."

The woman was close enough now that Cassie could see that the water had reached her knees and she was struggling to keep her balance. Just as Gage reached out to steady her, Cassie spotted a foot-high swell of water rolling toward them. Before she could scream a warning, the wave struck, sending them both tumbling. Gage regained his footing first. Thankfully, the child was still clinging to his back.

Swinging the beam of light back and forth, Cassie spotted the woman. She was on her feet again, but farther away. Her mind raced. If she could reach Gage and take the child, he could go after the woman. Placing her flashlight in a small cleft in the rocks where it would continue to provide a beacon, she slipped the straps of her backpack from her shoulders and hung it over a tree branch. Turning to where the path had been, she prepared to wade into the now waist-high icy water.

"Wait!" A voice preceded a shower of small stones, and a flashlight beam bounced across the path.

"Trent!" She turned, recognizing his voice. Behind him, sliding down the steep, rocky trail were Emily and Diane.

"The water is rising too fast. They need help." Cassie pointed to where Gage and the mother and son struggled toward them.

"Here!" Trent set his flashlight down on a rock before thrusting one end of a narrow nylon rope into her hands. "Tie it around something solid."

She interpreted his lurching steps as a sign he was fastening the other end around himself as he ran toward the spot where the trail disappeared into the water. With Diane's help she wound the rope around a tree trunk. Not trusting her knot-tying ability, she continued to grip the rope with both hands as Trent waded into the icy water. Emily followed him to the edge of the water. Then as he stepped into the waist-high flood, she picked up the rope and fed it slowly out as he shoved against the current.

"There's a woman and a little boy out there." Cassie panted with the exertion of trying to talk and make certain the rope didn't break loose. "Gage has the boy, but the water is carrying the woman farther out. They're the people who were at the last campground, and even though we ran, we couldn't get back this far before the water covered the meadow."

"We were worried you might have trouble getting past this point and would have to climb the slide. Trent had a rope, so we came back in case you needed help," Diane told her.

"I'm glad you did, but where did you get the rope?" Cassie asked.

"As we ran up the path across the road from our camp we went through Gage and Trent's camp. Trent grabbed it off the table where he'd left it earlier," Diane explained.

Cassie watched the brothers' dark shapes close the gap between them. Gage was only about twenty feet from shore when the two met.

She couldn't hear the words they exchanged, but she felt the heightened tension on the rope as Gage grasped it. Cassie strained to see the woman, but she was beyond the beam of light.

"Cassie!" She heard Gage call her name. With no more explanation she knew he wanted her to come for the boy. With the rope to cling to, she could reach the child, and Gage could turn back to search for the woman. She didn't hesitate, even though she'd seen how the water had reached Trent's waist, and he was around six feet tall. If necessary, she would swim! If the men didn't go after the woman at once, they might lose her in the darkness and deepening water.

"I'm coming!" she called, hurrying forward.

"I'll do it. I'm bigger than you." Diane slipped into the water ahead of Cassie and without looking back began pulling herself, hand over hand, toward Gage and the waiting child. Cassie stopped, watching her friend move farther and farther from the safety of dry ground. Diane was only a few inches shorter than the men, but the water swirled well above her waist, making her movements appear slow and clumsy. Cassie shuddered. Diane was a good six inches taller than she was.

It seemed to take forever for Diane to reach Gage, but Cassie knew only minutes had passed before Gage transferred the child to Diane's shoulders and her friend started the slow hand-over-hand return trip. At first Cassie's eyes stayed fixed on Diane, but soon fear drew her attention back to Gage. When she glanced beyond Diane and the burden she carried, she could no longer see either Gage or Trent. Frantically her eyes scanned the flooded meadow until she saw a dark shape she hoped was them.

"You're almost here, Diane." She turned her attention back to her friend who was now within a few feet of the shore. From over Diane's head, she saw another rolling swell of water rushing across the open space.

"Hang on!" she screamed and watched as the fast-moving wave lifted Diane, sending her tumbling. Emily's screams joined her own as Diane fell and the small figure on her back went flying into the water. Cassie's reaction was instantaneous. Without any hesitation to consider the possibility that she might be washed away, she plunged into the water, focusing only on the spot where she'd seen the child disappear.

Her hand struck something soft. She grasped it firmly and rose to the surface, kicking and fighting against the current. She heard the boy's gasping breaths and knew he was breathing.

"Can you swim?" She spit mud and water from her mouth to ask, while kicking to stay afloat. She twisted her hand into the fabric of his shirt to make certain he didn't slip away from her.

"Yes."

"Cassie! This way." Diane's voice was close.

"We have to reach Diane and the rope before another wave pushes us away. Turn on your side and scissor kick. I'll hang onto you."

"Okay, let's go." He struck out against the flowing water, and Cassie added her more powerful kick and one-armed strokes. Hanging on to the boy lessened her effectiveness, and silently she begged God for the added strength she needed.

They didn't seem to be making much progress, but it was only a few minutes until Diane's fingers brushed her hand. Then she was grasping the rope. Sputtering and half-crying she gripped the rope with one hand and clung to the child with the other as the three of them stumbled up the buried trail to dry ground where they collapsed in a soggy, breathless heap.

"Cassie! Are you all right?" Emily's worried voice penetrated at last.

"Yes, I think so." Cassie pulled herself to her feet and rushed to her sister. "What about Gage and Trent?"

"I—I don't know. I have Trent's flashlight, but I'm afraid to let go of the rope and turn it on. Oh! Look at your flashlight!"

Cassie glanced toward the rocky cliff where she'd left the light. Water lapped to within inches of it. She clambered up the rocks to rescue the flashlight, then climbed higher to scan the newly formed lake.

"Gage!" she called. After listening, she called his name again.

"We're here!" came a faint response. Tears pricked at the back of her eyes, and she nearly dropped the light as she scanned the water, searching for the two men. The beam didn't illuminate far enough to show her where they were.

"Pull on the rope." She thought it was Trent's voice that came to her this time. She shoved the light into a pocket in the rocks before clambering down. It wasn't powerful enough to show her where the men were, but hopefully they would see it and follow it to shore. Emily and Diane had the rope in their hands when she joined them. The boy picked up the rope behind Cassie.

"This will work better if we pull together." Diane took charge. "When I say one, pull with your left hand. Two, switch hands, pull with your right. One, two, one, two." They established a rhythm, and soon three shapes emerged out of the gloom to collapse at the water's edge.

"Mom!" Shalise heard her son call, and she struggled to her knees to meet his embrace.

Soon they were all rejoicing and hugging each other. Shalise felt arms around her and found herself hugging people whose names she didn't know, but whom she would love forever. Not all of the moisture on her face came from the floodwater. It felt like a flood of her own was erupting inside her heart. She couldn't let go of her son. She'd been so afraid she'd never see him again.

The wave that had knocked her off her feet had carried her a considerable distance before she was able to stand again. After regaining her balance she'd oriented herself by finding the point of light coming from the woman's flashlight, but she had wasted precious time searching for Kobie. The force of the water had kept her from moving closer, even after she discovered a dark shape she hoped was the man carrying her son.

"We'd better get moving." She heard that same man speak above the rest of the voices. She choked on an overwhelming surge of gratitude and love for him for risking his own life to save her and her son. Hugging Kobie to her, she surveyed the muddy, bedraggled group around her, and her gratitude extended to them all.

"Thank you," she struggled to say over the lump in her throat. Cassie's arm came around her, giving her a quick squeeze.

"You know what?" a young-sounding, feminine voice asked, then went on to answer her own question. "I don't know your names, and we've all been too frantic to tell you ours. I'm Emily Breverton, and the weepy one smushing you is my sister, Cassie. Diane Olsen is the one that followed the rope out to get your little boy. Gage and Trent Edwards are the guys who woke us out of a sound sleep to warn us a flood was coming."

Shalise rubbed a fist against a still teary eye and said, "I'm Shalise Richards, and this is my son, Kobie." She hugged her son again until he squirmed out of her grasp.

"We need to start climbing." Gage interrupted the introductions. "The water is going to cover this spot in a few minutes." The terror that had just begun to recede gripped Shalise once more and had her reaching for Kobie's hand to keep him by her side.

"My flashlight!" Cassie scrambled toward the rock where she had left it, which was almost cut off by the water, endangering her flashlight again. She snatched the light from its resting place and hurried back to the group.

"The trail is narrow from here on so we'll have to walk single file. Trent will lead and I'll bring up the rear." Gage got no arguments. Emily fell into place behind Trent as he turned his flashlight on, and the others lined up behind them. Shalise noticed that Cassie dropped back to walk just in front of Gage. She wondered if the young woman was romantically involved with the handsome young man—she'd almost fallen in love with him herself when she realized he'd saved her and her son's lives.

Shalise kept Kobie in front of her where she could keep an eye on him. Trent set a fast pace that kept the rest of them scrambling to keep up. Her legs ached, and she was glad for the conditioning she'd undergone the past few months. Silently she thanked her friend Dallas, who had made it her job to push and coerce her into taking a search and rescue course and to run with her almost every day. She also felt a surge of maternal pride seeing how well Kobie was keeping up without assistance from any of the adults.

As the path became steeper, her son's steps grew slower, however, and she wished she had the strength to carry him. Running after Gage, who at first seemed to be kidnapping her son, and then struggling against a relentless tide of water, along with the late hour, had sapped her strength. She didn't know how long they had been hiking uphill, but it seemed like hours.

The moon no longer provided much light, and streamers of clouds now blocked much of the light from the stars. Kobie tripped, and Shalise came close to stumbling too as she reached out to steady him. Only then did she realize the path was no longer made of dirt and pine needles but was rocky and jagged around fallen boulders, with steps made of various-sized stones.

At last Trent stopped, and she leaned gratefully against a large boulder. Kobie sat where he'd stopped in the middle of the rocky trail. Forcing herself to move, she sat down beside him and put her arm around him.

"Catch your breaths. This next section is really narrow. It may be slippery too, because there's loose shale in this area. We're almost to the junction where this trail meets the main trail coming up from the staging area," Trent said. "Once we cross this section we'll meet the main trail. It's a little wider, better maintained, and we'll be walking on dirt and pine needles again. We should be able to move faster once we're on it."

Shalise heard several groans. Her mind flashed back to a long-ago camping trip with her grandfather, and she had a sudden suspicion she knew what lay ahead of them. With the flood and the fear, she'd been disoriented, but now she remembered a hike to the reservoir with Grandpa. They'd visited the reservoir numerous times and usually followed the road to the trailhead, then hiked up the maintained trail. But one time Grandpa had suggested a shortcut coming back and had led her across a narrow, rocky ledge to a different path back to camp. That horrible path was the one she was on now! She remembered stopping halfway across the ledge and looking down at the tops of trees and the road like a ribbon far below. Something inside her had frozen, and she'd been unable to move. Her grandfather's voice had seemed far away, and she'd been unable to respond to anything he said as he tried to coax her to keep moving. She wasn't sure how he'd managed to drag her the rest of the way. She only knew she could never cross that ledge again. Panic made her breath come fast. She *couldn't* cross that ledge!

"The trail through this next stretch follows a narrow ledge at the top of a steep, shale slope for about twenty feet." Gage confirmed her fears, then went on. "There's a dangerous drop-off, and the flat, unstable stones provide no hand or toeholds, so we're going to need to be able to see where we're going. My flashlight got wet when I got knocked over back there, so we only have two flashlights . . ."

"My grandpa said my flashlight is waterproof. You can use it." Kobie struggled to his feet and took a step toward Gage.

Cassie turned her light toward the child-size pack still on Gage's back. Gage handed it to Kobie. After a few minutes of searching, the boy triumphantly produced a small flashlight. He clicked it on, and to Shalise's (but not Kobie's) surprise, a beam of light appeared. He thrust the light into Gage's hand.

"All right, Trent will go across first with one flashlight and the rope." Gage was already securing one end of the rope to a large tree. Panic was mounting rapidly in Shalise's chest. The path across the ledge was the only path to safety, but she couldn't set foot on it. During her search and rescue training course she had managed to avoid high places until the instructor began teaching the class to rappel. That was the one part of her training she hadn't completed satisfactorily.

"When Trent gets the rope tied securely on the other side, he'll yell and the rest of us will go across." Directing his instructions to his brother, Gage went on. "Trent, can you set up your flashlight so it shines across the ledge? I'll do the same on this side so everyone can see where to put their feet."

No! Shalise wanted to scream. *I can't cross that ledge. I can't let my baby do it either!*

Trent moved ahead, striding toward the ledge. Gage and Cassie followed him. All three flashlights picked out the narrow trail, then one beam swung out, revealing to Shalise a churning mass of water licking at an almost perpendicular slope. One misstep and there would be no rescue from the nightmare that had invaded the once peaceful canyon.

* * *

Web lifted his head and turned as though that would help him pinpoint the sound. It could have been the cry of an animal trapped by the rising water just as he and the Timmermans were. They'd seen several deer and smaller animals fleeing to higher ground, but he couldn't shake the feeling that the sound he'd heard had been human.

"Did any of you hear anything?" he asked, looking around the circle of dejected figures gathered around the fire he'd built to keep them warm when he discovered they could go no further. A rock slide blocked their way, bringing their limping, complaining trek to a halt.

"You mean, besides all that . . ." Bryan hesitated, "water?" Web knew the expletive the boy was careful to omit. He'd had words earlier with him over his crude language, and he was glad to know the warning had sunk in. He just hoped Bryan's father had gotten the message too.

"Not the water. I've gotten used to that," Web said, rising to his feet. "It sounded like someone shouting."

Chelsea raised her head, listened a moment, then said, "You don't think there's anyone else trapped here, do you?"

"It's possible. Quite a few tent campers and backpackers use this canyon, and I didn't get a chance to check all of the camping areas before the flood reached the trailhead."

"Will they drown?" Rachel asked in a horrified whisper.

"The force of the water wouldn't be as strong farther up the canyon as it was near the trailhead at the mouth, but anyone familiar with this canyon would try to make their way to this trail. It's the only way out, other than the road."

"Which is gone," Wade pointed out with a touch of bitterness, "and this trail goes nowhere." He referred to the slide that now blocked access to the upper third of the trail, implying that their situation was somehow the deputy's fault.

"I'm going to check around." It was probably nothing. The water and the destruction it created made enough noise to make him unsure he'd heard anything significant, but he welcomed an excuse to escape the quarreling, bickering family he'd so recently rescued. Their constant sniping at each other was wearing on his patience.

"You're leaving us here alone?" The woman's voice revealed a hint of hysteria.

"You're safe here," he reassured, trying to allay her fear. "The water won't reach this high, and there's plenty of wood to keep the fire burning until I get back."

"What if a bear comes?" the little girl asked, whose name he'd learned was Rachel.

"It'll take one look at you and run," her brother mocked.

"Bryan, you're coming with me." He didn't know what impulse made him order the boy to accompany him. Perhaps it was only compassion for the little girl who seemed to be the boy's constant target. To his surprise the boy didn't argue, but jumped to his feet and started toward him.

They retraced their steps across a small plateau meadow and hadn't gone far when the path curved in a wide arc toward the south. He remembered the steep, rocky climb that had preceded the curve on the way up. Once around the wide bend he noticed two things. First, the water now lapped at the top of the steep part of the trail. And second, a dim light could be seen off to the left.

"Hey! Look at that!" Bryan had seen the light too.

"I hear more than one voice too." Web felt a rising excitement. He felt personally responsible because he hadn't reached all of the campsites in the canyon before the deluge arrived. He'd certainly feel better if they found other survivors. "The trails join here," Web explained to Bryan as he hurried toward the spot where the two trails met. He wasn't sure what they would find when they reached the light, but he silently thanked Bill Haslam for introducing him to Hidden Canyon earlier in the summer. A little foreknowledge of the terrain made all the difference.

Thick pines blocked the light for several minutes. Then Web, followed by Bryan, stepped out of the trees onto a small, rocky plateau. A shadowy group of people stood a short distance away on the near end of a narrow ledge. Web counted. *Five!* One of which appeared to be a child.

"Come on, Mom. You can do it!" the child called. Alarmed by the child's words, he became aware that the group's attention focused on something beyond them, farther out on the narrowest segment of the ledge. Web narrowed his eyes, attempting to see what they saw. The clouds overhead shifted, allowing the silver crescent moon to add to the flashlights, illuminating the ledge where a woman stood paralyzed.

Web didn't need to see the woman's face to know her eyes were fixed, her ears immune to the sounds around her, and her legs incapable of carrying her one step further. If someone gave her the slightest touch, if her knees gave way, if she lost consciousness, she would fall.

CHAPTER 4

A half-dozen steps and Web was in the middle of the group trying to coax the frightened woman forward. He noticed that although the nylon rope stretched across the ledge was almost waist-high to the woman, she wasn't holding on to it. He gave it a slight tug, assuring himself that it was anchored on the other side. A young man turned startled eyes toward him, then seemed to relax at the sight of his uniform.

"Who is she?" he asked, and the others jumped at the unfamiliar voice.

"She's my mom." The boy who appeared to be about eight or nine was the first to speak. His voice trembled, hinting at tears, and a young woman he estimated to be about Bryan's age put her arms around him. Web heard the girl call the child Kobie and heard her assure the boy that the deputy was the answer to their prayers and that he would help them rescue his mother. He didn't consider himself an answer to anybody's prayer, but he certainly intended to reach that woman and take her off the ledge.

"Her name is Shalise Richards." A small woman, who appeared to be barely out of her teens, stepped closer and volunteered the information. "I don't know what happened. She was really brave until a few minutes ago when she seemed to suddenly go into a trance or something."

"I think she's acrophobic." A taller woman took her eyes off the woman on the ledge for a brief moment, then immediately turned back. "One of us needs to go after her before she loses consciousness or takes a hypnotic step closer to the edge. We've been arguing over who goes and who stays."

"I think I should go because the ledge is narrow and I'm the smallest," the first woman insisted. He noticed she was watching a small ripple of shale sliding down the slope. From the way she sucked in her breath and started toward the woman, he knew she read something in the shifting material that concerned her.

"What if she has to be carried?" This question came from the only male in the group other than little Kobie. The young man stepped in front of the short blonde.

"I'll go." Web unbuckled his tool belt and stepped past both of them. In passing he handed it to the woman who had volunteered to go. "Hang onto this," he instructed, glad that she voiced no protest.

"She doesn't know you. What if you frighten her?" the young man asked, worry clear in his voice.

"I'll do my best not to scare her any more than she already is." Feeling he needed to add more reassurance to the group of young people, he added, "I've dealt with acrophobia before." He remembered another frightening experience when he'd had to go after a newly hired welder on a high-rise construction site back in Detroit where he'd been on the city force before his deputy position in Utah. It had taken both a burly firefighter and him to haul the guy off a steel beam twenty stories high.

"My brother, Gage, is at the other end of this rope," the young man said as he stepped back, allowing Web to pass. "He's moving toward Mrs. Richards right now."

Web looked across the ledge to see a dark shape edging toward the frightened woman. Without hesitation, Web stepped onto the ledge too.

"The stone ledge is shallow. It's supported by a thin layer of soil and is beginning to crumble. The stone is shale, which crumbles easily and tends to be slippery," warned the small woman, who seemed to know an awful lot about geology. She had moved behind him to the edge of the ledge. "Stay as close to the bluff as you can," she instructed in a quiet voice, and he sensed she was far more aware of the danger than any of the other young people.

"Keep the rope taut," he cautioned those behind him as he grasped the nylon length and began the journey.

At first he moved quickly, but as he came closer to the frightened woman, the ledge narrowed and he slowed his steps. Keeping his voice low and unhurried, he began to speak. "Mrs. Richards—Shalise—I'm Deputy Bentley from Orchard Springs. I've come to help you get to the other side where your boy is waiting. Kobie is a fine boy. He's worried about you and wants you to come with him . . ." His voice rumbled on, soothing and coaxing. Normally he wasn't any good at talking to women, but he wasn't thinking of Mrs. Richards as a woman. To him she was only a badly frightened person who needed his help.

The clatter of falling pebbles drew his attention away for a moment and behind the woman he noticed the other man approaching. The man's steps were hesitant, and he seemed to be hugging the wall of rock on one side of him. The two men were but ten feet apart, with the woman between them, when Web saw a chunk of the ledge where the other man had last stepped drop out of sight. The clatter of rock sliding down the slope, gathering other rocks in its mad rush, reached them over the roar of the water. The other man didn't falter, but moved forward with smooth, careful steps as though nothing had happened.

Web was glad the frightened woman was facing him. She hadn't seen what he had seen, nor had the sound broken her trance. Had she been aware of the small rock-and-mud slide that carried away a piece of the ledge she stood on, she might have followed it into the floodwaters below.

There was no time to talk the woman safely through her fear. The rest of the ledge would likely follow the first broken slab within minutes. Web closed the gap in one swift lunge, pulling Mrs. Richards against his side. She was conscious long enough to struggle for just a moment, then collapsed, a deadweight in his arms. There was not room enough to bend and pick her up, so he began to back his way along the trail, dragging her with him.

"Shalise, you're safe now. We have to hurry though." The man who had been approaching from the opposite direction caught up to them. "Kobie needs you," he added.

Web added his own deep voice in an attempt to reassure the woman and gain her cooperation. The ground trembled beneath his feet, and he knew they weren't as safe as the other man had told her. *This whole ledge is going to slide off the mountain any minute!* He shook her slightly, and she obliged by opening her eyes. Seeing the white shimmer of her open eyes was all the incentive he needed to try harder to reach through her shock and gain her cooperation.

"Shalise, I'm going to take one of your hands and your friend will take the other. Then we're going to run." He hoped she understood and would be able to make her legs move. When he lowered her enough to stand and took her hand, she grasped it so tightly her nails cut into his flesh. She understood.

He didn't quite run, but his steps were as close to a lope as the ledge permitted. When they reached the end of the crumbling shelf of dirt and rock, he didn't pause. "Run!" he bellowed at the rest of the group and, without slowing his steps, swept the woman into his arms and raced for the other trail. He heard the man behind him repeat his order. Whether the others obeyed him or the other man, he had no idea, but they were all scrambling to leave the rocky shelf. Reaching the wider trail he paused to look back. The little boy was right behind him, and the dark-haired woman sprinted on his heels, urging him on. Bryan kept pace with the teenage girl and the young man he'd first seen trying to coax Mrs. Richards from the ledge. The second man and the blonde woman ran hand in hand, bringing up the rear.

"Kobie." The woman in his arms made a whimpering sound and struggled to free herself. Web set her on her feet and felt something tight in his chest when the woman reached for her son and the boy threw himself into her arms. Quickly he shut out the memory that attempted to intrude. That was another woman and another little boy. They didn't exist anymore.

When the others stopped beside him, he said, "We're safe here, but I'd like all of you to keep moving a little farther up the trail. There are a few more people about a quarter of a mile from here—Bryan's family." He indicated the teenage boy who accompanied him. The young people nodded their heads and once more began walking. He noticed that the woman he'd handed his tool belt to still carried it slung over one shoulder. Stepping to her side, he lifted it from her shoulder and clasped it back around his waist. Relieved of the weight, she straightened her back and flashed him a smile.

"Thanks for the help," she whispered. "By the way my name is Cassie Breverton, and this is Gage Edwards. I'll introduce you to the rest of these people as soon as we meet up with your group."

Gage clapped him on the shoulder before turning back to Cassie, and Web increased his pace to catch back up to the woman he'd rescued and her little boy.

Shalise saw the flicker of flames coming from a small campfire long before the weary group reached it. She relished the prospect of sinking down beside it with her son cradled in her arms. She was tired, but she suspected emotional turmoil played a greater part in the fatigue that slowed her steps and numbed her mind rather than the late hour and the physical demands of the flight to safety. She suspected she wouldn't have made it this far without the occasional supporting arm of the deputy who had dragged her off the ledge. She tried to thank him, but that seemed to make him uncomfortable.

She noticed two shapes huddled on opposite sides of the fire. Then as she drew nearer, she could tell one shadow was actually two people, a woman and a child. All three people remained seated, but turned their attention toward their group as they filed into the firelight. The big deputy waved his arm toward the log where the woman and child sat and indicated Shalise should sit too. Gratefully, she sank to the rough surface, and Kobie snuggled beside her.

Cassie launched into introductions while the deputy and the two brothers added wood to the fire. She briefly outlined their flight along the mountain trail, and Shalise shuddered, remembering the water that had carried her away from her son, then the ledge she'd tried to cross.

"All of us except Bryan were asleep when Deputy Bentley pounded on the door of our RV," said the woman who was seated farther along the log. She didn't raise her voice and appeared to be careful not to wake the little girl who slept at her side. The child looked a little younger than Kobie. "The path we followed was steep, and in many places we did more climbing than hiking. All I could think about was how badly my feet hurt. It wasn't until I looked back and saw the first wave of water lift the deputy's police car, then topple both it and our RV, that I understood how great the danger was. I can't bear to think about what would have happened if we'd still been in our RV. We owe our lives to Deputy Bentley," she concluded before introducing herself and her family.

Gage said something about scouting for more wood, then he and Trent left with one of the flashlights. The teenage boy, Bryan, Shalise thought the deputy had called him, jumped to his feet and followed. She watched until the darkness swallowed them up and she could only see their bobbing light growing smaller. Her arm tightened around Kobie, whose head had slipped sideways until it lay in her lap. She owed both his life and her own to Gage, the deputy, and perhaps to the whole group of young people. How could she ever thank them for risking their own safety to come after Kobie and her, strangers they'd only glimpsed passing on the road?

Deputy Bentley crouched down to say something to the woman sitting at the other end of the log. Shalise couldn't hear the words, but she saw the woman nod. Flames in the nearby fire ring leaped higher as one of the new logs caught fire, illuminating his face. It was a good face, not as handsome as Daniel's, but there was something comforting in the craggy features and the thick shock of hair that defied repeated sweeps of the man's large hands, falling across his forehead and not quite reaching his eyes. Something about the tired droop of his broad shoulders, coupled with the gentle cadence of words she couldn't hear, brought a wave of emotion rushing through her exhaustion.

Her hand strayed to her son's hair, stroking it in a way he wouldn't allow if he were awake. He'd been brave tonight, and she was proud of him, but she feared she'd let him down. A bubble rose in her throat, and the backs of her eyes stung. She struggled not to make a sound as the feeling overwhelmed her. What had happened? Not just tonight, but to all her tidy little world? Her husband didn't love her. She knew now he never had. They'd been completely wrong for each other. Why hadn't she known that? She'd lost everything she possessed of any value—except their son and her grandparents' old farmhouse. But even those seemed to hang in the balance. Her attorney told her just last week that Daniel had filed another suit to claim the house, and tonight she'd almost lost her son.

Her mind drifted to the young man who had snatched her from harm tonight. Gage Edwards was likely only a few years younger than

Daniel had been when they'd married, yet Gage's actions tonight had proved his maturity far beyond what her former husband had achieved. Huddled on a log, surrounded by darkness, she saw her marriage as she'd never seen it before. Once again she watched the firelight play on the face of the deputy who had also rescued her from the nightmare that had held her rooted to a crumbling ledge. For some reason her mind shied away from thinking too much about him. He was too real, too large, too . . . her mind stumbled at a word that wouldn't fully form in her mind.

Forcing her thoughts to other things, she focused on the man seated on another log on the opposite side of the fire. She wondered if he were ill and why he wasn't sitting beside his wife and daughter. She couldn't recall that Bryan had even spoken to him before he'd followed the Edwards brothers to search for wood.

Wade glared at the fire. Through the jumping flames he could see the deputy kneeling beside Chelsea. *She is probably gushing about the big ox being a hero or some such rot. I'm the one who dragged the stupid woman out of the RV. Although maybe I'm the stupid one. I should have left her there. Then there wouldn't be all this hassle about the divorce, and I wouldn't have to worry about how much of my hard-earned money some idiot judge is going to let her get away with.* A flicker of conscience chided him for his thoughts. He didn't want Chelsea to die. *Besides,* his thoughts turned wry, *if she were dead, she'd still manage to hold me back, since then I'd be stuck with Bryan and Rachel.*

Cassie wished she'd gone with Gage to find wood. Though exhausted, she still felt a restless energy that wouldn't let her sleep the way her sister and Diane were doing, sprawled on the sparse grass with both Cassie's and the little boy's backpacks for pillows. Her eyes sought out the other refugees gathered around the fire. The man seated a few feet away on a rotting log seemed detached from his family. Shalise and little Kobie huddled together, probably for both comfort and warmth. Deputy Bentley seemed to be examining Mrs. Timmerman's feet.

Of course! If the deputy had awakened the family to warn them of the coming flood, they hadn't had time to dress. Instead of the strong hiking boots she and her friends wore, Chelsea Timmerman was barefoot!

"Diane!" She nudged her friend, who moaned sleepily. "I need the first-aid kit."

"Okay," Diane lifted her head to mumble, then flopped back down on the pack. Cassie looked at her friend and sighed. Before she could shake Diane's shoulder again, Emily spoke.

"Let her sleep. That's Kobie's pack she's using for a pillow anyway. Here's yours." She thrust the nylon pack toward her sister.

"I just need the first-aid kit, then you can have it back."

"No thanks. Even though I'm too tired to take another step, I can't sleep. I wish Trent and Gage would come back."

"They'll be here any minute," Cassie whispered back to Emily. "They've been gone less than half an hour." She chose not to admit that she, too, was casting frequent glances toward the spot where the brothers and Bryan had disappeared into the dark. Picking up the pack, she walked around the fire to where the deputy now stood beside Mrs. Timmerman.

"I have a first-aid kit." She rummaged in the pack a moment, then triumphantly held up a small, square plastic box. The deputy took it from her hand, opened it, and turned toward the light coming from the fire to stare at the contents for a moment before selecting a small tube of antiseptic.

"We have a larger kit in the SUV . . ." She paused. "I guess the appropriate term would be *had.*"

"This will do," the deputy said. "Do you think you could find a roll of gauze and some tape in there?"

"Sure." Cassie picked up the box and began searching.

"We had a first-aid kit in our motor home too . . . along with shoes and jackets . . . and other things." Mrs. Timmerman stared at her left hand. Cassie noticed there were no rings on the hand and wondered if the woman's wedding ring had been left behind in the RV.

Cassie noticed the woman was shivering in the cold mountain air and very near tears. She was wearing thin satin pajamas, and Cassie suspected she'd been wearing the robe that was now wrapped around the little girl curled in her lap.

"That's the best I can do." Deputy Bentley rose to his feet.

"Thank you," the woman whispered.

"What about your children and your husband? Are their feet injured, too?" Cassie asked. The small amount of antibiotic cream and bandages wouldn't go far, but she'd share what she had as long as it lasted.

"Deputy Bentley carried Rachel most of the way," Mrs. Timmerman explained. "Bryan was still up. Wade was tired from driving so far. The moment he sat on his bed he fell asleep without undressing."

"I think there's a dry pair of socks in my bag," Cassie offered. "They'll help to keep your bandages clean and your feet warm." She began digging through the bag again and once more was successful in her search. "I'll put these on your feet." She knelt down. "That way you won't have to disturb your daughter."

"Thank you. You've been so kind."

"I'm just glad I grabbed my pack as Gage rushed me out of the tent, Mrs. Timmerman," Cassie chuckled.

"I am too, and please call me Chelsea."

"All right, Chelsea." Cassie smiled at the woman, then added, "Try to get some sleep."

"I don't think I can sleep until Bryan returns," Chelsea said with a glance over her shoulder. "Oh, I think they're coming."

Cassie turned to see three shapes emerge from the forest. Her heart lightened as she recognized Gage in the lead, burdened with an armful of small logs. She stood and walked toward them to help. In minutes the wood was piled near the fire, and two of the larger pieces were added to the blaze.

"Bryan, are you all right?" Chelsea asked.

"Sure," the boy answered, and Cassie thought she detected a hint of pride in that one word. She suspected Bryan was enjoying this adventure, maybe even learning something about himself.

"You three better stand close to the fire for a few minutes, then see if you can get some sleep." Web took the last chunk of wood from Bryan's arms. Cassie noted the way the young man shook his arms, as though they had been cramped by the weight he'd carried, before he turned with outstretched hands toward the fire. He probably didn't undertake tasks like carrying wood often, but she admired his eagerness to help.

"Uh-hum," Gage cleared his throat, and Shalise turned her head to see him standing with his back to the fire. "Trent and I have been talking and we feel the Lord has blessed us a great deal tonight. We'd like to thank Him for making it possible for all of us to escape the flood and that none of us were seriously injured. If any of you would like to join us, we'd welcome your presence."

Cassie stepped up beside the brothers, and after a few seconds Emily and Diane joined them. With her arm around her sleepy son, Shalise stepped toward the small group. The deputy was already standing near Gage, and though he didn't say anything, he stayed where he was.

"I'd like to be included." Chelsea didn't raise her voice or stand. The deputy backed up a step, as though widening the circle to include the woman and her sleeping child. Bryan looked uncertain, then moved a step closer to Trent.

Cassie couldn't resist a look at the teenager's father. Unlike his wife, Mr. Timmerman hadn't said a word when the boy returned, and he made no move to join their group.

Gage's prayer was brief, but his expression of gratitude touched Cassie's heart. She, too, felt overwhelming gratitude for their survival and safety. Gage's simple prayer seemed to echo her own tender emotions, bringing her a sense of spiritual closeness both to her Heavenly Father and to the small group of survivors gathered around the fire.

After the last amen faded away, she stood still, savoring the spiritual feeling that seemed to linger within the ring of light created by the fire. When she glanced up she noticed that Trent had joined her sister and Diane near the log where they had dozed earlier. The two girls were now seated on either side of him with their backs against the same log Wade still sat on. On the other side of the fire she watched Bryan help his mother to the ground where she could take advantage of the log as a backrest, rather than use it as a seat. He was surprisingly careful not to disturb the sleeping child in his mother's arms. A few feet away Deputy Bentley lifted the now sleeping Kobie from Shalise's arms and urged her to settle more comfortably against the log too. When she was in place, he didn't return the child, but sat beside her, still holding Kobie. It might have been the flickering light from the fire, but she thought she saw a tender, yet sad expression on the big man's face.

"That just leaves us." She turned to see Gage standing beside her.

"I guess so." She wondered if she should try to get comfortable beside her sister. Gage settled the question by placing an arm around her shoulder and leading her to where their siblings and Diane huddled together. He sat down next to Emily, then indicated Cassie should sit in front of him between his knees. She did as he asked and soon found herself leaning back against his chest. She should have felt awkward—she'd known Gage less than twelve hours, and she had always been slow to warm up to strangers, especially men. Funny, she didn't feel as though they had just met. The steady beat of Gage's heart transcended her thoughts. She turned her head, pressing her cheek closer to the steady beat. With his arms driving away the chilly night air, Cassie finally slept.

* * *

Gage woke with a start. Without moving, he surveyed the small clearing. The sun wasn't up yet, but already it cast enough light to chase away the dark night. He didn't see anything amiss, but he noticed the fire needed another log. As he began to rise to feed the fire, he became conscious of the weight against his chest. He looked down at the top of Cassie's head. He could hear her steady breathing and knew she was still asleep. Adding a log to the fire could wait—he didn't want to wake her. Warmth filled him as he watched her sleep. She was really something. He'd never met a woman like Cassie Breverton before.

His mind went back to the previous night's desperate climb to safety, and he acknowledged that all three young women had shown incredible courage. But Cassie had gone beyond courage to thinking, planning, and leading the others. He glanced down once more, catching sight of the curve of her cheek, and admitted he found her extremely easy on the eyes too. *What about Jena?* The thought intruded, shattering the simple pleasure he'd taken from holding Cassie through the night. Guilt stiffened his arms, and they fell away from the woman curled against him. Instinct told him he was being watched, and as he turned his head his eyes met his brother's.

Trent didn't say anything, but Gage knew he, too, was thinking of Jena, probably wondering as he was how Gage had ended up smiling with pleasure at waking up with Cassie in his arms when he was supposed to be in love with Jena.

* * *

Web awoke, straining to hear. Something had awakened him. The sound came again, and he recognized the drone of a small aircraft engine. He nodded in satisfaction. He'd expected the search to begin at dawn. He was glad Sheriff Howard hadn't waited for morning, though a glance at the sky told him dawn wasn't far away. The plane was drawing closer, which should have been his cue to build up the fire. He looked toward the dying embers, then at the woman and child huddled next to him for warmth. Unexpected peace filled him with a warmth he wanted to hold onto and think about. But the fire needed attention if they hoped to be rescued. With elaborate care, he eased Shalise back against the log and settled the little boy's head in her lap before standing.

Once on his feet Web stepped rapidly toward the pile of wood. He was joined almost immediately by Gage and seconds later by Cassie, who both seemed to be aware of the significance of the approaching plane. They didn't waste time on greetings, but set to work like a practiced team, fanning the fire into a dancing blaze that shot skyward. Just in case, Web tossed a green branch onto the fire, sending a plume of smoke higher than the flames.

As the droning sound drew nearer, he paused to scan the sky. When the plane was almost directly overhead a wing dipped letting him know they'd been seen. A chorus of cheers went up from the young people who were all on their feet looking upward now. They'd seen the signal too.

"Yes!" Bryan punched a fist into the air, then looked around. "Now what?" he asked. There was no mistaking the excitement in his voice. His hair was standing in peaks, and his clothes were wrinkled and dirty, but there was something in his face that, at the moment, made him look not much older than Kobie. "There's no place for a plane to land. Does that mean they'll send a chopper now?"

"Most likely," Web answered. "But it could be awhile."

"It went away!" Rachel began to cry. "I want to go home."

"It's okay." Kobie walked over to the little girl. "My mom said it's just checking to see if there are other people who need help. The pilot will radio search and rescue teams to let them know where to go and who needs help the most."

"That's right," Web said aloud while inside his opinion of Shalise climbed another notch. She was a good mother. He liked the respectful way she explained what was happening to her son.

"I want them to come get us right now." The little girl drew her mouth down in a pout. "I'm all dirty and hungry. I'm cold too."

"Poor little princess," her brother mocked.

"I've got something you can eat." Kobie's smile brightened before he dashed across the small clearing to retrieve his backpack.

"Just how long are we going to be stuck here?" Wade demanded. He took a step toward the others who were gathered around the fire, then coughed as a wave of thick smoke hit him. "I have important business in Chicago."

"Oh yeah, real important," Bryan sneered. "You're just afraid your girlfriend might find someone else before you get back."

"Bryan!" Chelsea spoke in a warning voice. Wade took a step toward his son, his fists clenched and fury showing on his face. Web shifted his weight, prepared to intercede should Wade attempt to strike his son.

"Look! M&Ms!" Kobie stepped between the combatants, waving a large package of the candy-coated chocolate pieces over his head, oblivious to the confrontation between Bryan and Wade. He hurried to Rachel's side. "My grandma gave them to me, but you can have some."

"Perhaps you can share with everyone," Shalise said. "I think we're all hungry."

"And thirsty," Emily added. "Don't you think it's ironic that we spent all that time and effort escaping water, and now we don't have any to drink?"

"Actually we do." It was Cassie's turn to retrieve her backpack. From its depths she produced a plastic bottle of water and three granola bars, which she quartered and passed around. The tiny squares of breakfast bars and a handful of candy were soon washed down with a squirt of water from the plastic bottle.

Web listened for more planes as he munched on his share of the meager rations. Occasionally he caught the drone of the small plane that had flown over earlier, but it seemed to be concentrating its attention on the other side of the main canyon. He wished he could communicate with the sheriff or the pilot of that plane, but his radio and supplies had been left behind in his cruiser. He wouldn't even have been able to light a fire last night if Bryan hadn't slipped him a cigarette lighter when his mother wasn't looking.

Gage walked up beside him. "How bad is the slide?" the younger man asked. Web knew he was referring to the slide blocking the trail out of the canyon.

"There's no way we can cross it."

"And there's no way a chopper can set down here." Gage answered back, gesturing at the small clearing where they sat dwarfed by towering pines.

"By now the water will have receded a great deal, but it will be days before we'll be able to walk out." Gage hadn't heard Cassie approach, but he nodded his head at her words, acknowledging that her judgment was correct.

"That means we've got to find a spot where the rescuers can reach us." Gage stared thoughtfully at the steep mountain towering above them. "There is a place . . ." Gage paused and Web turned to him, anxious to hear what he might suggest that could possibly lead them out of this nightmare.

CHAPTER 5

Shalise sat beside Chelsea Timmerman on one of the logs near the fire pit. They changed position each time a fickle breeze shifted the plume of smoke that was all that was left of their campfire. The sun was high enough now that the fire was no longer needed for warmth, but they were keeping a small blaze burning with enough green wood and grass on it to keep a steady stream of smoke in the air pinpointing their position.

They watched Kobie and Rachel play a short distance away. The children had accumulated a pile of pinecones and pebbles and were constructing some elaborate design in the dirt with them. They watched as Kobie fished a couple of M&Ms out of his pocket and offered them to Rachel.

"Your son has a kind nature," Chelsea admired, a note of wistfulness in her voice. "Bryan used to be like that, but once he became a teenager, he changed so much I hardly know him anymore."

"He's still a fine boy," Shalise assured the other woman. "He and Trent have done a great job of keeping us supplied with wood."

"How long do you think it will be before Gage and the deputy return?" Chelsea looked toward the opening in the trees where the two men had disappeared more than an hour ago.

"I don't know," Shalise admitted. "I think they're looking for a place where a helicopter could land."

"Do you think it's a good idea for us to be scattered all over?" Chelsea waved her hand in a vague gesture encompassing the whole canyon. Shalise knew Chelsea wasn't accustomed to roughing it, and being stranded on a mountainside was making her nervous. With

Gage and Deputy Bentley away searching for a place where they might be rescued, Trent and Bryan gathering wood, and the three young women on a berry-hunting expedition, their party did seem scattered, though there wasn't a great distance any of them could travel.

"Don't worry," Shalise attempted to reassure her. "If a helicopter shows up, they'll all hear it and come running. None of them are far away. Caught as we are between a flood and a rock slide, there's nowhere for them to go."

"I suppose you're right, but wouldn't we be safer if we all stayed together?"

"Oh, we're perfectly safe." Shalise reached for Chelsea's hand and gave it a squeeze. "The water is receding, and there's no danger of a mud slide here. I camped in this canyon when I was a young girl with my grandparents, and my son comes here often with his grandfather. I've never once seen a bear or a mountain lion around here." Even as she made light of the possibility of unwelcome wildlife, she wondered why Chelsea's husband wasn't the one trying to bolster her courage. She hadn't seen the couple exchange two words since she'd met them. She looked across the small clearing to where Wade Timmerman sat dissolutely stirring the fire with a stick.

"We're getting a divorce as soon as we get back to Chicago," Chelsea explained in a whisper. There was a catch in her voice. "Wade has found someone else, and I don't know what I'm going to do. I've never worked, and I don't know anything about our finances. I suppose we can live with my parents, but Daddy and Bryan don't get along."

"I'm sorry about the divorce," Shalise told her. "My husband filed for divorce just before last Christmas. He and his girlfriend got married a few days ago, and that's why I'm here. He promised earlier to take Kobie camping this weekend, and Kobie was so upset by his father's plans for remarriage, I thought it would be good for the both of us to go ahead with the camping trip on our own."

"Both my parents and Wade's insisted we take a last vacation together with the kids to see if we could work out our problems." She wiped away a tear. "It's been awful. Wade hasn't wanted to stop anywhere, and he's been grumpy and critical with the kids. They got so bored riding in the RV for two weeks with nothing to do that they started deliberately antagonizing him. They know just which buttons to push to set him off, but he doesn't have a clue how to deal with them."

"That sounds like Daniel," Shalise said with a bitter laugh. "He wouldn't exactly win any father-of-the-year awards either."

"Wade hasn't spent much time around our children before, and I don't think he knows how to talk to them or what they're interested in. He's put so much effort into his career, working long hours and weekends so we'd have everything we need, there haven't been many opportunities for him to get to know them." Chelsea seemed to be making excuses for her husband's lack of parenting skills. "When Rachel was two, we bought a house near our parents', which is about two hours from Wade's work. He has that long commute each day, so I thought I was helping him to have the kids fed and in bed before he got home every evening. I wanted to give him a chance to relax for a little while after his long day, but now I think I was wrong. Our marriage, our whole family, would have had a better chance if I'd let him be with the kids after he got home."

"You know what they say about hindsight." Shalise was silent for several minutes, then resumed the conversation. "Money was always our problem. I had a small inheritance from my grandparents and a trust fund my parents left me, and I almost always earned more money than my husband did since he seldom stayed with a job more than a few months. At first I naively handed over control of our finances to him, but after he spent almost all of the money I'd inherited by the time Kobie was born, I started getting more involved and at least controlled my own earnings. I was still caught unprepared during the division-of-assets part of our divorce proceedings to discover Daniel had emptied our savings, spent my inheritance, and sold assets I thought were mine—and there was nothing I could do about it. He's still trying to force me to sell my grandparents' house and acreage, claiming he's entitled to half of it."

"Do you think he'll win?" Chelsea looked worried.

"No, I don't, but only because my friend Dallas insisted I hire a really good attorney. And that's what you should do too."

"It's just so unfair." Chelsea's shoulders shook, and she wiped at her eyes. "I really tried to be a good wife."

"I did too, but I discovered I couldn't make our marriage work by myself. You not only need the best attorney in town to make certain you and your children are not shortchanged, but you need counseling too. I don't know what I would have done without my bishop to talk to when it all seemed too overwhelming." When Chelsea looked puzzled, Shalise explained. "A bishop is like a pastor, only my bishop isn't just my spiritual leader. He's also the president of the local search and rescue training unit. He might even be in that search plane we saw earlier, though he isn't a pilot and usually heads up a ground search and recovery unit. He enrolled my friend Dallas and me in his training program, and I think the rigorous training and his quiet counsel saved my sanity. It might have saved my life last night too, because without the training I wouldn't have been in condition to run or climb such great distances."

"I don't have a pastor," Chelsea said. "We've never gone to church. I used to go to Sunday School when I was a little girl, but Wade wasn't interested after we got married, and I never wanted to go alone. Our parents tried to get us to go to a marriage counselor, but Wade refused."

"Your attorney might recommend someone, or you could go to your parents' pastor," Shalise suggested. "If you think you might be interested in learning more about my church, I could arrange for someone to teach you what we believe."

"You belong to the same church as the young people who rescued you and your son, don't you?"

"Yes, we're all members of the Church of Jesus Christ of Latter-day Saints. You've probably heard us referred to as Mormons."

"I don't know much about your church, but I've seen your temple, which is a few miles from our home. And last summer there were quite a few stories in the newspaper about a new temple in Nauvoo. I remember reading something about Mormons believing that if a couple is married in one of those temples, their marriage is forever." Chelsea picked up a twig, twisting it between her fingers as she talked. She didn't look at Shalise, but Shalise heard the implied question.

"You're right. We do believe that God means for our marriages to last forever and that the family unit will endure even after we die. That is part of what made my divorce so difficult for me and Kobie. We want to be part of an eternal family, but we also believe God doesn't force anyone to do anything they don't want to do. Daniel had the right to choose whether or not he would honor the commitment he made to us, and he chose not to. That still hurts."

Wade pretended to pay no attention to the other people around him, but he watched Chelsea through narrowed eyes. She and the little boy's mother seemed to be finding plenty to talk about. He noticed the way the other woman glanced at him from time to time and surmised that they were talking about him. Chelsea was probably complaining, though a twinge of conscience made him admit he hadn't heard any complaints from her since they left the RV. He hadn't even noticed that she'd made the climb without any kind of footwear until the little blonde and the deputy started to bandage her cut and bruised feet. That was another thing that confused him. Getting a divorce was his idea, so why should he resent another man paying attention to Chelsea? He supposed it was because they weren't divorced yet, and she was still his wife.

Thinking of the deputy brought a scowl to Wade's face. Just because he'd warned Wade's family about the flood danger was no reason for him to set himself up as the one in charge. That bunch of kids that had been farther up the canyon had been doing fine without him, but they all acted like the deputy was Mr. Wonderful as soon as he showed up. *Even Bryan jumps to do whatever the deputy tells him to do—like scrounge for wood or stop teasing his sister. I'd bet fifty bucks Bryan would have just mouthed off if I'd sent him to do any kind of work.*

His attention shifted to the two children playing in the dirt, and he felt another stab of conscience. He should have been the one to carry Rachel to safety last night. He had noticed her bare feet when Bentley swept her up. He had to admit, too, that he'd been surprised by the distance Bryan had carried her considering the way the two fought over everything. At least he'd been the one to get Chelsea out of the RV and up the mountain far enough to escape that first rush of water, for which she hadn't bothered to thank him.

For a moment he wondered why Shalise and her son had been camping alone. He'd understood enough from the conversation going on around him last night to know they hadn't been camping with the others. Evidently she was a single mother and didn't have much choice if the kid had wanted to go camping. *Chelsea will soon be a single mother. Well, sure, but that will be different.* If Bryan or Rachel needed anything or wanted to go camping, he'd still be there for them. *You've never taken Bryan camping. You've never even watched one of his soccer games.*

Wade stood abruptly. Waiting around for someone to rescue them was driving him nuts. He needed to be doing something. Trying to appear casual, he strolled over to where the two children were playing. He frowned at the sight of Rachel covered with dirt from using her small hand to scrape a groove in the dust. Chelsea should watch her better, keep her out of the dirt.

It took a few minutes for their game to make sense. They'd built a village with stones for houses, pinecones for cars, and sticks for people. He bent over to pick up a flat rock, then brushing aside a pile of grass, he knelt beside his daughter. He'd show her how to align the streets by using the rock instead of her hand to scrape roads in the dirt.

"Daddy!" Rachel wailed. "You're messing everything up. You took the school and you're smashing the park!"

He realized too late he wasn't kneeling on just a random pile of grass, and the large rock he held was part of the children's game, too. His first impulse was to toss the rock on the ground and tell Rachel she shouldn't be playing in the dirt, but something made him hesitate. Dirt and rocks were all the kids had to play with. If he forbade Rachel to play anymore, she'd whine and fuss as she'd been doing for the past two weeks. Slowly he replaced the rock and rose to his feet.

Standing uncertainly beside his daughter, he didn't know what to say. Then he realized that he hadn't known what to say to Rachel for some time. He really didn't know when she'd changed from the adorable little imp who crawled into his lap each night with a storybook or begged for one more horsey ride before going to bed.

"It's okay," the little boy said. "You didn't hurt anything. It won't take long to make a new park." He was already at work spreading out the grass and replacing pebbles Wade hadn't previously noticed in one corner of the "park" to form a baseball diamond.

"There should be swings," Rachel pointed out, surveying the park from a critical angle.

"I'll see what I can do," Wade said. Rachel ignored his comment, but her lack of enthusiasm didn't deter his. If he could find twigs that branched at the right angle . . . He stepped toward a bush that grew a short distance away.

Chelsea watched her husband break off several small branches from a plant growing at the edge of the small clearing where they waited. She knew he was bored. Wade had never been one to sit around and do nothing. *This wait must be driving him crazy.* Once they would have found something to do together, but now they no longer even talked to each other. He'd only be irritated if she walked over there and asked him what he was doing. She turned back to Shalise.

Shalise was probably ten years her junior, but she felt a rapport with the younger woman she hadn't felt with anyone in a long time. She felt a pang of regret. When had Wade ceased being her best friend?

A shout interrupted her conversation with Shalise. Turning her head, she saw her son and his new friends emerge from the trees north of their makeshift camp. Bryan was walking beside Emily, and they appeared to be arguing. But it wasn't the angry, insulting exchange of words she'd grown accustomed to between her son and his father. His face was animated, and he appeared to be on the verge of bursting into laughter. Gone was the sullen, defensive boy who resented her questions concerning the friends he hung out with after school and who had goaded his father unmercifully for the past two weeks.

The younger Edwards boy led the way, his arms piled high with tree limbs. He spoke over his shoulder to Emily, who laughed, her voice ringing with gaiety in the mountain air. Chelsea watched him dump the wood he carried beside the fire, then turn to help Emily unload the stack she carried. Bryan let go of the small logs in his arms, then shouted, "Lookout," as they rolled and bounced on the ground. The other two girls, who had brought up the rear, crouched to release their loads as well.

"I can't move my arms." Emily stood with empty arms, curved as though still holding the load of wood she had carried. Bryan whooped with laughter, and Chelsea felt a pang in her heart. How long had it been since she'd heard her son laugh?

She glanced toward Wade and was startled to see him sitting in the dirt beside the two smaller children. He held something in his hands, which he passed to Rachel. All three seemed to be deeply absorbed in their activity. Rachel carefully set the object on the ground, then turned a beaming smile toward her father. Chelsea couldn't see Wade's face, but she noticed the way he straightened his shoulders. It wasn't the defensive posture she'd seen so many times in the last few weeks, but more a signal that he was proud in some way. She had a sudden urge to bundle up this group of young people and take them back to Chicago with her.

* * *

Something prompted Cassie to look toward the hiking trail, which she knew from checking it out earlier herself, ended a short distance from their camp in a jumble of rocks. Gage stepped into sight with Web right behind him. Gage was smiling, and his eyes seemed to focus on her before going on to the rest of their group. A sense of well-being filled her heart. She forgot her disheveled hair, hunger pains, and accumulation of concerns.

"It will be a challenge, but we can make it," Deputy Bentley said as he and Gage joined the group, now all gathered together in the small clearing. "We can get around the slide far enough to reach a small side trail. Gage and Trent are familiar with it—they've been camping here since they were small boys. It's steep, but it will take us to a high meadow where a helicopter can land."

"It's been a long time since we were up there, and it's not a maintained trail, so it could be quite different from what I remember. But this end of the trail looks good," Gage added.

"I remember," Trent put in, excitement in his voice. "You're talking about the place where we found snow still blocking the trail from the previous winter."

"Snow!" Chelsea glanced toward her daughter.

"I doubt we'll find any snow now, Mrs. Timmerman," Gage attempted to reassure her. "That trip was in June five years ago, and the snow was actually the last remnants of an avalanche from the previous winter."

"I can carry Rachel." It was the first time Cassie had heard Wade speak directly to his wife.

"The route we'll take is over some extremely rocky terrain," Web spoke again. "Fortunately most of us have shoes or boots of some kind." He turned to Cassie and asked, "Do you have enough bandages in your first-aid kit to improvise shoes for Mrs. Timmerman?"

"I think so," Cassie responded. "I have a couple pairs of thick socks that should help too."

"Rachel can wear my wading shoes," Kobie spoke up.

"That's right." Shalise turned to Chelsea. "Kobie has an old pair of tennis shoes in his pack. He brought them so he could play in the creek near our camp."

"I forgot to put them on before I waded in the water." He turned apologetic eyes toward his mother.

"It's all right. There wasn't time." She hugged her son until he squirmed in embarrassment.

"Will the search party know where we've gone?" Wade asked with an upward glance.

"Yes," Web told him. "They will be expecting us to look for a level place where they can land."

"We'll build another fire too, once we get there," Gage added.

Chelsea sat on one of the fallen logs while Cassie and Diane wrapped gauze around her feet. After they finished, they handed her two pairs of socks to pull over the bandages. When she stood she realized her feet wouldn't be as protected as they would have been in shoes, but she could walk quite comfortably. Hearing her daughter giggle, she turned to see Rachel take a few steps in Kobie's wading shoes.

"Come here," Web said, picking Rachel up and setting her on a large rock where he proceeded to pull the shoes off her feet. Using the last of the supplies from Cassie's medical kit, he stuffed the toes of the shoes with cotton and wound gauze around her feet to fashion loose socks. When he finished, he fastened the shoes back on her and stood her on the ground. Taking a tentative step, she smiled before scampering over to the pretend village she and Kobie had built.

"What else is in those packs?" Trent asked.

Kobie picked up his and dumped the contents on the ground. Trent smiled to see the treasures the little boy had carried halfway up the mountain. There was his flashlight, a comic book, two long red licorice sticks, a bright yellow jar of power bait, a whistle, and a collapsible cup.

Cassie's pack was now empty. Except for the few remaining items in the first-aid kit, her meager supplies were gone. Her flashlight, along with Trent's rope, had been abandoned back where they'd crossed the ledge. When it collapsed behind them, there was no way to recover the flashlight or untie the rope from the far side of the broken path.

Since Cassie and Kobie were the only ones with packs, it didn't take long to gather them up, put out their fire, and begin their hike. Gage took the lead this time with Cassie beside him and the others strung out behind. Trent brought up the rear. Both Bryan and Emily walked beside him until the trail narrowed and he stepped back to let them walk single file in front of him. Chelsea took up a position behind the smaller children, taking care to watch carefully where she placed her feet. Though the heavy socks and bandages helped, she knew she needed to take care to avoid stepping on anything sharp.

"It gets tricky here." Gage's voice floated back to her. She looked up to see a jumble of rocks blocking the trail. Raising her head higher, she shuddered at the sight of the broken mountainside.

"We won't attempt to cross the slide," Gage shouted. "If we follow beside it for a short distance, we'll come to a place where we can climb to another ridge and leave it behind."

"It seems foolish to leave where the rescue teams have already spotted us," Wade grumbled. Chelsea was surprised to discover he was beside her. She made her steps firmer, not wanting him to ridicule her or accuse her of holding them back.

"He and the deputy seem to know what they're doing." She ventured a tentative statement. Almost holding her breath, she waited for Wade to ridicule her faith in the men who had become their leaders. Instead, he reached forward to steady Rachel who was slipping on loose rocks as she struggled in her awkward shoes to keep up with Kobie.

"Look out!" Wade grabbed her arm, bringing her to a stop before her foot came down between two sharp stones.

"Thanks, Daddy!" Rachel flashed a hurried smile toward her father. Wade looked stunned. Chelsea wasn't certain whether it was the smile that surprised him or if it was the small courtesy of being thanked after two weeks of continuous complaints and insults.

"Maybe you better hold onto my hand," he offered. Rachel looked at his hand as though tempted, then back at Kobie.

"I think I better help my mom," Kobie whispered. "Now that my dad doesn't live with us anymore, she gets scared sometimes." He hurried forward to take his mother's hand. Shalise exchanged a smile with her son, and the two moved forward together.

Seeing her new friend leave her behind, Rachel looked disappointed for a moment, then reached up to place her hand in Wade's. After a couple of steps, she extended her other hand to her mother.

Gage led the group down one side of the jumble of rocks into a narrow ravine, then back up the opposite side. Leaving the slide behind, he led them along its edge, at the same time gradually climbing higher. Occasionally he glanced behind him, assuring himself that they were staying together.

A brisk breeze kicked up a small dust devil, and he noticed the air was growing cooler. A hush hung over the forest as though the birds and squirrels had retreated from the surrounding area or were hunkering down in their nests and burrows. Being a rancher, he'd long ago learned to look to the sky for answers. Just as he suspected, a black storm front was pushing over the canyon from the north. A distant roll of thunder urged him to push forward with greater speed. "Mrs. Timmerman is limping severely," Web said in a low voice, catching up to him. "Her husband is carrying their little girl and isn't in a position to be much help to her. I think I'll drift back and see if I can help her."

"What about Shalise? Is she managing all right?" Gage took his eyes from the trail that wound through a narrow gorge to glance behind him.

"Yes, I don't think you have to worry about her. She seems pretty tough, and her son is keeping up fine. He even tries to help her through the rougher patches." Gage detected a hint of admiration for the pair in the older man's voice.

The next time he looked back, he noticed the big deputy was carrying Chelsea Timmerman on his back. Her husband looked red-faced and grim. Gage wondered whether Wade was frustrated, maybe even a little jealous that another man was carrying his wife, or just exhausted from their rapid hike with seven-year-old Rachel on his own back. Gage suspected Wade wasn't accustomed to the kind of strenuous activity the flood had forced on him. He and Trent could take turns carrying the little girl, but he suspected Web was the only man in their group capable of carrying her mother for any great distance. Trent stepped forward and said something to Wade, but when Wade shook his head, Trent stepped back beside Bryan and Emily.

It would soon be raining. Gage could taste the difference in the air. The wind had picked up too, adding to their labor as they pushed their way along a game trail that emerged at the top of the cleft in thick brush and trees. He began avoiding those stretches that might leave them exposed to lightning along the ridge line or under the taller trees.

Above the rush of wind and the loud claps of thunder, the beat of rotors reached his ears. Everyone stopped to stare when the rescue helicopter swooped overhead, and Gage pointed in front of him, hoping the pilot would understand. Seeing the chopper lent them all new energy, and they picked up their pace.

Wind whipped over the ridge with the ferocity that Gage had often seen precede a storm in the mountains. Tree branches twisted, and the first splatters of rain kicked up dust as they hit the ground in front of them. They were less than a quarter of a mile from the meadow now, but he knew they were too late. The storm was upon them, and it would prevent the helicopter from landing.

Rotor blades whipped through the air overhead again, barely visible due to the ferocity of the storm, but still brought the hikers to a halt. The pilot gestured with his hands, confirming Gage's assessment and Gage felt his heart sink. The air was becoming too turbulent for the chopper to stay aloft. The pilot signaled once more, pointing toward the meadow they were struggling to reach. A gust of wind sent the craft careening sideways, and Gage knew the rescue crew had no choice but to abandon them until the storm abated. Their small group would have to remain on the mountain another night.

CHAPTER 6

"They're leaving us!" Emily wailed as the helicopter disappeared, racing ahead of the storm.

"Do we have to stay here forever?" Kobie asked.

"I want to go home!" Rachel began to cry. "I'm hungry and I don't want to stay here."

"Don't cry, Rachel." Kobie hurried toward her while pulling at his pack. When he stood beside her father, looking up to where she sat on Wade's shoulders, he handed her one of the long, red licorice sticks, which she accepted eagerly.

Web lowered Chelsea to the path, then helped her to a fallen log. She eased herself to a sitting position before looking back to see Wade set Rachel on the ground too. Rachel made her way to her mother's side to sit on the log while they rested, and Chelsea watched her take large bites of the licorice. She found herself both envious of the candy Kobie had given her daughter and immensely grateful that her child had something to eat.

"How long will this storm last?" she wondered aloud. "None of us has eaten since sometime before the flood except for a few bites of granola bar and a little candy."

"It's the thirst I'm having a hard time with," Bryan muttered.

"A whole canyon full of water and there's nothing to drink," Emily seconded his remark.

"We'll be okay," Web attempted to reassure the group. "If I understood that pilot right, he dropped supplies for us at the place we meant to meet up with the rescue chopper."

"Do you think he left supplies?" Cassie asked Gage.

"I think so, but there's only one way to find out. Let's go." He pushed forward, and, with a few complaints about the weather, the others fell in line behind him. Wade swung Rachel onto his shoulders again. Chelsea clamped her lips closed, refusing to groan as her battered feet took the first step. Diane stepped forward to place an arm around her waist while Web supported her other side. Once again she was grateful for the deputy's strong arm.

Wade is handling this better than I expected, Chelsea thought while observing her husband a few steps ahead of her. His face was red, and he was breathing hard, but he wasn't complaining or lashing out at Rachel for needing his help. Physically he wasn't in the same condition as the Edwards brothers or the deputy. He wasn't exactly overweight, but the long hours he spent in his office or commuting, along with the fact that he'd soon be forty, didn't add up to the youthful stamina of the other men.

He looked tired, and she wished she could carry Rachel part of the way, but she knew that wasn't possible. She was in far worse physical shape than Wade. She'd become bored after Rachel started school and had found it difficult to fill the long hours while her husband and children were away. Between a weekly cleaning lady and the yard service company, there was little house or yard work left for her to do. In addition to long telephone conversations with her parents, her days were filled with lunch dates with her friends, afternoon naps, and too much snacking. She'd thought of volunteering at Rachel's school or joining a spa, but she'd never gotten around to it. She wasn't fat, she assured herself, but like her husband she was carrying thirty pounds more than she needed, and her lungs and muscles were unaccustomed to this much exertion.

The rain was increasing in intensity and the temperature had dropped. She couldn't remember ever being so cold and miserable before in her whole life. Rachel was hunched over Wade's shoulders with her head leaning against his, as though trying to make herself as small as possible. A quick glance over her shoulder showed her Bryan marching along beside Emily and Trent. He appeared completely unfazed by the torrent of cold water streaming down upon him. In fact, he seemed to revel in both the experience and his new friends.

"Just a little bit farther, Mrs. Timmerman," Web's voice rumbled almost in her ear. He seemed to sense her increasing discouragement.

"I'm all right." She tried to reassure him—and herself—but it was taking more and more effort to keep moving. The trail had become slippery, and with the wind-driven rain slashing against her face, she stumbled more often, and her feet felt like heavy blocks of ice, almost impossible to lift. The wet socks and bandages were becoming heavier with each step. Her hair stuck to her face, and with Web and Diane clutching her arms for support, she didn't have a free hand to push it out of the way.

"Daddy!" Rachel's shrill scream pulled Chelsea from her misery. Forgetting her injured feet, she lunged toward her child, only to slip on the slick mud and crash to her knees. Diane saved her from injury, but Web had let her go to help Rachel. She watched in horror as Wade staggered and Rachel flew from his shoulders. Wade's arms windmilled as he fought to catch Rachel and steady himself. It was Web who caught the falling child.

"Rachel!" Chelsea crawled toward her child.

"She's all right, just shaken up a little bit." The deputy turned so Chelsea and Rachel could throw their arms around each other.

"Daddy dropped me," Rachel sobbed. Chelsea felt a stirring of anger. Wade should have been more careful. If he were too tired to carry Rachel any longer, he should have asked one of the other men or Bryan to carry her for a while. She'd even heard Trent offer to take a turn.

"No, I don't think he dropped you," Web said, placing Rachel on the wet grass beside her mother. As he walked away, Chelsea busied herself making certain her daughter was uninjured.

"Dad? What's the matter with Dad?" Bryan's voice penetrated Chelsea's absorption with Rachel. She turned her head to see a knot of people gathered around Wade. Water streamed down her face, and she couldn't see clearly, but he appeared to be sitting hunched forward, with Web and Diane on either side of him.

Struggling to her feet and pulling Rachel along beside her, she limped toward the group gathered around her husband.

"Wade?"

He looked up, his face contorted with pain. At once her eyes went to his right hand, which crossed his chest to clutch at his left shoulder and she understood. Wade's father had been in his early forties, only a few years older than Wade was right now, when he'd suffered a heart attack. Wade had never known his grandfather who died from a heart attack at an early age as well. She sank down beside her husband and reached for his wrist. After counting his pulse for a minute, she looked up at the people gathered around her husband.

"Is there any way to get that helicopter back here?" she asked, even though she knew the answer before the deputy shook his head.

Wade tried to rise to his feet.

"Lie down, Mr. Timmerman." Diane placed her hands on his shoulders and urged him back. She began questioning him in a soft voice about where the pain was centered and the severity of it. She repeated a check of his pulse.

"I'll be all right. Just need to rest. Is Rachel hurt?"

"She's fine," Diane assured him.

"What is it? What's the matter with Dad?" Bryan elbowed his way to the front and sank down beside his mother.

"He needs a doctor." Her voice was a thready whisper.

"How close are we to some kind of shelter?" Web turned to Gage.

"There's not much anywhere close." There was hesitation in Gage's voice.

"We just passed something that might work," Trent volunteered. "I noticed a couple of large trees that wind or lightning brought down not long ago. They're leaning against a rock ledge, forming a sort of lean-to."

"Yes! I remember seeing that." Gage turned to Web. "If we can get Wade into the shelter under those trees, we can get him warm and dry. Then I can hike ahead to see if the search and rescue people left us any supplies."

"The sooner he's out of this rain the better," Diane said. "But he shouldn't try to walk. He needs to be kept as still as possible."

Wade moaned and slumped toward the ground. Chelsea guided his head to her lap. Ignoring the rain pouring on her head, she sat on the muddy trail cradling him in her arms. She held him as she'd held Rachel through the previous long night. *Wade is strong. Surely he isn't going to die here on a mountain top hundreds of miles from home. I don't want to lose him.* Then she remembered that even if he didn't die, he would soon be gone. He was leaving her for another woman.

Reining in her emotions, she reminded herself that things would be no different from the way they had been the last five years. She'd seen very little of him during that time. She'd given up trying to compete with his career and had no strength left to fight another woman. She had been angry with him for so long, but she didn't want him to die. The rivulets of water running down her face weren't all rain—something inside her own chest was twisting painfully, telling her she'd been wrong to think it was over. She still cared about Wade.

"Trent, take Bryan with you and get any rocks or debris that might be under those trees that fell. Your brother and I should be able to carry Wade." Web took charge in his usual, blunt way. He knelt beside Wade, explaining that he and Gage would form a chair with their arms to carry him and that they would soon have him out of the rain.

"I'll find a comfortable spot for you," Diane promised as Web and Gage lifted him. She hurried after Trent and Bryan while Chelsea trailed behind.

"Is Diane a nurse?" Shalise asked Cassie in a quiet voice that barely carried above the rain. "She seems to know what to do."

"She plans to become a doctor. This is her last year of undergraduate study, and she hopes to be accepted into medical school next year."

"If there are any supplies waiting for us, Wade needs them now." Shalise stepped closer to Cassie and kept her voice low. "We're all cold and wet, and we can expect the temperature to drop even more tonight. Hypothermia could become a problem for all of us, but especially Wade and the children."

"You're right," Cassie agreed. "The men are going to be busy for a while. But Gage said it's a short distance to the meadow, so I think I'll continue on up there. If there are supplies, I can have them back here before the men finish moving Mr. Timmerman."

"I'll go with you," Shalise volunteered.

"What about Kobie? Should I ask Emily to watch him?"

"Yes, thank you. He's pretty concerned about the little Timmerman girl and will probably want to stay close to her. It might be good if Emily keeps an eye on both of them. I think Chelsea and Diane are too busy to give them a thought."

Emily, who had been standing back looking uncertain, joined her sister and Shalise. After Cassie explained the plan to her and asked her

to tell Gage where they'd gone, the two women turned back to the
trail while Emily started after the others, intent on catching up to the
two frightened children. With only the two of them, both in good
shape, wearing sturdy hiking boots, Cassie and Shalise were able to
move much faster.

"There it is!" Cassie pointed ahead. Shalise looked through the
slanting rain to where the trees ended and breathed a sigh of relief. An
open area, smaller than the flooded meadow they'd crossed last night,
spread before them. A brown canvas lump rested a hundred feet from
where the trail ended.

"Let's go!" she shouted above the din of the rain and stepped from
the slight shelter of the trees. Thunder crashed in a deafening roar.
The storm seemed to be increasing in fury, or maybe it just seemed
that way because they were now without shelter. "Stay low," she
cautioned as she bent nearly double. She certainly didn't want to
invite lightning to find them in the open.

It only took seconds to reach the supplies, but it took longer to
drag the heavy pack back to the safety of the trees.

"Whew!" Cassie gasped as she paused to catch her breath and
wipe rain from her face. "What do you suppose is in here?"

"Food, water, blankets, a compass, rope, a small shovel, and a first-aid
kit. Maybe a flashlight. There might even be a battery-operated radio."
Shalise ticked off the essential items.

"Whoa! You ever been stranded on a mountain before?" Cassie asked.

"No, but I took a mountain rescue class last winter so I got
pretty familiar with rescue equipment." Shalise was busy dividing the
large bundle into two smaller packs. With the rope that had secured
the bundle, she formed loops to enable them to carry the loads on
their backs.

Both women staggered as they slipped their arms through the
loops and swung the packs to their shoulders.

"It's a good thing it's all downhill," Shalise attempted to joke,
staggering under her load.

Cassie slipped once and had to be helped up by Shalise, who then
lost her footing and fell too. When they finally got themselves upright
again, they moved more slowly, grasping shrubs and tree branches to
help them stay erect.

"Cassie!" Gage called her name. Her load seemed to lighten as she saw Gage emerge from the driving rain. He hurried to her side, but he didn't take the pack she carried. Instead he lifted a wet branch and motioned for them to duck beneath it. "Through these trees." Once past the tree he placed one arm around her, lending her support as he led her to the makeshift lean-to. After entering the sheltered area, he slipped the ropes from her arms and knelt at once to search through the pack. She leaned wearily against a tree trunk, feeling bereft of energy without Gage's support.

"We would have passed right by if Gage hadn't been watching for us," Shalise exclaimed as Web stepped forward to relieve her of her pack. Once free of the heavy burden, she made her way to Kobie. She didn't speak, but simply extended a hand to squeeze his shoulder, letting him know she had returned.

The area under the fallen trees was larger than she had expected. The center, close to the ledge the trees leaned against, appeared to be dry. There Wade Timmerman lay stretched out on a bed of pine boughs, with his wife and children hovering near and Kobie sitting next to Rachel. A small fire burned nearby, and Shalise assumed Trent had saved whatever dry wood he found for the fire as he cleared out the space to use for a shelter. He and Emily sat beside the children, conversing quietly.

Shalise turned her attention back to Web and Gage, who were sorting through the supplies she and Cassie had retrieved. Gage selected a couple of tinfoil packets and a plastic pouch marked with a large red cross. Both men walked toward the man lying on the ground where Gage handed the medical pouch to Diane. He then opened another foil packet to reveal a large, blanket-sized sheet, which he held as a shield while Web removed the fallen man's wet shirt and pants. In minutes Wade was securely wrapped in one of the foil emergency blankets.

"How is he?" Shalise whispered to Web when he and Gage returned to the packs spread on the ground.

"Not good, but as long as he stays quiet the pain recedes. Diane thinks he's suffering an angina attack rather than a full-blown heart attack. She thinks if we can keep him warm and quiet, he has a chance."

"That's good to hear." Gage joined their conversation. "Do you see anything we can use to make this place a little more weather proof?"

He continued to sort through the items on the ground. He opened a long pouch, then reached inside for a smaller pouch. "Water!"

Trent reached over his brother's shoulder for a handful of the small water packets and was soon distributing them to everyone. The children giggled when they held the wobbly water bags in their hands. Shalise noticed that Chelsea took only a few sips, then used the small plastic straw that was taped to the bag to dribble a few drops into her husband's mouth.

"All right, everyone." Web stood and spoke loudly enough to get everyone's attention. "Thanks to Shalise and Cassie, we have a few supplies to work with now. We have two large plastic ground cloths. I suggest we use one as a wall on the north side of our camp and one as a roof. There are enough emergency blankets that if we use two to sit on, we'll still have one for every two people to wrap around themselves tonight. We don't have anything to heat water in . . ."

"My cup won't burn. Grandpa made hot chocolate for me in it once." Kobie dug his tin cup out of his pack.

"Okay," Web laughed. "It seems Kobie is the only one of us that came prepared. We have soup mix packets, so anyone who wants to make a cup of soup should ask to borrow Kobie's cup."

"We have several dozen small packages of crackers and cheese, a few cans of Vienna sausages, and two large bags of trail mix," Cassie listed the menu choices. "We can start on those while we take turns heating the soup and chocolate."

"What about a radio? Is there one in the pack?" Shalise asked.

Gage shook his head. "Not the kind we can use to call for help. It only emits a signal that pinpoints our location." They were on their own until the storm ended and a helicopter returned for them.

Shalise wandered closer to where Diane knelt beside Wade, wondering what there might be in the medical kit that would be of any use to him. She knew the medical supplies in those emergency kits tended toward bandages, antiseptic, and splints—none of which would be helpful to a possible heart attack victim. She watched Diane give Wade aspirin to chew and remembered from her own first-aid training that aspirin was usually administered to heart patients. She admired the young woman's calm, efficient manner and whispered a silent prayer of gratitude to Heavenly Father that Diane had assumed caring for the stricken man. If his care had been left to her, she wasn't certain she would have remembered about the aspirin. When she got back home she was definitely going to register for another emergency class.

Wade slept after swallowing the aspirin. When he awoke, he didn't feel the pain, but he held himself still, fearing that the slightest movement would bring it back. The wind and rain seemed to have ceased, though he could still hear the occasional drip of rain filtering through the canopy of trees. There was enough light to see the group he'd become a part of—through fate and expediency—huddled together near a small fire that had died to little more than embers. Another time he would have laughed at their strange space-alien appearance, all wrapped in shiny foil. A glance at his own body told him he was wearing foil too, and not much else.

He didn't remember a whole lot beyond the agonizing pain. He'd been vaguely aware of Web and Gage carrying him to this place. He remembered, too, that each time he'd awakened, Chelsea had been beside him. Diane had given him aspirin tablets and ordered him to chew them. Someone must have reached the supplies the deputy had said were waiting for them, because he recalled Chelsea had trickled a few drops of water into his mouth and had moistened his mouth with a damp cloth each time he awoke. Yet this time she wasn't beside him, and he wondered where she was.

A muffled sound brought his head around to see her lying beside Rachel a short distance away. They were both asleep, though Chelsea was making little moaning noises almost as though she were crying in her sleep. She was probably cold and uncomfortable lying on the ground. With the firelight playing on her face, he noticed she was still a beautiful woman, even with her hair frizzed around her face and dark smudges beneath her eyes. He was surprised he'd noticed. Without makeup or a fashionable hairstyle, she appeared younger, almost like the eighteen-year-old girl he'd fallen in love with years ago.

Chelsea shifted in her sleep and drew Rachel closer to her side. Rachel, too, looked younger by the faint light of fire coals, more like the happy two year old she'd been before they'd bought the house out on the point. His glance went to the pants and shirt spread near the fire, and he recognized them as his own. He wondered if the swing he'd made from bits of sticks and vines was still in his pants pocket. He basked once more in the glow he'd felt when Rachel had accepted the swing and voiced her approval of the simple handmade toy.

Taking care to move as little as possible, he searched the darkness for his son. He found him seated beside the deputy with an emergency blanket covering them both as they leaned back against a large rock. The three young women were huddled together on the other side of the rock, not far from the two men he'd learned were brothers. His attention turned back to Bryan. He wasn't a bad kid, and he obviously looked up to these new friends. In fact he'd made himself useful ever since they'd met up with them, and he'd certainly cleaned up his language. Sweat and rain had flattened his punk hair, and he bore little resemblance to the irritating kid who had taunted and annoyed his father during the past two weeks. If anyone had told him a week ago that his son would soon be friends with a cop and a bunch of religious people, he would have laughed.

Wade realized that Bryan was no longer a child and suddenly he felt cheated. He'd done none of the things he'd once been so anxious to do with his son. They hadn't even been to a ball game together. He had a vague recollection of Chelsea telling him Bryan was interested in soccer and had tried out for a team. Wade had no idea who sponsored the league or if his son had even made the team. It had been years since he'd taken Bryan to the lake in Wisconsin where Chelsea's family owned a cabin. His son was a stranger. After two weeks of traveling across the country in the confined space of the RV, he still knew nothing of him—except that he had a smart mouth.

He feared it was too late now. Bryan was seventeen, and Wade had done nothing to encourage him to apply to a good college. He didn't even know if Bryan's future plans included college. Two days ago he would have bet Bryan had no plans beyond his next pair of earrings. In a little more than twenty-four hours, he'd caught glimpses of a young man he hadn't known existed. Now there would be no chance to let his son know he was proud of him or to guide him through the difficult choices the next few years would bring the boy.

He thought about Mandy. If he survived, would she stand by him? Not likely. Mandy was brilliant and ambitious. She'd be a partner in the firm one day, and she certainly wouldn't waste her time on a man whose bum heart would only slow her down. He was washed up just like his father, even if he survived. The prospect of early retirement, being unable to drive, afraid to travel, weighing each bite of food he took, giving up steaks and desserts, and spending endless hours in hospitals and doctors' offices wasn't living. He would hate becoming his father. At the moment his empty stomach came close to convincing him he'd miss steaks and chocolate milk shakes more than Mandy.

"How are you doing?" A voice interrupted his thoughts. He turned his head the short distance necessary to see the speaker. Gage Edwards crouched at his side.

"Better," he told the younger man.

"But you can't sleep," Gage said.

"You don't seem to be sleeping either."

"True. I noticed the fire was almost out and decided to see if I could find some dry wood under one of the other trees around here. When I returned with a couple of small logs, I noticed you were awake," Gage told him. "I thought if you were in pain, I could get you some more aspirin."

"Aspirin isn't going to help the pain I'm feeling." Wade's voice held a note of bitterness.

"Want to talk about it? I'm not sure I can give you any helpful advice, but sometimes just telling another person about something I'm worried about helps me think it through and find the right solution."

Once more Wade's gaze traveled over to Chelsea. She wasn't as beautiful or brilliant as Amanda Rogers, but she wasn't stupid either. She wouldn't stay with him just because Mandy wouldn't want him anymore. It wouldn't be fair to Chelsea anyway to keep her tied to a man who didn't love her—though the past twenty-four hours had shown him she mattered to him more than he'd thought.

Strange he should worry about fairness now. He could suddenly see that not much in life had been fair to Chelsea. She hadn't had a chance to go on to college, and he didn't have any idea what she might have chosen to do if they hadn't married so young and if she hadn't been plunged into motherhood when she was scarcely more than a child herself. He wasn't certain which pain he felt was worse—physical or emotional.

Sensing Wade's reluctance to talk about what was bothering him, Gage decided to change the subject. He placed one of the logs he'd found on the glowing coals, then stirred them until the new wood caught fire. After seating himself where the small blaze would warm his back, he spoke again. "The helicopter will be back shortly after sunup. They'll have a stretcher, which will make moving you easier."

"I'm sorry I've become such a nuisance," Wade offered quietly.

"You're not a nuisance. We all want to help you any way we can. I just wish we could help your family more. Cassie and Shalise talked Rachel into lying down, but neither your wife nor Bryan would leave your side until Chelsea fell asleep right here beside you. Later, Bryan and Web moved her beside Rachel, and Bryan finally fell asleep while talking to Web. They're terribly concerned about you."

"I haven't been much of a father or husband for years—and now it looks like I put it off too long. As soon as we get back to Chicago, Chelsea and I will be getting a divorce. Bryan has made it pretty clear over the past few weeks that he has no use for me. And Rachel and I were just getting to know each other again when this happened." Wade made no attempt to disguise his self-disgust.

"I'm sorry about your marriage." Gage looked him in the eye. "But I don't think it's as beyond hope as you seem to think it is. Chelsea still cares about you."

"She knows I've been seeing another woman." Wade found it hard to maintain eye contact with the younger man, but he felt a need to be honest with him. He didn't want Gage to harbor any illusions about his heart attack bringing him and Chelsea back together.

"How serious is this other relationship?" Gage asked. "I know it's none of my business, but I find myself caught in a similar situation."

"You're not married, are you?" Wade felt anger and disappointment churning to the surface, even though he could see the hypocrisy in his reaction. He'd seen a budding romance between Gage and Cassie, and for some reason it disturbed him to think this man might be leading on a young woman Wade had come to like and respect.

"No, I'm not married, but I've been thinking quite seriously about marriage for almost a year." Gage ignored the accusatory tone of Wade's question. "Jena's father owns a large ranch that adjoins my father's smaller ranch. She and I have been friends since we were children, but during the past couple of years while Trent has been away, we've become closer. We've talked about marriage, though I haven't actually proposed. Her father is encouraging us to marry. His health isn't good, and he's made it clear he'll rest easier if he knows I'll be helping Jena run his place. We have a lot in common, though we don't share the same religious beliefs. I thought that was enough and that I could be happy with Jena—then I met Cassie."

"Yes, Cassie." Wade sighed. "You're right. Your problem is somewhat like mine although your situation is more excusable than my own. Chelsea and I married right after she finished high school, and I was in my last year at the university. Bryan was already on the way, and we were young and in love and thought we could beat the odds. Seventeen years of struggling to get through graduate school and move up in my profession left little time for my marriage. We drifted apart, partly because of so little time together and partly because our interests have gone in different directions. When I'd take Chelsea to company socials, she'd be bored, and I would be embarrassed by her lack of education and poise.

"A few months ago the company hired a woman who was assigned to work with me on a major project. Because of that we got close, and before long I realized she was everything my wife was not. Mandy is tall, slender, brilliant, perfectly groomed, and ambitious. Other men are green with envy when we walk into a restaurant or any gathering together. With her I feel successful and alive. I guess what I'm saying is I feel confused. I'm thinking and feeling things I hadn't considered before. I don't know. I just need some time to sort it all out."

"That's really why I can't sleep and why I left camp for a while," Gage admitted. "I wanted some time alone to think and pray. After that helicopter arrives a few hours from now, I'll probably never see Cassie again. But I know where she goes to school. I could see her if I decide to. So that's my dilemma. In the morning do I say good-bye to Cassie, a woman I could easily love and will never forget and then go back to Jena? Or do I tell Cassie I have feelings for her and then go home to break off my relationship with Jena?"

"I'm not the man who can help you." Wade felt reluctant to admit he had no advice for the friend he wouldn't see after tomorrow either. "I was just lying here feeling sorry for myself because I'm a stranger to my children, Mandy will dump me when she learns I've got a weak heart and won't be able to keep up with her, and there's nothing left between Chelsea and me." He paused, then asked almost as a joke, "Did praying help any?"

"Yes." Gage absently tossed a pinecone in the air several times. "Yes, praying did help. I feel calmer. I'm still not sure which direction my life should take, but I know I'm not ready to propose to Jena. I also feel that after this is over I should see Cassie at least one more time to discover whether the attraction we feel now is real or just part of the heightened emotion we've all experienced the last couple of days."

"Do you think you could say one of those prayers for me?" Wade discovered that he was only half teasing.

"That's something Trent and I wanted to ask you about. We could give you a blessing if you'd like. In fact, that's the only advice I can share with you—put both your health and your relationship with your family in the Lord's hands."

Chelsea awoke to a low murmur of voices. She recognized it was coming from Wade and Gage, but she couldn't make out the words until Wade asked something about saying a prayer. When Gage offered to give her husband a blessing, she held her breath, expecting him to make a flippant remark. He'd never been interested in attending church, and she doubted he'd ever offered a prayer in his entire life. She didn't want him to hurt Gage's feelings now. Wade had no way yet of knowing the things Shalise had explained to her about their beliefs and could easily misunderstand.

Instead of laughing or making some crack, Wade seemed to be considering Gage's offer.

"I've never thought much about praying or God or anything religious since I was a boy," Wade finally said. "But I've never come so close to death before—twice in less than twenty-four hours. I heard someone say once that even agnostics and atheists become believers when they come face-to-face with death. And I have to admit that at this point, I would welcome a blessing."

.

CHAPTER 7

Gage left Wade's side and returned a few minutes later with Trent. The two young men placed their hands on his head, and Gage began to speak. Chelsea leaned closer, not wanting to miss a word. She couldn't hear all of Gage's softly spoken words, but enough to know Gage was seeking the Lord's help as much to resolve Wade's mental turmoil as his physical pain. She heard him say her name and the names of her children. As she listened to Gage pray for healing and comfort, for Wade and for his family, she felt a measure of peace enter her heart.

Right after Gage finished praying, Diane left the blanket she shared with Cassie and Emily to check on Wade's condition. Chelsea drifted back to sleep to the murmur of quiet voices surrounding her husband. When she awoke again, light was creeping into their shelter. Rachel was still sleeping, so she tucked the insulated emergency blanket closer around her daughter before making her way to her husband's side. She felt almost shy facing him this morning.

"Did you sleep well?" she asked.

"Pretty well." He didn't elaborate, nor did he mention the blessing Gage had given him, so she didn't say anything either, but busied herself preparing a cup of hot water. She offered him a couple of sips. She didn't give him more because Diane had said that allowing him to eat wasn't a good idea until he reached a hospital. After holding the cup for him to sip the warm liquid, Chelsea tripped on a trailing stip of gauze as she tried to step away. The bandages and socks on her feet had become tattered and ripped. Web caught her before she fell, and as she began to thank him, she paused.

"Listen!" She stood frozen with Web's hand still supporting her.

"What is it?" Rachel asked from her silvery cocoon.

"It's the helicopter!" Kobie shouted. "It's coming to give us a ride home."

"They won't be able to see us here!" Emily groaned. "If we run, do you think some of us could get to the meadow in time to keep them from leaving us again?"

"They won't leave without us," Web assured everyone. "But the sooner we make contact, the sooner Wade will be at a hospital."

"We're on our way," Bryan shouted. He was only a few steps behind Gage and Trent, who were already pounding up the trail. Cassie and Emily followed, but Diane stayed behind.

Shalise put her arm around Chelsea. "I heard only one helicopter, so we won't all be able to leave at the same time. They'll take your husband and family first, so this might be our only chance to say good-bye. I'd like to stay in touch." She held out her hand. "This is the name and address tag from Kobie's backpack. It got a little wet, but it's still readable."

"Thank you." Chelsea wiped a tear from her cheek. "You and Kobie have been so kind to Rachel and me. I don't think I could have made it without a friend."

On the other side of the shelter, Diane checked Wade's pulse. "I'm not sure whether you had a heart attack or not. The doctors at the hospital will be able to tell you something definite. I suspect you had an angina attack, which is certainly serious enough."

"What's the difference? Either way my life is pretty much over."

"No, angina is often a warning. You may have blocked arteries that need to be cleared, or you might need a pacemaker. But this could be the warning that gives you an opportunity to prevent a heart attack," Diane argued.

"I don't want to live as an invalid." Wade continued feeling sorry for himself.

"You'll only be an invalid if you make yourself one." Diane seemed to be losing patience. "I heard Gage give you a blessing early this morning. Every blessing he promised you is yours if you have the courage to reach out and take it." She rose to her feet and walked from the shelter with her head erect.

Chelsea felt a wave of shock sweep over her. Diane had been so patient with Wade until now. Her care for Wade had convinced her that Diane was right to seek a career in the medical field, but she wasn't sure what had just happened. Wade had been quite upbeat since Gage had given him that blessing. He'd even been pleasant to her when she'd given him a few sips of soup. But as soon as everyone grew excited about being rescued, he'd slipped back into a black mood.

"I think our would-be-doctor just discovered something about life and death that most doctors don't understand until they're much further along in their training," Shalise commented with an odd smile.

"What do you mean?" Chelsea asked.

"A doctor can only heal a person as much as he believes he can be healed. Faith, determination, desire, attitude—whatever you want to call it—makes the difference. Medicine gives a person a fighting chance, but if the patient doesn't fight for his own life, not even the best doctor in the world can save him. And that's true of marriage too."

"Did you fight to save your marriage?" Chelsea didn't know why Shalise felt Wade's fatalistic attitude toward his health applied to their marriage.

"Yes." Shalise seemed to have no trouble seeing the connection.

"But Daniel still left you."

"Yes, he left me. I couldn't make our marriage work when Daniel didn't believe in it, but I have the peace that comes with knowing I did all I could." Shalise bent to pick up her son's backpack, then once more looked into Chelsea's eyes. "I didn't quit, but once Daniel moved on with his life, I did too. My marriage died, but I still have a life to live and a son to raise."

"I did nothing," Chelsea spoke in a whisper, looking toward the spot where her husband lay. "I let him move on without me. I didn't strike one blow. Most of the time I didn't understand what he was talking about while he was going to graduate school, then beginning his career. I didn't think it mattered, and I was more interested in learning to be a mother. When he told me he wanted a divorce so he could marry Mandy, I knew I couldn't compete. She has a doctorate, lectures at seminars, and is beautiful. I gave up."

"It may not be too late." Shalise grinned. "The past couple of days you've proved yourself a lot tougher lady than you thought you were."

"I did, didn't I?" She grinned too. "It's been a hard lesson, but I think I've learned some new things about myself. I've been a passive dreamer instead of a doer. Without the rest of you, if I had even survived that flood, I would have died of fear or hypothermia out here. I need to be more capable and independent like you and those young girls. Instead of letting life just happen, I'm going to be out there fighting for what I want." She cast a determined glance her husband's way, then concluded, "Wade Timmerman is about to go home to a different wife, and she won't be Amanda Rogers!"

* * *

Gage watched the chopper lift off with seven members of their group and felt a wave of melancholy. Before Friday everyone but his brother had been a stranger. Now he felt as if his family were being broken up. As hard as the past two days had been, they had also been a couple of the most memorable days of his life.

He was glad Wade would soon be at a hospital and that their entire group had survived their ordeal, but it was hard knowing their paths would probably never cross again. Watching Cassie board the chopper, then turn to wave in his direction, had been the toughest of all. He'd hoped she would be among those who waited for the second flight, but the pilot had thought it best for Diane to stay with Wade during the flight, and the other two girls had chosen to go with their friend. An ache in his heart told him he'd never quite stop missing Cassie. A stab of guilt made him wonder how he could feel so strongly for a woman he'd only known two days when he was seriously considering marrying Jena, someone he'd known almost his whole life.

He looked around at the diminished group. There was only Shalise and Kobie, his brother, Web, and himself. At least they had a decent meal to eat while they waited for the chopper to return for them. Volunteers had made sandwiches and donated drinks, salads, and chips for them once the story had gotten out to the media that a dozen campers were stranded on the mountain by the flood—a flood that had devastated farms and ranches for miles and generated several dramatic rescues of campers and livestock. Four people had lost their lives. At least the sparsely populated ranch land between the canyon and the first town had provided a place for the water to spread out, keeping it from destroying the heavier-populated areas.

The pilot had teased Web about being a hero. A national affiliate had picked up a local reporter's story about the deputy who had risked his life to clear the canyon, then was caught by floodwaters himself. The reporter had been waiting at the airport when the helicopter pilot had returned the previous day and reported sighting a dozen people, including one in uniform, making their way up the mountain from the flood area. The story had set off a media frenzy, which convinced the pilot to land at the hospital instead of the airfield to avoid a mob.

Gage helped himself to another sandwich. As he ate, he gazed upon the peaceful meadow and the surrounding mountain peaks he loved almost as much as he loved the rippling grasslands of Wyoming. He wondered if life would go on as planned once he got back home or if he'd always feel he'd left a part of himself on this mountain.

No one had much to say while they ate, but after they finished, Kobie lay his head on his mother's lap and drifted to sleep. Shalise then leaned back against a smooth birch tree and closed her eyes. She wasn't asleep, however; she was still too keyed up to sleep. She'd sleep later, after she and Kobie were safely back in their own home. She felt immensely grateful her grandparents had given her the house and that, according to the chopper pilot, Orchard Springs had been mostly untouched by the flood. In her mind the old ranch house was truly a haven from all the problems in her life. Her fingers stroked the hair at her son's nape, and she smiled. Her impulsive decision to take Kobie camping hadn't turned out as she'd expected. She'd never been more terrified in her life than during their flight from the flood that had invaded the peaceful canyon. But there had been good moments too.

She'd been proud of Kobie's courage and the way he'd befriended little Rachel. She'd never noticed before how much he resembled her grandfather. She felt grateful, too, for Daniel's father, who had taught his grandson about the mountains and forest. The new friendships she'd made these past two days were more things for which she was grateful; there had been an instant bond between her and Chelsea Timmerman. For most of the past year she'd thought little of being grateful for anything, but now she felt overwhelming gratitude for her life, her son, and her home to return to.

She looked up to see Web and the brothers from Wyoming deep in conversation. Those three were also among the people she had to thank her Heavenly Father for when she knelt tonight beside her own bed. They had been brave and resourceful beyond belief. She feared it would sound trite if she said it aloud, but they were her heroes. She would never forget the calm and peace that had penetrated her fear when the big deputy placed his arms around her and guided her to safety away from that nightmare ledge. Web looked up and his eyes met hers, sending an element of awareness through her that she hadn't felt for years. He dropped his eyes and looked embarrassed. He'd felt it too. She didn't know why that pleased her so much.

"I think I hear the chopper coming." Gage gazed toward the sky. She craned her neck to see if she could see the helicopter, but she could neither hear nor see it.

"You're not from around here, are you?" She heard Trent direct the question toward Web and strained to hear the big man's answer.

"I work for the local county sheriff." He sounded half-asleep.

"But before you came here? Where did you grow up?" Trent continued his questions.

"Detroit." Web showed no interest in discussing his background. Why his taciturn answers to Trent's questions left her feeling disappointed she didn't know. The man's past wasn't anyone's business but his own. Still, she'd like to know more about the big man.

Web figured Trent would give up on his questions if he feigned sleep. After the fatiguing events of the past two days, he didn't have to pretend too much. He had never felt comfortable talking about his past.

From beneath lowered lashes Web saw the boy had fallen asleep in his mother's lap. He liked the picture they made, but he felt a tug of jealousy too, and he wasn't certain whether it was because he and his little brother hadn't had a mother they could lean on like that, or if he was just a little jealous of anyone who got that close to Shalise Richards.

Shalise Richards is a good-looking woman, kind and caring. Her ex-husband must be crazy to have left her. The thought was quickly banished from his mind. She was the kind of woman he sometimes found himself dreaming about, but never acting on that attraction. He didn't know what to say to a woman and wasn't the kind of good-looking, smooth-talking man that caught women's attention.

He and Shalise lived in the same town, but he didn't recall seeing her before. He'd heard about her husband—or rather ex husband. He had a reputation for being a ladies' man with a great sense of humor most men admired. He'd heard a couple of deputies talking about his marriage to a singer they referred to as "hot," but Web was willing to bet she didn't hold a candle to Shalise's looks or just plain good sense.

"Hey, what did I just say?" he heard the laughter in Trent's voice.

"Uh, I'm not sure," he admitted with a self-deprecating shrug. "We were talking about where I grew up . . ."

"Then you tuned me out." Trent attempted to sound offended.

"I didn't mean . . ."

"It's okay. I'd rather look at Shalise Richards than listen to me too." Trent laughed as the big, tough-looking cop turned bright red.

"Knock it off, Trent. Interrogating me about my love life is bad enough, but embarrassing Web is going too far." Gage gave his brother a playful shove.

"That's the trouble with brothers," Trent lamented, elbowing Gage in the ribs. "They just don't appreciate brotherly concern. If you have a brother, I'm sure you know what I mean."

"I had a little brother." The quiet sorrow in the big man's voice brought the brothers' scuffling to a stop.

"Do you want to tell us about him?" Trent asked in a more subdued voice.

"He's dead." Web lifted his chin and seemed to be examining the sky. "He was about Kobie's age when he died."

"I'm sorry," Trent spoke seriously. "I didn't mean to bring up bad memories."

"Not bad memories exactly," Web admitted. "The past couple of days I've watched Kobie and remembered the good times Frankie and

I had. Then I've watched the two of you and wondered what it would be like if we were still together."

"Some of the best experiences in my life have been with Trent," Gage added, joining their conversation. "A little brother can be a pest at times, but I don't think there's any other relationship quite like the one between brothers. I'm sorry you didn't get to experience having yours with you longer."

"Yeah, it makes me kind of sad to see that little boy over there and think of him growing up without a father or even a brother." Web looked toward the sleeping child. "A boy needs a man to show him the ropes and look out for him. My brother and I never knew our father, but I tried to make it up to him. I guess I was too young or just not good enough."

"Hey, don't be so hard on yourself. From what I've seen of you the past few days, I suspect you were the best big brother you knew how to be." Trent moved closer to Web. "It's only natural that you miss your brother—Gage and I really hated being apart for nearly four years—but once we were together again, it was like before we went on our missions, only better. I think it will be a little like that when one of us dies. The one who remains will miss the other one for the rest of his life, but we'll both be comforted by knowing we'll be together again in the next life."

"Do you really believe . . ." Web paused as the heavy beat of rotors swooping over the mountain top drowned out his words.

"Yes, I know you and your brother can be together again if that's what you want." Trent raised his voice as the chopper circled briefly away from them to position for landing. He might have said more, but the returning noisy engine eliminated further conversation. In minutes they were scrambling aboard the chopper. Web found himself seated behind Kobie with an empty seat beside him. While Kobie gazed out the window, saying good-bye to what had turned out to be the adventure of a lifetime, Web looked at the empty seat and wondered what it would be like if his brother were sitting there beside him. He couldn't get Trent's words out of his mind nor deny the hope those words had ignited. Was it truly possible? First chance he got, he'd ask Bill Haslam what he thought the chances were he'd ever see his brother again.

* * *

"No, Mom, you and Dad don't need to come get the children. Bryan is more mature than you think. He'll supervise Rachel just fine. Just meet them at O'Hare. Their plane should arrive at 4:10." She didn't mention that Bryan had taken responsibility for his sister ever since their arrival in Logan. Her mother was convinced Bryan was completely irresponsible because he dyed his hair, wore earrings, and sported pants large enough for two heavy men to wear at the same time. Nothing Chelsea could say would change her mother's mind. But her mother didn't realize what she had recently discovered. Both Chelsea and Bryan were much stronger than any of their family knew.

"We don't need you to wire us money. Wade still has his wallet." Again, she didn't elaborate.

"But dear . . ."

"I'm fine. Please, don't worry." She really didn't want her mother to come, she realized. She'd turned to her parents for help with every crisis in her life, and she was grateful for their willingness to help, but somewhere deep inside she knew if she didn't stand on her own now she never would. She'd leaned on her parents when she should have been strong enough to stand by herself. She'd been such a coward, hiding in her house or running to her parents instead of facing the problems in her marriage and reaching out for what she wanted. Shalise was right. The weak, dependent Chelsea was gone. Out there on that mountain she'd discovered she could be strong when she needed to be.

She hadn't even broken down while she and her children waited for a cardiac specialist to examine Wade—or during the surgery that followed to clear the blockage. She was also proud that she'd signed the surgery consent form, even though on the phone Wade's mother had advised against it. Then when Cassie and Emily's grandparents had arrived to take them on to Salt Lake, Chelsea hadn't panicked when they left.

Once she knew Wade was out of danger and resting, she'd sent Bryan to find a hotel room for them where they could clean up and rest. Then she'd handed him a credit card and sent him shopping with his sister for a change of clothes for all of them. He'd made sensible choices and even kept Rachel entertained.

"Mom, you're worrying needlessly. Logan is a nice city with a low crime rate and a fine hospital. I'll be fine here by myself. It'll only be a couple of weeks, then we'll both fly home. Just meet the kids' plane and keep them until we get back. I love you." She added a hurried good-bye and hung up.

She took a deep breath and mentally patted herself on the back. It had been tempting to let Dad handle the insurance details and allow Mom to come hold her hand. She just had to remember her whole future depended on what she did now. Taking a deep breath, she picked up the phone one more time to dial a number she'd memorized a long time ago, but seldom used. Wade's company frowned on personal calls, but this wasn't exactly a personal call. The sooner his company knew not to expect him back for at least thirty days, the sooner she could put her plan into action.

Wade awoke slowly to find himself in a dimly lit hospital room. He'd awakened before, he recalled, but had drifted back to sleep. He turned his head far enough to see he wasn't alone. Past the maze of tubes and wires that all seemed to emanate from various parts of his body, he saw Chelsea curled in an armchair. At first he thought she was asleep, then he noticed she was studying a clipboard in her hands.

"Chels," he croaked. She looked up, then seeing he was awake, put down the clipboard and walked over beside his bed. He couldn't put his finger on what was different about her, but he knew at once that something was. Maybe it was the jeans. He hadn't thought she even owned a pair. Her mother didn't approve of them, but even only half-awake he approved of the way they looked on her. Memory of the flood came back, and he assumed the jeans were all she'd been able to find to replace the clothes she'd lost.

"Water," he croaked through parched lips.

"The doctor said a few ice chips are all you can have for now." She scooped a tiny sliver of ice onto a spoon and held it to his mouth. It didn't anywhere near satisfy his raging thirst, so she doled out another one. That wasn't enough either, but after the second chip she set the spoon back down.

"Where are we?" he managed to ask.

"You're in a nice, modern hospital," she answered, and something in her voice told him she was being evasive.

"And where is this hospital?" He wished he hadn't asked. He didn't want to hear her say the name of the famous cardiology hospital where his father was a frequent patient.

"Logan, Utah."

He was in a small-town hospital? He couldn't believe it. *Wait! I remember being airlifted from the mountain.* Perhaps he was just being stabilized before being sent on to Chicago.

"How soon will I be sent on to Chicago?" he asked.

"Dr. Cameron said you'd be able to travel in about two weeks."

"Two weeks!"

"Yes," she responded with a smile, touching his hand. "He said the surgery went remarkably well. There was no damage to your heart, but you will need to watch your diet and get more exercise from now on."

Surgery! Chelsea had let some small-town doctor talk her into allowing him to operate on his heart? No, Chelsea wouldn't agree to something like that on her own. It must have been his mother's decision, which meant his heart was so bad there hadn't been time to fly him to Chicago. "Where are my parents?" he asked.

"Home, I suppose," Chelsea responded nonchalantly. "You know your father can't travel, and your mother never leaves him alone."

"You did tell Mother I'd had a heart attack, didn't you?"

"But you didn't have a heart attack." Chelsea patted his hand as though he were a small child needing reassurance. "Dr. Cameron said Diane was right. You had an angina attack, which was painful for you, but didn't leave your heart damaged. He said you should consider it a warning that you could have a heart attack if you don't take care. He operated with something he described as a small balloon that he sent along your artery to remove the blockage and open it wide enough so that blood will flow through easier. He said it's quite a common procedure and that your recovery will be fast, though you'll have some restrictions on food and activities for a little while. After that you can live a normal life as long as you watch your diet, exercise, and have regular checkups."

"Did my mother approve of the procedure?" he asked after a few minutes silence. Something didn't add up. His mother was dead set against any type of heart surgery. His father's doctor had given up even suggesting bypass surgery for his father. He watched Chelsea carefully, waiting for an answer.

"I didn't ask her," Chelsea stated with surprising calm. He was amazed he didn't have another heart attack right there!

Wade stared back at her with a look of horror on his face. He seemed about to sit up, but Chelsea restrained him with little more than a touch. She would have preferred this conversation wait until Wade was stronger, but she couldn't lie to him.

"Don't get excited," she whispered in a soothing voice. "That wouldn't be good for you." She would wait to explain how during that last long, cold night on the mountain she'd done a lot of thinking about what might be best for each of them. And she'd made some decisions. One of those decisions had been to get her husband back—not only from Amanda Rogers, but from his parents and his career. She'd also concluded that getting Wade back meant she had to get herself back, beginning with standing up to their families.

They'd married young with both their parents' enthusiastic support, and now she could see she'd never really moved beyond the insecure girl who had married the son of her parents' best friends, playing out her marriage according to their rules. Their parents' support had made life easier for them, but now she wondered if their marriage might have been stronger if they hadn't bought the "perfect" house on a quiet, tree-lined street in the same neighborhood where they'd grown up. Would they both have found greater fulfillment and grown together, instead of apart, if they'd found a house and friends closer to Wade's work and worked out their problems between just the two of them? It suddenly occurred to her that perhaps Wade's obsession with his career and even his relationship with another woman were his way of reaching for independence from his parents.

"Where are the kids? And how soon will Mother get here?" He seemed angry and a flash of insight told her that he had no reason to think her capable of handling this emergency.

"I'll have to call a nurse to sedate you if you can't discuss this calmly," she warned. Her severe tone seemed to surprise him. "Bryan and Rachel are on their way home," she continued in a gentler voice. "They'll be staying with my parents until you're well enough to travel, but your parents can't travel. Your office has been notified that you won't be in until you've recovered. My parents will be busy with the children, so for the next two weeks it will be just the two of us."

From the look on Wade's face, she guessed he considered that promise some kind of threat.

CHAPTER 8

Gage shut off the engine and looked around at the ranch yard before stepping out of the cab of the new truck he'd purchased in Logan. The grass looked browner and the bunkhouse needed painting. The wind whipped the sheets his mother had clipped to the clothesline. She insisted wind-dried sheets smelled fresher than those she placed in the electric dryer. Just over the hill he picked out the poplar trees surrounding the old house that had been his grandfather's, then the ranch foreman's, and which now sat vacant—waiting for him. Try as hard as he might, he'd never been able to picture Jena in that house. As he stared across the distance separating him from the old house, he found it much too easy to imagine Cassie organizing that house and setting it to rights.

A sound drew his attention, and he turned back to the ranch house to see his mother and younger sisters peering out of the front-room window, waiting to be certain he was the driver of the strange vehicle before running to meet him. He removed his hat and waved.

"Gage!" he heard his father's voice. Turning toward the sound, he saw his father give the reins of the horse he'd been working a quick wrap around a corral post before starting toward him. His long, ground-eating stride appeared casual, but Gage knew better. In seconds his father reached him, and Gage jumped to meet him in a fierce bear hug.

"You're here," his mother said from behind them, then hugged him with almost as much strength as his father had. His sisters clamored about him, and the ranch hands came forward to shake his hand.

"You're sure Trent is all right?" his mother fussed. "I wish he'd come home again before starting school."

"Mom, there wasn't time. You know that." He placed an arm around her shoulder. "Don't worry. He's fine, and we stopped in Salt Lake to get him outfitted all over again. I met his roommates—you'd like them."

"Are any of his roommates good-looking?" his fourteen-year-old sister asked.

"Now Mary Beth," his mother shook her head, and twelve-year-old Katherine giggled.

"Debbie and Tara and their families will be here for dinner tonight." His mother brushed away a tear and beamed happily. "We've been on the phone with them every day since we heard about the dam breaking. I called them as soon as we heard you'd been rescued, and your sisters and I started right in planning a welcome-home dinner."

"Any excuse to get your grandkids out here," Gage teased. The greatest frustration of his mother's life was that her two older daughters lived in Denver and Cheyenne, and consequently she wasn't able to see them and their families as often as she'd like.

"You bet!" she acknowledged, then swatted him. "Don't you think it's about time you settled down and provided me with a few grandbabies I can spoil right here on the ranch?"

"You've got the brats." He winked at Katherine. "They won't mind a little spoiling."

Mary Beth pulled a face.

"Jena's coming," Katherine announced, her face turned toward the long, dusty lane leading to the ranch house. "I knew she couldn't wait until tonight."

"All right, girls. Let's get back in the house and finish preparations for dinner." Gage watched his mother hustle his little sisters back inside the house. He knew she was trying to tactfully provide him with some privacy to greet Jena. Unfortunately, he didn't feel prepared to be alone with her.

"I guess we better get back to work too. If we're going to knock off early for a celebration dinner, we'd best finish the chores now." His father made an awkward excuse and started for the barn, both hired hands who'd accompanied him following behind him. He paused once, and Gage thought he might come back to add his usual admonishment to be careful, but after a slight hesitation he continued walking toward the corral. His dad liked Jena, but he wasn't convinced Gage and Jena belonged together. He'd voiced his doubts about Jena's lack of interest in the Church more than once. Gage suspected his father had some concerns about his oldest son leaving to run the Bar C before Trent was through with school and ready to settle down on their own ranch. It had taken the events of the past week to convince him his father's concern was entirely for Gage's future happiness.

Gage sighed. He had his own doubts now and wasn't sure he was quite ready to see the woman that just a week ago he was contemplating marrying. He knew now that their religious differences mattered more than he'd previously thought. And he also feared even more that he'd not be able to give Jena his whole heart. The experience he had gone through in the canyon hadn't changed him as much as it had reminded him of truths he already knew, strengthening his feelings toward the gospel. Being around the Timmermans and Shalise Richards had also brought to his attention how great the commitment between a couple needed to be in order to survive the challenges they faced.

Dust swirled around Jena's car as she stopped beside Gage's new truck. He took a step toward her as she flung open her door and raced toward him, her long chestnut curls flying in the wind. He caught her as she flung herself in his arms, and he twirled her around until she pounded on his chest and demanded to be put down.

"Okay, okay!" He laughed and set her on her feet. She immediately grabbed his hand and tugged him toward the porch swing.

"Tell me everything," she demanded breathlessly as they settled side by side in the old swing they'd played in as children, and which had over the past year become the setting for more than one lingering kiss. "I heard about the dam breaking and knew that was where you and Trent were camping. There was a story on the news about two fishermen whose bodies were found in the Bear River. That really scared me."

"It was a frightening experience, but I never doubted I would make it out alive. My fear was for some of the others trapped by the water." He glanced toward the window to see Mary Beth leaning out of it so she could hear better.

"Come on out," he motioned to her. "I might as well get this over with. I only want to tell this once. Bring Mom and Katherine too."

"I'll get your father." Mom's voice came from the open door. The screen door closed with a bang as she hurried toward the barn. In minutes she was back with Gage's father.

"You knew Trent and I were camping at Hidden Canyon in Utah," Gage began. "We'd been alone there all week, so when other campers began arriving on Friday, we watched them set up and knew where each group was located. Three girls from Kansas who were on their way to BYU camped just below us. You know Trent—he offered our services to help them set up camp and invited them to eat dinner with us. Not long after we walked them back to their camp, we heard the dam break and knew everyone in the canyon was in danger. We were quite high, and the first rush of water shot right past the mouth of the smaller canyon where we were camping. We ran to warn the girls and a woman and her young son we'd seen arrive just before dark. Eventually we met up with a county deputy and a family he'd rescued." He continued telling his family and Jena about the experience, ending with Wade Timmerman's heart attack and their rescue by helicopter.

Gage was careful not to say too much about Cassie. He'd only known her two days, and it was too soon to tell whether the connection that had blossomed between them was real. Besides he didn't want to hurt Jena. Even if it was Cassie's face, not Jena's, that had filled his mind all the way back to Wyoming, he wasn't sure at this point of his feelings for either woman.

Noise and confusion reigned the remainder of the day, and there was no way to avoid telling the story again as his older sisters and their husbands and children gathered around. In spite of his noisy family he found his thoughts drifting at frequent intervals to Cassie. He wondered if she were settled in her apartment and if she might think of him occasionally, or if he'd ruined everything by kissing her before hurrying back to his truck.

Trent had learned the girls' address from Emily earlier, and Gage had stopped to tell all three girls good-bye. He'd felt awkward standing at their door, then found himself almost tongue-tied when Cassie opened it. In jeans she'd been attractive, but when she came to the door dressed in a skirt and knit sweater and with her short, blonde curls brushed and styled, she'd taken his breath away. He'd only spoken with her for a few minutes, ostensibly to reassure himself that she, her sister, and Diane had made their way safely back to Provo. Then he'd focused on a tiny white scar at the corner of her mouth he hadn't noticed before. He'd been looking at the faint mark, wondering how she'd gotten it, then suddenly he was kissing her.

It had happened so unexpectedly, he wondered if he should apologize, but he didn't because there was no doubt she'd kissed him back. He didn't exactly regret the kiss, but now in the big family room of his parents' home, he felt guilty each time he caught Jena watching him, which was most of the time. That kiss had haunted him all the way back to Wyoming, and he had a hunch it would continue to haunt him for a long time.

He found himself feeling grateful that his nephews and nieces allowed him no time to be alone with Jena. He didn't know what to say to her. When she filled a plate for him and sat beside him on a lower step of the staircase, the children crowded around him, and a toddler plopped herself between them.

"Did the water drown all the squirrels?" six-year-old Delta asked.

"No, I think they ran away really fast, just like Trent and I did." He smiled into her huge round eyes.

"Was the little boy scared?" Delta's four-year-old brother asked.

"A little bit, but Kobie was really brave and tried to help Rachel, who is younger."

"Is Rachel my age?" Delta asked.

"Pretty close, I think, maybe a year or so older." Gage ran a finger lightly down his niece's cheek.

Only after the children were asleep and it came time to walk Jena to her car were they alone. She turned her back to her car and leaned against it, lifting her arms to his shoulders.

"I missed you," she whispered, looking up at him expectantly and rising up on her toes. He bent his head and briefly touched her lips with his. There was no urge on his part to linger, and he wondered if that were his answer. He wanted to say he'd missed her too, and in a way he had. She'd been on his mind a lot the first few days of his and Trent's vacation, but he hadn't missed her the way he'd missed Trent the four years they'd been apart, nor had he experienced the almost physical ache he'd experienced on the long drive home as he considered the possibility that he might never see Cassie again.

He kissed Jena again, this time more soundly. His future was here in Wyoming, he told himself. Cassie was intent on becoming an engineer, and there was no telling where her career might take her. The sooner he put her out of his mind, the happier he'd be.

* * *

As September drifted into October, Gage knew his feelings for Jena weren't all they should be. He sensed she knew it too, but he couldn't bring himself to say anything to her. She even took extra pains to invite him to dinner and to be particularly sweet and attentive to him. The trouble was, he *wanted* to love Jena. They'd been friends most of their lives, and he cared about her and her happiness. She also fit neatly into his plans and dreams for his own future. She would make a good wife, and together they would continue the tradition of keeping the Bar C one of the premier working ranches in the state. She'd expressed a willingness to be baptized, and in time her faith would be as strong as his. On the outside it appeared to be the perfect situation. If at times he doubted this, he kept his doubts to himself.

They occasionally drove into town for dinner or a movie, and life seemed to go on as it had before, but he found himself reluctant to formalize their relationship. Each time he planned a special occasion to ask Jena to marry him, something always seemed to come up to put off his proposal.

He and Jena both took part in the fall roundup. He kept himself too busy to think during the days, and at night he fell into bed too exhausted to even dream. Long after his father's stock was sorted out—with breeding stock shuffled to the fenced areas and the stock to be sold trucked to distant destinations—he continued to help Jena and her father. Ranch work was hard and demanding, but he knew it was guilt that kept him working beyond what was needed. He hadn't written to Cassie or called her since returning home, but in spite of his best efforts to banish her from his thoughts, he heard her laughter on the wind, saw her face in the clouds, and felt her strength beside him as he wrestled recalcitrant yearlings into trucks or dragged stubborn cows from the brush-filled arroyos. *If Jena is my future, I have no right to think of Cassie,* he constantly reminded himself.

Trent called home frequently, but sometimes Gage took the initiative and called his brother. The fall demands of the ranch kept Gage too busy to spend much time on the computer, but he knew Trent stayed in close touch with their parents and sisters through e-mail. When Gage took the time to check his own e-mail, there was almost always a short note from his brother.

He urged his horse on. The roundup was finally over, and he was making one last check of a few brushy draws before heading back to the trucks. His mind wasn't on cattle, but kept returning to Trent's last e-mail message to the family. He'd asked Mom if he could invite Emily and her sister for Thanksgiving dinner. But that wasn't all. Last night there had been an e-mail message from Cassie as well. He'd stared at her name, and all the feelings he'd struggled to bury with hard ranch work had resurfaced with a vengeance.

Gage knew Trent and Emily saw each other almost daily and sometimes studied together, so he naturally saw Cassie frequently as well. Trent hadn't said he and Emily were serious about each other, but Gage thought they might be. If their relationship were serious, how would he handle being thrown into proximity with Cassie again? He'd stared at the sender line for a long time wondering if he should just delete the message. But he knew he was just stalling and that he wouldn't delete the message without reading it. At last he clicked the mouse over her name, and a brief note appeared on the monitor.

Cassie told him Trent had given her his brother's e-mail address so she could pass on a message from the Timmermans. Her note was brief, slightly formal, and caused his heart to ache. She wrote that she and Chelsea had stayed in touch and that Wade was doing well. He'd lost twenty-four pounds, was feeling great, and he wanted Gage to know his advice had worked. *What advice?* Then he remembered the brief discussion the two of them had shared and that he had suggested that Wade pray about his situation.

Cassie had gone on to tell him the Timmermans had moved to a condo closer to Wade's work and that Chelsea had decided to go back to school now that Wade was home early enough for her to attend an evening class a couple of times a week. There was no mention of divorce or Mandy Rogers. He wondered if Wade meant that he'd prayed about his marriage and that he'd gotten an answer that he should give their marriage another chance. He hoped that was the case.

Cassie's message was impersonal, but he'd read it more than twice. At first he hadn't been able to get beyond the fact that Cassie had written to him, but as he'd searched out the last of the cattle throughout the rest of the day, he'd thought more and more of Wade's message. If Wade, who wasn't even a member of the Church and who admitted to little religious training, had turned to God for answers, why hadn't he? Oh, he'd prayed, but had he really listened for the answer? Would he still be haunted by memories of Cassie if his decision to stay with Jena and the Bar C were right?

Out of the corner of his eye, he caught a flash of red hide disappearing into the brush of a deep gully. Wheeling his horse to the left, he started down the steep slope. Reaching the bottom, he saw the cow, followed by one of the Bar C ranch hands, making its way up the opposite side of the gully. He watched until the horse and rider following the cow were out of sight.

Stepping down from his saddle, he wrapped the reins around the thick limb of a straggly scrub oak, then took a few more steps farther into the brush and scrawny trees that still boasted a few leaves. There he looked around awkwardly, then knelt. It was time to take his own advice.

His prayer was brief; he didn't want to keep Jena or her father waiting for him. He didn't receive any lightning-bolt kind of answer, but he felt confident for the first time in months that the answer would come. And this time he would act on that answer, whatever it might be.

High clouds drifted overhead, hinting of snow, but so far winter had held off. Drawing his horse to a stop on the crest of a hill, he removed his hat, letting the ever-present Wyoming wind sweep through his hair. Below he could see Jena loading her horse into one of the trailers for the final trip back to the ranch buildings. The rolling hills spread before him, and the dry grass undulated in the wind, forming a backdrop for the woman and her favorite mount, a big red roan gelding. He ached for the beauty of the scene below. He'd always felt an affinity for this land, and the Bar C was the finest ranch in the entire state, in his estimation.

"There's nothing finer than the Bar C." He hadn't heard Pat Brady ride up behind him. He glanced at Jena's father's face, looking for signs of stress. He'd questioned the wisdom of having Pat accompany them today, though he had to admit Jena had been more than careful about taking the hardest tasks herself, and her father had seemed to need to take a small part in what was clearly his last roundup.

"It shows the care you've lavished on it for the past half century," Gage complimented, keeping his eyes focused on the endless miles of range that spread as far as he could see to the mountains.

"And my father before me," Pat said with obvious pride. He fumbled with his shirt pocket, then frowned as he remembered that the pack of cigarettes that pocket had held for fifty years was no longer there. "It pleases me to see the way you're drawn to this land. For years I regretted that I didn't have a son to pass it on to. But lately I've become content, knowing a son-in-law could love this land as deeply as I do and that eventually it would pass to my grandsons."

"This land is in Jena's blood too. You can trust her to care for it as well, maybe better, than any man I know." Gage felt Pat underappreciated his daughter.

"She'll do better with a good man beside her." Pat sounded impatient, and Gage understood the man was anxious to settle his daughter's future. Time was running out for the man who had been born and raised on the Bar C and who had devoted his life to making it one of the premier ranches in the West. The cancer eating at his lungs had only been slowed for a time, not permanently stopped. He had only one child to continue his work and passion.

An ugly thought crossed Gage's mind—was it Jena's future that concerned her father? Did Pat value his land more than his daughter? And was it fair to turn over the management of the ranch to Jena's husband rather than directly to her? He'd known Jena since they were children, and he couldn't remember Jena ever wanting anything other than to run the ranch. Pat had never officially made her the Bar C foreman, but Gage knew she filled that role and filled it well. He'd never once heard Pat acknowledge his daughter's hard work nor promise her the ranch, but he had heard him lament the absence of a son to inherit the place. Was marrying him the only way her father would ever turn the ranch over to her? Did Pat care whether Jena's husband loved her, or was his only concern the acquisition of a son-in-law who could run the Bar C?

And what about him? Were the vast acres of the Bar C more important to him than Jena's happiness? He didn't know if he could answer that question honestly. He truly did care about Jena, but it wasn't the kind of caring that would see them through the ups and downs his parents had weathered. Would they stumble and drift apart as the Timmermans had done? Would his children put the ranch above everything else, including the gospel? His experience in the flooded canyon should have convinced him life was far more important than temporal things.

Sure he sometimes missed his old truck and the camping gear he'd been collecting for years, and it had put a large dent in Trent's college funds to have to replace his wardrobe, computer, and the books he'd considered important to his college career. For some reason, perhaps it was the message passed on by Cassie, his thoughts kept returning to Wade Timmerman. Wade was a man who put a lot of importance on financial success and the trappings of that success, but he'd never once expressed any regret over the loss of his expensive motor home. Remembering that before-dawn discussion they'd shared after Wade collapsed, he realized two brushes with death had altered Wade's priorities.

Thoughts of Wade inevitably turned Gage's mind back to Cassie. With her, he'd had a small taste of being with a woman who sought God when trials came her way. Could he live his life with a woman who saw no need for God in her life, who would raise his children outside of the Church? No matter how much he liked and admired Jena, would he always wonder if she, like her father, valued the ranch above the happiness of her family? What kind of marriage and home could they expect to have without love and shared faith at its center?

If he had to ask whether it was Jena or the Bar C he loved the most, wasn't that a pretty strong indication something wasn't right? It was time to admit he didn't love Jena the way she deserved to be loved.

His heart didn't feel light, the way it usually did when he received an answer to his prayers. The calm assurance was there, but he dreaded the talk he would have to have with Jena.

Pat gave a sigh, then nudged his horse forward. Gage had almost forgotten the man beside him, who was also gazing across the miles of rich grassland as though it were his last glimpse of heaven. With an ache in his heart, he followed the older man down the hill. Watching him relax his usual straight posture in a slight slump and brace himself with one hand on the pommel, Gage felt a wave of regret for what he must do. Jena stepped forward when they got to the foot of the hill and reached for her father's reins. Gage dismounted, then lent Pat a hand dismounting and making his way to the truck hitched to a large horse trailer.

After seeing Pat seated in the cab of the Bar C truck, Gage removed his own horse's saddle and coaxed the mare into his horse trailer. When he finished, he walked over to Jena, who was leading her father's horse to the trailer where her horse patiently waited. With the two of them working together, they soon had the horse loaded and the last of their equipment stowed.

"Would it be all right if I come by later tonight?" Gage asked. "Once I get some of this trail dirt washed off, maybe we could drive into town for dinner."

"I'll look forward to it," Jena said. Lifting her hat from her head, she swatted at the dust coating her pants. "Dinner sounds good, but right now I think I'd settle for a tall, cold drink. I'll have one ready by the time you get back to the Bar C."

* * *

Two hours later Gage was driving up the poplar-lined lane leading to the Bar C. He'd barely had time to shower and don his best Wranglers. He was surprised when Jena answered the door wearing a skirt and looking dressed up. She usually dressed casually when they went out. Tonight her skirt was short, and she'd piled her hair on top of her head. Beaded earrings dangled from her earlobes. She looked young and pretty and bore little resemblance to the tough cowhand who had just finished ramrodding a long, dirty roundup. Suspecting her expectations for this night were far different from his, his heart sank.

Over dinner they talked mainly about cattle prices and range improvements. Gage didn't know how to say what he had to say. He looked around at the small café with a bar at one end and decided it wasn't the place to bring up anything personal. Jena moved over next to him in his truck on the long ride back to the ranch, and Gage found it difficult not to squirm. He didn't want to hurt her, but all evening the conviction had grown stronger that it would be wrong to continue letting their relationship slowly drift toward permanency, and it was equally wrong to let her expect he would eventually ask her to marry him.

It wasn't until they returned to the ranch that he came up with a way to say what was on his mind. After helping Jena from his truck, he suggested they walk for a few minutes. She agreed and reached for his hand. They walked in silence until they reached a large stump that was all that remained of an old poplar tree that had once been part of the row of trees that lined the lane leading to the ranch house. They sat side by side on the stump. Jena squeezed his hand, and he knew even more he had to tell her how he felt. Anything less would be encouraging her to go on thinking he intended to marry her.

"Jena," he began in a halting voice, "we've been friends since we were children, and I think we both hoped our friendship would become something more. Even though we've worked together and shared some good times, I think friends are all we're destined to be." Pausing, he waited for Jena to speak.

"Friendship is more than many couples have." It was almost an argument, and there was sadness in her voice, but he was glad she didn't attempt to claim she was in love with him.

"I want more," he whispered the words. "And I want you to have more too."

"There's no time for me to find more." There was a catch in her voice, and he lifted an arm to circle her shoulders. "Gage, I'm so sorry. I've been terribly unfair to you. But to be honest, I really tried to love you. I kept telling myself it would happen, that it shouldn't be hard to fall in love with my friend. Until this summer I believed we could be happy together, and I knew Daddy had hoped for years that we would marry. When I learned that he had no intention of leaving the ranch to me, that he would sell it before leaving it to a woman—even his own daughter—I set out to get you for a husband. I took advantage of your loneliness after Trent left, but I found I couldn't push a physical relationship that would betray your values—or my own. I offered to join your church hoping that would bring us closer, but I've known for several months that even though we're friends and no one could run the Bar C better than you, marriage between us would be a mistake. It's just so hard knowing that if we don't marry, I'll lose everything."

"You're a beautiful woman with a lot more than a ranch to offer. You'll find someone right for you," Gage tried to comfort her. She shook her head, and he could see tears glistening on her cheeks.

"Dad doesn't have much time left. His doctor said a couple of months at the most. He's been so happy believing we would marry and provide him with a grandson, he's already written his will, leaving the ranch to you."

A jolt went through him. *The Bar C will be mine?* He straightened and asked, "To me specifically, or simply to your husband?"

"To you. He knows you're too honorable to take the ranch without marrying me. He was excited about our date tonight and convinced himself you intended to propose. He'll be furious and blame me when I tell him we broke up instead. He'll say it's because I haven't taken his advice to dress more provocatively and encourage a closer physical relationship, or because I didn't join your church."

"Jena, that is all wrong. Whether you joined my church, slept with me, or did anything else to entice me into marriage, our marriage wouldn't bring either one of us happiness. We each have a right to marry a person of our own choosing. I know your father has some stubborn ideas about a woman not being as capable as a man of running the Bar C, but you're his daughter, and you've been running it single-handedly for almost two years." Gage couldn't believe Pat would pass over his only child.

"He doesn't believe I've done it alone. He's convinced that you made most of the decisions and that you've been the guiding factor in all I've done." She sniffed, and he knew that his tough, strong friend was close to breaking down.

"Don't worry, you're not going to lose the Bar C. I'll think of something," he promised.

"Miss Brady," a low voice came out of the dark. Gage recognized Bernard, one of the older hands who had been on the ranch as long as he could remember. His wife, Ruth, was the housekeeper who had pretty much raised Jena.

"It's your father. Ruth sent Martin to warm up the plane, and she's on the phone with the hospital right now." Martin was Ruth and Bernard's son, who also worked for the Bar C and doubled as a pilot whenever needed.

"Let's go." Gage grabbed Jena's hand and began a sprint to the ranch house. The moment they walked through the door Jena took over supervising Pat's transfer to the small plane her father had purchased a long time ago to check the far corners of the Bar C and keep tabs on his cattle. It frequently came in handy for trips to Cheyenne or Denver, as well.

Jena was fully qualified to fly the light plane, but she chose to have Martin pilot the plane so she could sit with her father.

"Gage . . ." her voice trailed off.

"Don't worry about the ranch. I'll help Bernard and see that everything is taken care of." He helped her into the plane, then turned to assist Martin's wife into the seat beside her husband. He was glad Jena would have another woman along.

"Gage . . ." Pat's hoarse whisper ended in a choking gasp for breath.

"Don't try to talk." He gripped Pat's hand in a reassuring gesture.

"Glad . . . you . . . Jena . . ." his voice trailed off, and Jena placed an oxygen mask over his mouth and nose. Gage was crushed with a load of guilt. Pat clearly thought he and Jena were engaged, but this was no time to straighten out the misunderstanding.

"Don't worry. Everything will be fine." He didn't know whether he was speaking to Pat or Jena—or both. He stepped back, and Martin revved the engine for takeoff.

After checking that all was secure on the Bar C, Gage drove home. He'd barely finished telling his parents about Pat's relapse when the phone rang. His father silently handed the receiver to him.

"Hello."

"Gage, he's gone." Jena began to cry. "He made it to the hospital, but died about twenty minutes after we got here."

* * *

The next morning Gage showed up at the Bar C just as the sun was coming up to begin working the horses and to assist Bernard with the other chores. Jena arrived late in the afternoon. Her eyes were red, and his heart went out to her as he walked her into the house that felt too large and too empty without Pat. She stood still, looking lost and lonely in the hall of the big house. Placing an arm around her, he held her while she cried.

"Do you need help with the funeral arrangements?" he asked as he seated her on a sofa and sank down beside her. She shook her head.

"No, Daddy made arrangements to be cremated and for the ashes to be sent here later. He wants them scattered on the Bar C. He doesn't want any kind of memorial service." Her voice was desolate, and he couldn't help being angry on her behalf. It had never occurred to Pat that a funeral wouldn't have been just for him, but for Jena too—to give her a chance to perform one last service for him and to obtain formal closure for herself. Even in death he'd been unable to think of Jena's needs.

"Dad's attorney will be here tomorrow morning to read the will and officially turn the ranch over to you." He felt her stiffen and turn away as she gave him the information. With a sick heart he remembered what she had said about her father's will. There had been no time to persuade Pat to change his mind.

"I can't take your home from you. The ranch is yours," he told her. "We'll find a way to break the will."

"Daddy wanted you to have it. If he'd believed I could handle it, he would have left it to me," she argued.

"That's not quite true and you know it," Gage countered. "Pat never wanted me to own the Bar C. He only wanted me to be a caretaker until the day he had a grandson to take it over."

She said nothing for a few minutes, then stood. "I'd like to be alone. I'm going to my room now." She stopped before reaching the door and without turning around said, "You'll let Trent know?"

"Yes," he promised. Telling Trent wouldn't be easy, both because his brother would hurt for their friend and because Gage would also have to tell him he wasn't marrying Jena. Not marrying Jena meant one of the brothers would have to find work on another ranch he could never hope to own, or do some other kind of work his heart wouldn't be in.

CHAPTER 9

Gage gave the wire one more twist, then stood back to check the line of fence that disappeared over the hill. It looked good, and he was glad to have the job done; building fences wasn't his favorite activity. He pulled his hat from his head and whacked it against his dusty pants a couple of times before settling it back on his head. For November the weather was unseasonably warm.

It took only a moment to gather up the posthole digger, wire cutters, and various tools he'd used and dump them in a small compartment at the back of his four-wheeler. Straddling the small tractorlike vehicle, he let his gaze drift across the new fence to his neighbor's rolling grassland, now brown, but still capable of providing a lot of forage for the Bar C cattle. He'd always particularly loved this spot. Jena would begin trailing her herd to this lower pasture any day now, just as he and his father would soon bring their herd of heifers that would freshen in the spring to this sheltered valley for the winter.

Something close to melancholy caused him to brake one last time to look out over the valley. He knew now why he'd never gotten around to replacing the fence that separated the two herds before. Somewhere in the back of his mind he'd always dreamed of the valley without a fence dividing it. Telling the dream good-bye was harder than telling Jena good-bye had been. Of course, he hadn't literally told Jena good-bye—she was still his neighbor and friend, and he'd continue to help her as much as he could. But their courtship was at an end.

A capricious wind rippled the long grass, and a hawk circled in the sky, reminding him of what might have been. He hadn't completely gotten past the ache that had struck him when he'd signed the papers refusing the legacy Pat had left him, but his conviction that he was doing the right thing never wavered. It had only taken a few seconds to sign his name and give up his dream. Pat's attorney had been surprised at his adamant refusal to accept a bequest worth millions, and Jena had told him he was being a gallant fool. But it had all been simpler than he'd expected. By refusing to accept the ranch, it had reverted to Jena as next of kin. The Bar C was now legally hers.

With that thought, he squared his shoulders and turned toward the house. There would be just enough time to shower and change into clean clothes before Trent arrived for Thanksgiving. He smiled, admitting to both excitement and a bit of nervousness. Trent wasn't coming alone. Emily and Cassie were coming with him.

* * *

Cassie drove carefully. She still wasn't certain how Emily and Trent had persuaded her to drive all the way to the Edwards's ranch for the holiday weekend. It was true she felt sympathy for Trent, who didn't have a car of his own, and she wanted him to be able to spend the holiday with his family. And yes, she understood that Emily wanted to meet his family, but why did she have this fluttery sense of excitement in the pit of her own stomach?

Well, maybe it was because she was looking forward to seeing Gage again. Gage! Why did everything come back to Gage? She hadn't been able to get him out of her mind for weeks after he kissed her good-bye and drove away three months ago. She'd been hurt and disappointed when he never contacted her again all through September and most of October. Then a few weeks ago she'd forwarded an e-mail message from Wade Timmerman to Gage, and suddenly the exchange of e-mail messages was a daily occurrence—one she had to admit she looked forward to each evening.

"Turn here." Trent pointed to a narrow road that led across thick prairie grass and meandered toward a mountain showing darker green interspersed with the white and gray of deciduous trees, the bright fall foliage gone. After bumping over a couple of cattle guards, she saw a cluster of poplar trees with their naked branches pointing to the sky. When she drew abreast of the trees, she saw that they sheltered a house that appeared to have been recently painted white. Completely encircling the house was a wide veranda that would be an inviting, cool place to relax at the end of a physically demanding day.

"Just over this hill is the main house," Trent announced, breaking into her thoughts. Struggling to quell the butterflies in the pit of her stomach, Cassie pulled up beside a pickup truck that looked like the one Gage had been driving when he'd briefly stopped at her apartment to tell her good-bye. Dust billowed behind the used SUV she'd bought with the insurance check for the one destroyed by the flood. Both she and her passengers paused to let it settle before opening the doors.

"They're here!" a voice shouted. Cassie stepped out of the vehicle and was immediately surrounded by people and dogs. With everyone speaking and moving at once, she stood still, uncertain of which way to move.

"Cassie!" Suddenly Gage was there beside her, and everything else seemed to fade away.

* * *

Shalise balanced a slice of pizza in one hand and a can of soda pop in the other as she made her way to Dallas's sofa.

"Bet you never had a Thanksgiving dinner like this before!" Dallas plopped down on the other end of the sofa.

"No, I can't say that I have," Shalise agreed. *What an understatement!* She bit down again on the cheesy slice. All of her previous Thanksgiving dinners had featured a roasted turkey, mashed potatoes, stuffing, cranberries, and pumpkin pie. But then, she'd never been entirely alone for Thanksgiving before. Kobie had been invited to his grandparents' home for the holiday dinner, and since Daniel and his new wife were expected, Shalise had turned down her former in-laws' invitation to join them too. Her best friend, Dallas, had taken pity on her and invited her to have dinner with her, but before she could begin fixing the meal, she'd been called out to search for a missing hiker, and Shalise had gone along.

"At least it's turkey pizza." Dallas sighed and took a huge bite of the wedge she held in her hand. "I'm just glad we found that guy."

"Me too." Shalise's head began to nod. Finding the confused, elderly man and returning him to his family had been gratifying, but participating in the search had been rewarding in other ways as well. Not only had the hike along the river been strenuous enough to leave her no time to think about her own lonely Thanksgiving, but it had given her an opportunity to see how quickly the river's flood plain was recovering from the devastation that hit it almost three months ago. It would be several years before the range land recovered, and it could take several more seasons for the ranchers to recover financially from the necessity of buying feed for their herds so early.

She leaned back against the sofa. She'd rest her eyes for a moment. Her last thought before she drifted off was that she'd gotten through Thanksgiving. Now she could look forward to Christmas. Kobie would be home with her for the most important holiday of the year. Daniel and his parents could see him, but they'd have to come to her home at her convenience.

* * *

Web threw the bags and boxes that had held his dinner in the trash barrel behind the duplex he rented. It had been a long day. He'd been at an accident scene when the call had come announcing an elderly hiker was missing. By the time his report had been filed, someone else had been assigned to the search, and the local search and rescue unit got involved. He'd responded to two more accidents involving drivers who had attempted to drink instead of eat their holiday meal, then he'd been called to handle traffic at a fire where someone's dinner had gone up in flames. He'd volunteered a couple of hours of overtime so the dispatcher could run home for dinner with her family, then picked up dinner for himself at the diner.

He looked across the small yard to the mountains that appeared purple in the fading light. Above one peak a star sat in lonely isolation. He watched as another, and then another, joined the darkening sky. He felt lonely for the first time in years.

Being alone hadn't been so bad after he'd left Detroit. He'd wanted to block out the memories and accept that he was alone and always would be. Then he'd been caught in that flooded canyon and found himself caring about someone again. Sometimes he wondered if Wade Timmerman had recovered from his heart attack and if he'd divorced his wife like he'd planned to do. He shook his head, thinking the man was a fool to divorce a woman like Chelsea. Occasionally he wondered about the young people as well. Gage was a good man who had more to him than he knew. That Diane was a sharp one. She'd make a good doctor. He thought about the little boy, Kobie, most of all—and his mother. He'd seen them both a few times around the schools where Shalise worked and Kobie was a student. Once in a while he said hello to the boy, and they'd talked for a few minutes one time when the boy had been with his grandfather at the gas station. But he hadn't had any reason to speak to Shalise, and he didn't think she'd noticed him the few times he'd seen her. It was probably just as well. He would have just stammered and made a fool of himself if she'd spoken to him.

* * *

"I don't think you should have gravy on your potatoes," Wade's mother fussed. "You really shouldn't eat the potatoes either."

Wade glared at his plate, then looked at his father's, which was practically empty. It only held a thin slice of white meat and a few raw veggies. His father had starved for ten years and hadn't gotten one bit better; he wasn't going to fall into the same trap. The doctor in Utah had told him he could eat small portions of whatever he wanted as long as he exercised too, so that was what he intended to do. He reached for the gravy boat.

"Aren't we going to have a blessing on the food before we dig in?" Bryan asked. His plate was so full, he should have just asked for a second plate, Wade observed.

"Sure, why not?" Chelsea's father beamed at his only grandson, obviously pleased that the boy had brought up the subject. He'd expressed approval earlier of the slacks and polo shirt Bryan had showed up in for dinner, and Wade had been privy to a whispered comment or two between the two grandfathers concerning Bryan's missing earrings. Wade hid a snicker. His father-in-law wouldn't be so pleased if he knew the reason for Bryan's change in appearance. He wasn't even sure how *he* felt about it.

Wade's father-in-law offered grace before they began to eat. Just as Wade was beginning to think he'd be able to eat in peace, his mother asked if he'd been in to see his father's cardiologist yet.

"No, I'm seeing a doctor closer to where we live now," he answered.

"Oh, Wade, you can't trust your health to just any doctor." She stared at him in dismay.

"Mother, my doctor is a perfectly good doctor. He was recommended by the surgeon who took care of me in Utah."

"But Wade . . ."

"I would prefer not to discuss my health at the table, if you don't mind." He set his mouth in a firm line and refused to answer any more questions.

Giving up on him, his mother turned to Chelsea. "I know that under the circumstances you wish to be prepared in case you need to work, dear, but you know we'll help out if Wade is unable to support his family. This really isn't the best time for you to be away from your family so much. You needn't exhaust your strength going to school when Wade and the children need you to look after them."

"I enjoy school." Chelsea went on eating. She appeared unperturbed by his mother's comment. He was glad of that. A few months ago, she would have left the table in tears, then driven him nuts for weeks trying to make up to him for all of her supposed neglect. Actually he was enjoying Chelsea's classes as much as she was. Those were the nights he and Rachel watched ball games on TV, ate popcorn, and held video game tournaments. Once in a while Bryan joined them, but most of the time Bryan holed up in his room or went over to a friend's house. He and Bryan didn't openly fight now, but they were each a little wary of the other.

Before his grandmother could turn her attention to Bryan, Chelsea's father attempted to change the subject. "Well, Bryan, do you have a college picked out for next year?"

Bryan nodded his head and kept eating.

"That's good, son." The older man nodded his head in encourage-ment. "Ivy league or state?"

"BYU." Bryan reached for a second helping of turkey dressing.

His grandfather wrinkled his brow and looked confused. "What did you say?"

"BYU. It's in Utah. I met some really cool kids this past summer. That's where they're going. Braden Gibson, he's a kid I know at school, is going there too and we'll probably room together." He turned to his grandmother. "Did you make pumpkin pie? Do you want me to whip the cream?"

"Now wait a minute." Wade watched his father-in-law puff up. Bryan was going to get it. He'd warned his son to keep quiet, but obviously it hadn't done any good. "Are you talking about that Mormon school? No grandson of mine is attending some Mormon school!" He said "Mormon" like it was a dirty word. Wade's mother-in-law bolted from her chair and ran for the kitchen. She returned seconds later with a pumpkin pie piled high with whipped cream. She hastily dished a slice onto a dessert plate and handed it to Bryan.

"Actually, Grandpa, most members of The Church of Jesus Christ of Latter-day Saints prefer to be called Latter-day Saints, or LDS." He took a mammoth bite of the pie. "Thanks," he said to his grand-mother between bites.

"Don't get flippant!" James Niederhauser roared. "You're not going to that school."

"Now, dear," Colleen warned, fluttering around her husband. "Don't lose your temper. I'm sure we can talk calmly about this."

"Why, goodness," Wade's mother joined in. "There's nothing to talk about. Of course the boy can't go clear across the country and be exposed to a bunch of heathens."

"Mormons, Mother, not heathens." Wade found he couldn't resist jumping into the fray. "Actually, they're very devout Christians, not heathens at all."

"You know some of those people?" His mother turned on him, her tone of voice revealing how scandalized she was at this news.

"Grandma," Bryan had to cover his mouth to keep from spitting pie, but his laughter still bubbled out. "There are over eleven million Latter-day Saints. Dad is bound to know a few of them."

"Next you'll be telling me *you* know some of them," Grandma Timmerman challenged him in a disdainful voice.

"Actually, I do." He put down his fork and lifted his chin. He spoke to his grandmother, but he never took his eyes off his grandfather Niederhauser. "It was a bunch of 'Mormons' who saved our lives last summer. The doctor that operated on Dad is a 'Mormon.' My 'Mormon' friends have been teaching me about their church, and I've been meeting with two of their missionaries. Last night I asked to be baptized. If Mom and Dad won't agree to let me become a 'Mormon,' I'll just wait four months until I'm eighteen and won't need their permission."

James Niederhauser pounded on the table, while Wade's own father gasped for breath. For once Wade's mother was too shocked to say anything, and Colleen looked as though she might faint.

Wade felt a lot of things, but surprise wasn't one of them. Bryan hadn't been the least bit secretive about his interest in the Mormon faith, and Wade and Chelsea had discussed this possibility. They'd both admitted to some interest of their own, but this predictable reaction from their parents had been the reason they'd shied away from actually doing anything about it. Wade couldn't help admiring his son's courage, though he wished he'd chosen a better time and place to make his announcement.

"No! Absolutely not!" James roared. "Now, if no one else has anything to say, we'll go on with our dinner."

"If Bryan gets to be a Mormon, I want to be one too!" Rachel spoke up.

"No one at this table is going to be a Mormon!" James shouted.

"Calm down, Dad," Chelsea told him, laying a hand on his arm. She appeared completely unruffled and her voice was firm. "Bryan is almost an adult, and he's proved himself to be a dependable, mature individual. I think decisions concerning religion and the college he wants to attend are for him to decide. You, and all of us, certainly have a right to discuss his choices with him, but not to dictate them. I'm sure Bryan will be happy to tell you all about his reasons for becoming a Mormon if you choose to ask him later. If you like, we women can go watch the football game, so you men will have plenty of privacy to discuss religion while you clean up the dishes." She daintily wiped her mouth and stood to leave the room. The other two women looked hesitantly at their husbands, then followed Chelsea from the room. It took a strategic poke in the ribs to send Rachel after them.

Wade suppressed a smile. He liked the woman his wife was becoming. In fact, he suspected he was falling in love with her all over again. He began stacking plates. A surreptitious peek at his son told him something he hadn't noticed before. Bryan was a lot like his mother—and that wasn't bad.

CHAPTER 10

A song about a reindeer running over someone's grandmother blared from the radio. Shalise brushed a lock of hair behind her ear and smiled as she scooped the last pieces of gingerbread from the cookie sheet. Her son liked that silly song. In fact he seemed to have developed a sense of humor based on silliness since he started the fourth grade. She didn't mind. He could be as silly as he liked as far as she was concerned. She was just grateful he was her cheerful little boy again and that he was looking forward to Christmas with all the excitement and enthusiasm only a nine-year-old could possess.

While waiting for the gingerbread to cool and her son to come home from school, she picked up a letter she'd left lying on one end of the kitchen counter to read again. It was from Chelsea. She read again of Bryan's determination to be baptized and smiled when Chelsea wrote of her son's continued friendship with Trent and Emily. Emily had passed on the news that Gage and Cassie were planning to marry in the spring, just as soon as Cassie finished school. She smiled again, thinking of the bond that had formed between the stranded campers the short time they'd been together. It seemed that bond would continue on through eternity for Gage and Cassie. They were planning to fly to Kansas for Christmas so Gage could meet Cassie's family. This would be a special Christmas for them. She couldn't help envying them a little bit.

An ache filled her heart as she remembered last Christmas. Daniel had moved out a week before Christmas, and she had been served with divorce papers as she returned from work two days before the holiday. While she'd struggled with her own hurt and grief, her son had adamantly insisted Daddy would come home for Christmas.

On Christmas morning there had been a large box waiting on the front porch addressed to Kobie from his father. She'd helped him drag it inside and place it beside the tree, but he hadn't opened it. He wanted to wait until Daddy came. Eventually he'd opened the smaller gifts she'd placed under the tree, but showed little enthusiasm for the trucks and books she'd selected. He spent most of the day kneeling on the sofa with his face pressed against the window watching for Daddy's car to turn off the highway and start up the lane. He'd raced to answer the phone each time it rang, but the voice on the other end was never his father. Tears wet the child's cheeks when she at last carried him to bed late that night, long after he'd fallen into exhausted slumber. Her own tears had wet her pillow when she stumbled to her own lonely bed.

Sometime during the week after Christmas Kobie had dragged the heavy box to his room where it sat unopened until just after they returned from the mountains last fall. He'd been sad, then angry when he viewed the pieces of a bicycle. Even after she spent a whole Saturday reading instructions and struggling to assemble it—finally resorting to enlisting the help of the farmer who rented the back forty acres of her farm—Kobie refused to ride it. He parked it in the garage and steadfastly ignored the little mountain bike. He'd forgiven his father for so much, but something had shattered when he viewed what he considered his father's gift of a broken bicycle.

This Christmas would be different. She and Kobie would decorate their gingerbread house after he came home from school, and she would take him to the pond to skate this evening by the light of the bonfire the high school kids were planning to build. All weekend they'd listen to silly songs and Christmas carols, then she'd sit in the audience and smile while Kobie played one of the "wise guys" in the Christmas pageant at the church. Daniel's parents would come by with too many gifts on Christmas Eve, and they'd drink hot chocolate and eat sugar cookies.

The mantel clock chimed the hour as she moved to the kitchen window. Drawing the curtain back with one hand, her gaze went to the slope beyond the orchard in time to see the school bus round the hill. It grew larger then disappeared behind the trees. Going to the refrigerator she pulled out a gallon of milk. Kobie would want milk with the warm bits of gingerbread she'd trimmed from the house pieces. She poured two glasses, one for Kobie and one for herself, before returning the jug to the refrigerator.

She peeked out the window once more, but Kobie wasn't yet in sight. The lane was over a quarter of a mile long, and most of its length was hidden by the orchard. Daniel had wanted to sell all of the land surrounding the house, including the two twenty-acre orchards on either side of the lane. They had been abandoned as a cash crop years ago and left to grow wild, but to a little girl struggling to adjust to the loss of her parents and her new life with her grandparents, they had been a magical forest. She couldn't part with them.

Since the city limits had begun moving steadily in their direction, threatening to swallow up their small town and the surrounding farmland, Daniel had insisted the land was being wasted. He envisioned selling both orchards to a developer, tearing down the old farmhouse she had inherited from her grandparents, and moving into an elegant new home to be built on the old farm. They'd fought over her refusal to sign the papers he brought home a month before he'd walked out. He'd never liked living outside of town, and he considered the farmhouse a demeaning residence for someone with his talent and ambition. He'd never understood her attachment to the home where she'd been raised after her parents died in an accident when she was six.

A knot of bitterness lodged in her heart as she remembered how close she'd come to giving in to Daniel's demands. He'd made her feel guilty for depriving her son of the opportunity to grow up in a beautiful house and for failing to secure a college fund for him. She knew now that if she had agreed to sell the land, the money would have disappeared just as the money in their joint savings account had disappeared before Daniel left. She grew angry again, remembering the fight he and his attorney had waged in their attempt to claim the farm—or at least a fifty-percent interest—in his portion of their divorce settlement. He'd even demanded custody of Kobie and insisted that the child was the true inheritor of the land, and that he, the boy's father, should control the child's assets. He cited his MBA and management of his own consulting business as credentials superior to Shalise's experience teaching history to high school students.

She sighed and swept her fingers through her hair. Once more she felt gratitude for her friend Dallas. Dallas Delahaney was a counselor at the high school where they both worked. She'd been the one to recommend an attorney and insist Shalise hire him to protect her interests, while Shalise was still wringing her hands and telling herself that Daniel would come back.

After months of legal wrangling she finally admitted she had never really known her husband. She'd never known how much money meant to him, nor how little the Church and their marriage mattered to him. The final blow was learning he'd been seeing another woman several months before he filed for divorce, and that he'd used the money from his joint account with Shalise to put a down payment on the house he and the woman shared. Lingering resentment still hovered near the surface of her heart, telling her she'd been a fool to blindly trust him with control of their assets—and control of her heart. Oddly, it was only when she nearly lost both her own life and Kobie's when Canyon Crest dam broke, that she began to realize the past was over, giving her the determination to build a new life for her and her son.

Daniel had attended church during their short courtship, and he'd promised to take her to the temple as soon as he worked out a few problems. But after they married, his church attendance had become sporadic, and though she paid tithing on her salary, he found excuses to put off paying tithing on the money he earned. She'd paid their living expenses out of her salary, while his was supposed to be going into a joint savings account and investments for their future. She'd been too unconcerned about money to wonder about Daniel's near obsession with getting rich.

Shaking off memories of her ex-husband and the hurt and anger those memories always evoked, she walked over to the window to look out again. There was still no sign of Kobie.

Glancing at the clock, she wondered what was taking him so long. He'd had plenty of time to walk up the lane. Of course, he didn't know that she was waiting for him to help assemble their gingerbread house. He'd probably taken the path through the orchard and found something among the trees that captured his attention.

She mixed icing and gathered the bags of candy she and Kobie would use to trim the little house. Her eyes kept straying to the window, and when half an hour passed she stepped out on the porch to call his name. She waited, but no child's voice responded to her call.

Uneasily she stepped back inside the house. He might have missed the bus, but if he had, why hadn't he called? She eyed the telephone for several minutes before making up her mind. She dialed the number she'd long ago memorized. The school secretary answered. His teacher had already left, but Mrs. Evans said she was almost certain Kobie had gotten on the bus.

"The parking lot was crowded today," the secretary explained. "You know how it is. The last day of school before the holidays. A lot of parents pick up their children. We watch, but . . ."

A cold chill went down Shalise's spine. "Is it possible . . . ?" She hated to ask, but she'd heard stories about noncustodial parents who snatched their children from school, and Daniel had been furious when she refused to let Kobie accompany him and his new wife on a ski trip to Sun Valley for the holidays. "Do you think Daniel might have picked him up?" She choked on the words.

"No, I don't think so," Mrs. Evans answered, but Shalise could hear the hesitation in her voice. "Daniel always comes to the office first and requests permission to see Kobie or talk to his teacher."

"What!" Shalise gasped. "Daniel has been going to Kobie's school?"

"He's only been here a couple of times," the secretary spoke defensively. "He has papers that say he has a right to be informed of Kobie's scholastic progress."

"But not without my knowledge!"

"He said it was all right with you, and we didn't have any reason to think he would lie. I've known him all his life . . ." Mrs. Evans was getting upset now. "Should I call the police?"

"Kobie's probably playing in the orchard and has forgotten about time." She knew she was trying to reassure herself more than Mrs. Evans.

"Children his age sometimes leave the bus with a friend, and with Christmas just two days away. . ." The secretary tried to offer another alternative, but deep inside Shalise knew the woman didn't believe that was what Kobie had done any more than she did.

Hanging up the phone, she dashed to the closet for her parka and boots. In minutes she was trudging down the lane toward the bus stop. Less than two inches of snow covered the ground from the previous day's snowfall, and an occasional thin spot glinted with gravel where she'd driven her car to and from the main road. Kobie had been in the passenger seat beside her in his new snow togs when they'd left home this morning. A breeze swept through the bare branches on either side of her, reminding her that night came early in December. She shivered as a sixth sense told her something was terribly wrong.

The lane gradually curved, and she was soon out of sight of the house. A few feet further on, tears stung her eyes as she noted small boot tracks with the toes pointed toward home, then swerving from the lane toward the fence that ran parallel to it. On the other side of the fence a single trail of tracks led into the trees. Kobie loved the orchard as dearly as she did. He couldn't resist tramping beneath the trees even when snow obliterated the familiar path. Silently she thanked God that her small son was somewhere in the orchard and not on his way to some mysterious destination with his father. She only needed to follow his tracks.

Pausing, she called his name, but no boyish shout bounced back to her. Some silent warning urged her to hurry, and she was running by the time she reached the old-fashioned stile that crossed the fence.

In her hurry she stumbled, nearly falling from the wooden steps. She righted herself and plunged into the trees, following the tracks left by two child-size boots. She hadn't gone far before she saw that he had fallen. Puzzled, she stared at the ground. The boot prints disappeared. There were no tracks indicating he'd gotten up and continued on the trail. That didn't make sense. Turning to look behind her she wondered if he'd retraced his steps, but only one set of small tracks was visible. She looked around with a sense of unease and called his name again.

Sweeping her parka hood back, she stood still and listened. Not even the wind stirred the naked branches overhead. All was silent. Her heart raced, and she felt an inexplicable fear.

"Kobie!" she screamed. There was something ominous in the deep silence of the little wood. She took a few steps then halted. Although the small boot prints had disappeared, there were a number of deep indentations with indistinct edges. They may have been footprints, but she wasn't sure. A memory flashed in her mind of a winter day long ago when she'd longed to play outside, but had no winter boots. Her grandmother had placed several pairs of Grandpa's socks on her feet over her shoes, then stuffed each foot in a plastic bag. She'd made tracks like those she was seeing now, only these were much larger. Fear clutched her throat.

She couldn't just stand there doing nothing—staring at what might or might not be footprints. Sudden anger superseded her fear. Daniel! Daniel was trying to frighten her. If he had taken Kobie, she'd have him arrested! He'd been angry when she refused to allow their son to go with him, but she'd never once considered he might just take Kobie. *I'll follow* . . . She lunged forward, then abruptly stopped once more, staring at red spots dotting the snow. Lifting her eyes she saw a trammeled area where bold streaks of red colored the white blanket of snow.

Stumbling forward she knelt beside a small puddle to stare in horror. Every instinct told her she was looking at blood. Her mind grappled with the evidence. Perhaps Kobie had been injured when he fell. He might have bumped his nose.

Regaining her feet, she hesitated, uncertain which way to go. The strange tracks led into the trees in the direction of the road. Her first instinct was to follow, but if she returned to the house she could call the sheriff's office and have Daniel's car stopped.

A sound registered slowly. A vehicle was making its way up the lane from the road. Hope set her legs in motion, sending her running back toward the lane. Daniel was bringing Kobie back! Sudden tears filled her eyes, causing her to stumble as she reached the stile. It had only been a cruel joke. Renewed anger swept through her slender body, and she shook with the force of it. How could someone she once loved and trusted be so cruel?

She heard the squeal of brakes and, blinking back tears, she raised her head ready to confront her former husband with all of the scathing anger that gripped her soul—only the man stepping out of a white Blazer was

not Daniel. This man was taller with broader shoulders and he walked
with a kind of confidence that bore no similarity to the cocky swagger
she'd once found amusing in Daniel. His coat and cap were emblazoned
with the sheriff's department logo, and the light bar atop his vehicle clearly
identified him as a law officer. She gasped for breath unable to speak.
Deep in her soul she thanked God for sending Web Bentley to her.

"Shalise?" Web queried as he moved toward the obviously
distraught woman. "Mrs. Evans at the elementary school said Kobie is
missing . . ." He let his words trail off as he reached for the woman
who looked as though she might faint. He hoped she wouldn't—he'd
never been much good at dealing with hysterical women. He wasn't
much good with women period. Though he'd certainly like to help
this one. He'd helped her off a ledge once; he fervently hoped he
could help her again now.

His hand settled around her arm, and as he looked into her
upturned face, he felt a moment's relief that though her eyes looked
wet and shiny, she wasn't crying. She appeared angry and out of
breath. And beautiful. She came just to his shoulder and had hair the
color of warm honey, hair that was sleek and smooth and curved
forward to brush her cheek. His mind recalled her hair pulled back in
a ponytail and her face scratched and smudged the last time he'd been
this close to her. Surely it was the tears she wouldn't allow to fall that
made her blue-gray eyes appear so large.

"Daniel, my ex-husband, took him. Please use your radio to let
the highway patrol know so they can stop him before he leaves the
state!" Her eyes flashed with barely checked rage, but in spite of her
anger she spoke coherently.

"What makes you think your ex-husband has the boy?" He tried
to keep his voice even. He didn't like any kind of domestic dispute,
but wrangling over custody instead of helping a child deal with the
changes a divorce dumped on the poor kid's life seemed like selfish
stupidity to him. Custody battles always seemed to heighten
emotional reactions, so he had to know if Shalise had a valid reason to
suspect her ex-husband. The last thing he wanted was for Shalise to
lose the careful control he sensed she was fighting to maintain. He
remembered how strong she'd been while they were trapped by the
flood and hoped she still possessed some of that strength.

"Daniel wants custody of Kobie so he can sell the property Kobie will eventually inherit. But the judge gave me custody and that made Daniel angry. He thinks if he takes Kobie places and looks like a loving parent in public, the judge will change his mind. He's particularly angry now because I wouldn't agree to let him take Kobie to Idaho for a ski trip during the Christmas break." Her voice rose as she spoke.

"But what makes you think he took him?" He had to glean as much information as possible before she lost that fragile control.

"Look!" She swept her arm toward a set of kid-size tracks leading toward the fence that paralleled the lane. "He got off the bus and came this far. He likes to wander through the orchard instead of coming straight up the lane to the house. Only . . . he only went a little way, then he fell. There's blood . . . and—and the tracks disappear. Someone picked him up . . . and there are tracks leading toward the road."

A little alarm began going off in the back of Web's mind. If there was blood, this might not be a simple parental snatch. A cold shiver slithered up his spine, bringing memories he hastily shoved back into their dark hole.

"Show me where he fell." He took a step toward the fence and was pleased to note that her footsteps had not obscured the child's anywhere except where they had both crossed the stile.

"Please, call first." Blue-gray eyes surrounded by thick black lashes distracted him for just a moment until he read the pain in them.

"All right," he agreed, though he would have preferred to follow the kid's tracks into the old orchard first. But if Kobie had been snatched by his father, it would be better to act fast before they reached another state. He grabbed the CB speaker inside his truck and spoke briefly with Sheriff Howard before turning back to the woman who stood where he'd left her, staring into the trees in the gathering dusk.

They walked single file along the path without speaking until they came to the spot where the child had fallen. He motioned for her to stay put and went on alone. She'd been correct in the way she'd read the signs—Kobie had fallen. And since there were no further tracks made by small boots, she was probably also correct in assuming someone had picked the child up and carried him from the scene.

He approached the spots of blood cautiously. Something about them made him uneasy. If the child had injured himself in the fall, the blood should have been closer to the place where he'd tripped. He knelt for a closer look. The area where specks of blood colored the snow looked trampled, though there were no footprints. The larger spots appeared to have been brushed over. Closer to the tree something caught his eye, and he leaned forward for a better look. The faint impression in the snow looked like a paw print. The animal wasn't large, so he felt reasonably certain it hadn't attacked the child.

"Shalise," he called over his shoulder. "Does your son have a dog?"

"No, but you might find signs of dogs. The farmer who leases the farm has two large dogs who sometimes come here. Kobie asked for a puppy for Christmas, and his father wanted to get him one, but I said no. I didn't think now was a good time to get one since Kobie and I are gone most days. I promised he could get one next summer when we're home more so it can adjust before the next school year."

Web scowled at the small paw print, but decided against saying anything to Shalise about what he'd found. It just might be that her former husband had used a puppy to entice the boy into leaving with him without saying good-bye to his mother. A tuft of gray hair caught in the bark of a nearby tree trunk told him there was a good possibility he'd guessed right.

While looking for further evidence of a dog or a man around the tree, he almost missed the clear strand of fish line circling the tree's trunk. He reached for the line then changed his mind. He rocked back on his heels and studied the muffled tracks for several minutes. They were unmistakably the tracks of a big man who had taken time to shroud his boots in something like burlap to cover his tracks in the snow. Both the camouflaged footprints and the heavy-duty, nylon fish line were part of the crime scene, and he'd leave it for the crime lab boys to check out. But he was getting a picture he didn't like.

Taking great care not to disturb anything, he rose to his feet and glanced back toward the woman standing beside the spot where her son had fallen. She looked small and dejected with her shoulders hunched and her hands deep in her pockets. Something about her aroused his protective instinct that had led him into law enforcement, only it had never seemed quite so personal before. Slowly he walked toward her. He knew her eyes were following him, but he avoided meeting them. Instead he concentrated on the snow on either side of where the child had fallen. At last he saw it, a faint hairline leading from one tree, past where the child had floundered in the snow, to another skeletal tree on the opposite side of the path. The child hadn't fallen, he'd been tripped!

"Tell me about your ex-husband." He modulated his voice to conceal his growing suspicion. "Would he hurt Kobie?"

"Physically, you mean? No, he wouldn't actually hurt him, hit him, or anything like that. But he's neglectful. He's gone off and left him alone several times when he was supposed to be watching him."

"Has he ever punished your son harshly or hurt a family pet?"

"Not deliberately. He's self-centered, but the only time he hurts anyone is when he's so intent on what *he* wants, he refuses to see that someone else has needs too. Once he sent Kobie to his room for being noisy when he wanted to work on a project. Six hours later I came home from work to find Kobie asleep on the floor of his room with tear streaks down his face and wet pants. He hadn't even had any lunch. Daniel was absorbed in something on his computer and had forgotten all about sending Kobie to his room. As for pets, we've never had any."

"I need to call in what I've found, then follow those tracks through the orchard. Perhaps you should return to the house," Web spoke abruptly, then began walking with long, rapid steps back toward the lane without waiting to see if Shalise would follow. He didn't want her to hear what he had to say to the sheriff.

"I'll stop at the house after I check out the tracks," he called over his shoulder as he lengthened his stride. He'd check on this Richards guy. Shalise would probably have to be checked out too. Most often when a crime involved a child, the parents or some other relative were involved. He tried to ignore the gut feeling that told him they were dealing with more than a frustrated, noncustodial parent—unless this Daniel Richards was not only a jerk, but twisted and sick as well.

CHAPTER 11

Shalise stopped her pacing to peer out the window once more. Other than the patches of light reflecting from the windows of the house, all was dark and still. Web had kept his word to stop at the house after following the tracks through the orchard. He'd told her the trail continued to a partially concealed turnout where years ago her grandparents had sold apples and peaches to passing motorists from a wooden fruit stand. He confirmed that a vehicle had been parked there since the last snow storm. After letting her know other officers were on their way to check out the spot where Kobie had disappeared, he'd told her he was going back out to meet them.

"He's not in the orchard," she'd protested. "Why aren't you searching for Daniel's car?"

"There's a four-state APB out." Web spoke in a careful manner that set Shalise's teeth on edge. She appreciated his consideration in stopping to inform her of what the department was doing, but she wished he wouldn't act as though he were walking on eggshells around her.

She watched him turn away to walk toward his vehicle, leaving her feeling useless. She wasn't sure she could bear waiting for the deputy to return or for the telephone to ring. She should be out there, doing something. She lifted the curtain to better search the blackness. A fine sifting of snow covered the front porch, and once or twice she caught a glimpse of a light deep in the orchard. She closed her eyes and prayed.

The phone rang, and she scrambled to reach it before it could ring again.

"Hello," she gasped into the mouthpiece.

"Shalise?" She recognized her former mother-in-law's voice, though the other woman sounded close to tears. "Has something happened to Kobie? Two deputies were just here looking for him. They seemed to think Daniel and Kobie were here."

"Have you seen them?" Shalise gasped. She had no doubt Daniel's mother would tell her the truth. Though Darlene Richards was a little flighty and tended to smother those she loved, Shalise had never doubted the woman's love for her grandson, nor her heartbreak at the breakup of her only son's marriage. She'd been furious when she learned Daniel planned to remarry and take Kobie to another state to live. Her testimony concerning her son's inability to settle down and his emotional immaturity had helped the judge form his decision to award custody of the boy to Shalise—and had driven a wedge between Daniel and his parents. Daniel resented the continued closeness Shalise shared with them.

"No, I haven't seen Kobie since you brought him over Sunday afternoon," Darlene reported. "Daniel stopped in later that day, and he let us know he was angry because you wouldn't let him take Kobie for Christmas, but I told him a little boy belongs at home beside his own Christmas tree on Christmas morning. That's where he expects Santa Claus to leave his presents, and he should be there to find them. A ski resort is no place for a child on Christmas. Why, if Daniel took Kobie off to some ski resort, Gramps and Grammy wouldn't even get to see him. We missed him last Christmas, what with Daniel starting all this foolish divorce business. But the dear boy will have his Grammy this year—"

"He's not here. I don't know where he is," Shalise cut in. "He never came home from school."

"And you think Daniel has him," Darlene deduced.

"Yes, I think Daniel might have picked him up. He wants Kobie, and he thinks he was cheated in our divorce settlement. If he takes Kobie to another state, he might get custody there. He might even think that if he has Kobie, I'll sell the farm and give him the money to get Kobie back." Her anger spilled out.

Her former mother-in-law, who was generally never at a loss for words, was quiet for so long that Shalise feared she had offended her.

Though Darlene had sided with her in the custody suit, there was no doubting the woman's fierce love for her son.

"Daniel might take Kobie for a few hours just to scare you, but he wouldn't keep him." The older woman's voice was stiff, but it carried a wealth of sadness. "Daniel's greedy and he wants the money he could get for selling your farm, but he isn't mean. And he loves Kobie. He loves me too, and he wouldn't hurt me by taking my grandson away. He's been angry with me since I sided with you at the custody hearing, but he still wouldn't do something like that. Besides, if he took Kobie, he'd have to hide, and Lena wouldn't stand for that. Her career is just taking off, and she has every intention of being where the rich and famous are. She'd leave Danny in a minute if she thought he might hold her back, and he knows it."

Was Daniel's mother right? Lena had a powerful voice and had received an offer from a record producer a short time ago. She planned on being in Nashville in less than a month to begin recording, and Daniel was enamored with his new wife in a way he'd never been with Shalise. He wouldn't jeopardize being in Nashville with her. But if Daniel didn't have Kobie, where was her baby? Daniel had to have him. It was the only explanation.

She looked over at the table where a few hours ago she'd been happily preparing to help Kobie make and decorate the gingerbread house they'd been planning for weeks. He'd seen one in a magazine and had become excited when she'd described the ones she and her grandmother had made all those years ago. She'd agreed to bake the gingerbread using her grandmother's recipe, and they'd gone shopping together for decorative candies and a little ceramic Santa to set on the chimney top. Kobie's enthusiasm had fired a similar excitement in her for the project.

She rose to her feet and walked over to the table. Picking up the two glasses of milk, she poured them into the sink, then walked back to study the table. She should have put everything away, but doing so seemed like giving up, accepting that Kobie was gone. No. She made up her mind. She wouldn't put away the gingerbread. She'd leave it on the table as well as the candy until Kobie came home. She'd bought enough Skittles, gumdrops, and miniature candy canes to decorate several gingerbread houses, knowing that more would wind up in his tummy than on the little house. They would be right there on the table waiting for Kobie when he came home. She clenched her hands and sniffed. She wouldn't cry, nor would she consider the possibility that Kobie might not be home in time to make his Christmas gingerbread house.

Wandering through the front room, she stopped beside the tree Gramps and Grammy had helped them decorate. She smiled wistfully at the memory of Kobie leaping over boxes of ornaments to grab his favorites and rush them to the tree. She and Darlene had laughed until their sides hurt when they'd noticed all of the ornaments were on the lower half of the tree. They'd teased him a bit, and Gramps, seeing his grandson's crestfallen face, had picked Kobie up and held him so he could reach the top half of the tree. Within minutes it no longer resembled the sparsely decorated tree they had found so humorous. Kobie was so proud of that tree. If he walked in the door right then and saw she hadn't turned on the lights, he'd be disappointed. She reached down to plug them in.

For a long moment she stood staring at the lights. Where was Kobie now? In some impersonal hotel room? Would Daniel and Lena even have a Christmas tree? Or fill a stocking for him? Daniel had always left that sort of thing to her. He'd never shown interest in any part of Christmas other than his friends' parties. The only party he hadn't been interested in was the one at the church. A lump rose in her throat. Kobie was supposed to be one of the three wise men at the annual pageant and party tonight. Would he be back in time? She had to believe he would. With determined steps she marched to the door to flip on one more switch. When Kobie came home the house would be a blaze of Christmas lights, indoors and out!

* * *

Web didn't like it. Everything pointed to a snatch by the father, but he didn't believe it.

A couple of the other deputies who knew Daniel Richards thought it was just the kind of stupid stunt Richards would pull. They reminisced about the time Mr. Olsen flunked him in geometry and Richards had gotten even by putting a dead skunk in the teacher's car. And they howled with laughter about the time when a girl he'd been dating sneaked out with some guy from the college in Logan, so Richards paid her little brother five bucks to swipe some of her underwear, which he flew from the flagpole at the high school the next day.

The other deputies described Richards as an amiable guy who'd always gotten by on his good looks and charm. Even in high school, he'd won student offices and played on teams because everyone liked him, not because he'd really worked at anything. Some of his classmates suspected he occasionally conned one of his girlfriends into writing a paper for him or sharing her answers on an exam. Like many teenagers, he'd indulged in a little illegal partying, driven too fast, and been known to swipe a few cigarette packs and candy bars from local stores. But he'd never been in any serious trouble and was well liked in the community.

Apparently Richards had been spoiled rotten by overly indulgent parents and had discovered early that every time he flashed a smile at some female, she'd fall over backwards to take over where his parents had left off. Web pieced together a pretty good picture of Shalise's ex-husband from the stories his fellow law officers volunteered. It seemed Daniel Richards had married pretty Shalise Kobert two weeks after she turned twenty-one, then gained access to the trust fund her parents had left her and ran through it in less than three years.

The general air of unconcern within the department angered Web. Sheriff Howard seemed to think the whole business was an irritating nuisance that would never have happened if the elder Richards had only had the gumption to paddle Daniel's behind a few times while he'd had the chance. Several other deputies were laying odds how long it would take Daniel to figure out that caring for a kid was work and hustle him back to his mother.

Running his finger down the list of motels and hotels in the Sun Valley area, he wondered if Lane Johnson and the other deputies were right about this all being a silly hoax and he was just being a sucker for big blue eyes. Of course, Shalise's eyes weren't exactly blue—they were nearer gray, almost the color of a silky, long-haired cat his little brother had hauled around when they were kids.

Johnson claimed he'd dated Shalise a few times when they were back in high school. He'd asked her out a couple of times since her divorce too, but she wasn't ready to date yet and had turned him down. Web found himself resenting Johnson's air of propriety toward Shalise and suspected his fellow deputy didn't know Shalise anywhere near as well as he thought he did.

"Richards is a jerk." Johnson leaned against a file cabinet, his hands in his pockets, as he explained to Web his take on the case. "And now that he's married again, she'll get over him. Never could figure out why a smart, good-looking woman like Shalise fell for the guy in the first place, but it happens all the time. Good looks and charm, a certain smile, and the babes fall all over guys like him. Don't get me wrong. Richards really isn't so bad, just irresponsible. Besides, his loss could be my gain." Web took exception to Johnson's knowing grin, but tried to keep his reaction to himself.

"I wouldn't call interfering with legal custody or scaring his ex-wife half out of her mind mere irresponsibility," Web murmured, but Johnson just laughed.

"Welcome to the club," he smirked, implying Web's interest in the case was fueled by a personal interest in Shalise. "Two-thirds of the guys in this town have fallen for Shalise Kobert at one time or another, but good old Daniel is the only one she ever gave a green light. Even now, I'll bet she'd take him back faster than you can blink an eye if that little singer he married were to toss him back. You can stay here and call all the motels and rental agencies in Sun Valley if you want, but the cops up there know their job. They'll find him." He whistled as he strolled out of the office.

Web didn't waste time worrying about Johnson's remarks. He wasn't interested in Shalise Richards in the way Johnson had suggested. It wouldn't have done him any good if he had been. He didn't know the first thing about talking to women, and the few stumbling attempts he'd made to let a woman know he was interested had ended in disaster.

His shift ended, but something about little Kobie's disappearance wouldn't leave him alone, so he continued to make calls. Everyone else had dismissed the splotches of blood in the snow as a nosebleed. After all, the kid had obviously tripped. There had been no trace of the clear, plastic fish leader near where Kobie had fallen, but he knew he wasn't mistaken about that faint line in the snow. The others might dismiss the filament around the tree near the smears of blood as a remnant from a game some kid had played last summer. And yes, he knew stray dogs were a dime a dozen in the county, especially in the areas just outside of town. But he still felt unsettled.

When calls to all the motels and hotels in the Sun Valley area produced no results, he turned to the computer on his desk. He'd been hired by the county sheriff's office partly because of his computer background. This rural county had recently received a grant to upgrade their law enforcement computers to a system that would allow greater access to state and federal files. His own desire for a rural life far from the grief he'd known in Detroit had prompted his acceptance of the position. He typed in his password with a few quick keystrokes. When access to the National Crime Information Center flashed on the screen, he went to work.

Kobie was too old to be the object of a snatch by a frustrated would-be parent. Childless kidnappers always went for infants and smaller children who were too young to remember their real parents. His heart ached with dread as he clicked open the files that always filled him with the most grief.

Thieves and burglars weren't the only criminals who established a pattern in the commission of their crimes. Serial killers and pedophiles signed their work too. First he searched the NCIC bank of known child sex offenders for any that used a dog or puppy to lure their young victims. The list was sickeningly long. One by one he began tracing the whereabouts of the offenders. Many, but not nearly enough, were behind bars.

Eliminating those who had checked in with parole officers or who had been questioned by police within the past few days narrowed the list further. Those who operated exclusively in the east or in big cities were cut too. He paid particular attention to known or suspected offenders within the western states.

Though the car driven by the man who had taken Kobie could have been rented, he next ran a check on which pedophiles on his list owned cars and their makes and models. The tire prints he'd found belonged to a full-size automobile, such as the late model Buick driven by Daniel Richards—one more reason everyone else in the department was convinced Richards was responsible for Kobie's disappearance.

Picking up his phone he made a call to the Logan airport, assuming it to be the most likely place for a stranger in the area to rent a car. Methodically he contacted car rentals at every airport from Boise to Salt Lake City, carefully adding each vague possibility to his list.

"Bentley!" He turned to see the sheriff standing in the doorway. "Why are you still here?"

Hesitating just a moment, he decided to share what he'd found with his boss. "Look at this." He indicated the printouts on the desk. The sheriff moved closer and accepted the paper Web handed him. Howard studied the papers for several minutes before dropping them back on the desk.

"You're wasting your time," he growled. "The Richards kid is with his father."

"But if he isn't?" Web questioned softly. He watched the other man's face and knew he was reviewing the few facts his deputies had gleaned about Daniel's and Lena's departure and saw the hesitation there. The couple hadn't canceled utilities or emptied their bank accounts, and Daniel wasn't the sort to walk away from a home valued at close to a quarter million dollars. Neither the highway patrol nor the Sun Valley police had found any trace of them. The sheriff wasn't as certain as he'd like to be.

"I suppose you're right." Howard sighed. "It won't hurt anything to check a little further afield, but I can't afford a lot of manpower. It's snowing again, and I'm going to need every available officer investigating accidents." He picked up the papers and peered at them once more.

"What's this?" he asked jabbing a finger at a line.

Web read details he'd previously skimmed over. In the past nine years three children in Oregon, one in Arizona, another in New Mexico, and four in Texas had been discovered dead by strangulation. They all bore the marks of thin cords about their necks. They had also all been molested. A cold sickness lodged in his belly. Thin cord? Could it have been clear filament like fishing line? Why hadn't he considered the nylon filament part of the kidnapper's signature style? Studying the cases more closely, he discovered the crimes were unsolved, but a suspect had been arrested then released in one of the Texas cases.

Swiftly turning back to the computer, Web punched in a new code. Court records were brief since the suspect had been released, but he didn't doubt he could piece together more details from newspaper accounts.

He was aware of the sheriff's knuckles turning white against the edge of his desk as he read over Web's shoulder. Lester Ferrindale had been arrested four years ago for suspicion of murder in the case of José Navarona, a six-year-old Texas boy whose body was discovered two days after his disappearance, rather than the weeks or months later the other children's bodies had been found. A classmate waiting behind a hedge to pounce on his friend had witnessed the abduction and had scratched in the dirt the license plate number of the car he'd seen the boy climb into carrying an injured puppy. He couldn't describe the driver other than to say he was big. The car had been a rental, and the rental company's records proved ambiguous, so Ferrindale had been released for lack of evidence, even though the man was 6'2", weighed 210 pounds, and samples taken from the rental car proved to be dog hair.

A quick check of the NCIC files showed no subsequent arrests and that the address Ferrindale had listed four years ago no longer existed, if it ever had. A man fitting his description had stayed at a motel four miles from where the New Mexico boy disappeared last year. He'd checked out of the motel six hours before the boy was reported missing, and the police had been unable to trace him for questioning. In that case too, the plates on the car the man had driven when he registered at the motel were traced to a rental agency. The car, abandoned in Taos, had been rented with a stolen credit card. The man's description closely matched the Texas mug shot.

Web pulled the list of car rentals back onto the screen. Several men fitting the vague description of Ferrindale had rented full-size automobiles from rental agencies at the Salt Lake City airport, but only one had been traveling alone. He began a trace on that man's ID.

Howard rolled the report he held into a cylinder and whacked it against the palm of his other hand for several minutes before speaking. "I still think Richards took his kid. He probably doesn't even know that what he did is considered kidnapping. I doubt he intends to keep him. He's pretty ticked off at Shalise and probably thinks that by taking the boy he's just getting even. In case I'm wrong, consider the case yours. Follow up on whatever angle you think best, but keep me informed."

Web amended the APB he'd sent out to surrounding states to include the possibility that someone other than the father may have taken the child. Then Sheriff Howard turned back to his own duties and ordered the two dispatchers to keep a pot of coffee hot and to order in sandwiches and soup from the café across the street for any of his people that needed something warm between calls. His expression was grim as he stepped out the door into a swirling snowstorm.

Web hadn't had dinner, and his eyes were bleary from watching the screen, so he didn't mind the interruption when one of the dispatchers, Mrs. Waverly, set a cup of soup on his desk. Almost absently he lifted it to his lips and took a swallow. His mind was still on his computer screen and at first her words didn't sink in—until she mentioned Shalise, then suddenly his attention focused.

". . . been calling every half hour. Poor thing. That boy is everything to her. I could just shake that Danny. He has no business worrying her like that, and I told her so. The very idea! Telling her he was going to Sun Valley when all the time he planned on Vegas. When he gets back here, I . . ."

"Daniel Richards is in Las Vegas?" Web jackknifed upright in his chair. "How do you know he's in Vegas?"

Mrs. Waverley looked startled, then smugly patted her hair. "The Las Vegas police called just before the sandwiches arrived. I patched them right through to the sheriff, but he's up in a canyon where reception is poor. I'll give him the message as soon as he calls in."

"The boy?" Web held his breath.

"I'm sure he's fine. Daniel wouldn't hurt him. I was just going to call Shalise and let her know everything is going to be fine, then I thought you might want your soup while it's hot so I came in here first."

Web struggled to maintain his patience. "Did the Las Vegas police department say anything about the boy? Did they confirm that his father has him? Is he being returned?"

"No, but why wouldn't they send him back? Do you think they'll want Shalise to go get him?" She frowned.

Why couldn't the other dispatcher have taken the call? Mrs. Waverly was the least competent dispatcher he'd ever dealt with—and the worst gossip. It was all Web could do to refrain from saying something he knew he'd have to apologize for later. "Look, go back to your desk." He struggled to keep his voice even. "I'll call Las Vegas. If you get any other calls concerning the Richards boy before Sheriff Howard gets back, put them through to me. Got that? And don't call Mrs. Richards. If she calls here you are not to tell her anything. Just put her call through to me. Is that understood? Now get me whoever called on the line." His voice lost its even tenor long before he reached the end of his speech, and he watched in dismay as Mrs. Waverley, blinking back tears, rushed from his office.

In less than two minutes his phone rang, and he was listening to Captain Denning in Las Vegas explain that two patrolmen had spotted Richards's car nearly an hour ago in a casino parking lot. He'd sent detectives right over, and they'd found Richards had registered under his own name at the hotel. After a short search they'd located the man and his wife having dinner. The child was not with them nor in their room. The detectives had taken the couple to the precinct house for questioning but planned to release them shortly unless the Utah police had something substantial on which to hold them.

"Richards is demanding to speak to his ex-wife," Denning concluded. "He's angry, but I think he's concerned about the kid too."

"Stall him a little while," Web retorted. "I need to break it to her first that Kobie isn't with his father." After getting the captain's agreement, he hung up and headed for the door, snagging his coat off its hook on his way out.

As soon as he rounded the curve in the lane, he saw the lights. They outlined the porch and trailed across the eaves. The front-room window provided a frame for a brightly lit tree. Something about the Christmas card perfection of the gaily decorated old farmhouse and the falling snow brought an ache to his heart. He wished his mother had been like Shalise. But his mother would never have thought of turning on lights to welcome him home. He'd never known a Christmas like the one he could see Shalise had planned for her little boy. Unlike Shalise, his mother had never baked gingerbread or strung lights on a fir tree when he was young. The cynic in him suspected his mother had only remembered him and Frankie when she filled out the forms that guaranteed a steady stream of checks from the state.

He tightened his grip on the steering wheel and forced himself to turn his thoughts back to what he'd say to Shalise. A bunch of colored lights had never gotten to him before. He hadn't been sentimental about Christmas for many years. He'd only been six when he'd realized he'd never get a visit from Santa Claus or have his own Christmas tree. The ache had continued for a long time, but he was a grown man now who didn't need to get maudlin about holidays. Christmas was just another day. Unfortunately, he feared this Christmas wouldn't be just another day for Shalise Richards.

CHAPTER 12

Shalise heard the growl of an engine before she saw headlights cut through the falling snow. A vehicle was making its way up the long lane leading to her house.

"Please let it be Kobie coming home," she closed her eyes and prayed as the lights drew closer. Her fingers curled into tight fists, and her breath froze deep inside her chest. When she opened her eyes, she could see a reflection of Christmas lights on the light bar on the top of a sheriff's department truck parked in front of her house. If they'd found Kobie, would they call or just bring him home? Surely they'd bring him home! She began running toward the door.

A knock sounded on the heavy, wooden door, and her legs felt weak, incapable of carrying her as she stumbled toward it. She fumbled with the door latch in her haste. When she finally flung the door open, her eyes searched frantically for what wasn't there. Webster Bentley stood before her, alone.

"Kobie! Where's Kobie?" The hint of hysteria in her voice frightened her. She couldn't fall apart. Her son needed her.

"We haven't found him yet." Web stood on her front porch shifting his weight from foot to foot and eyeing her as though he expected her to suddenly start foaming at the mouth and turn rabid.

She wanted to scream and cry, but she wouldn't. Losing control wouldn't help her son. She had to be strong.

"I—I'm sorry. Please come inside," she invited while struggling for a calmness she didn't feel. Web looked far too serious, and her fears began to escalate. *If he weren't serious would that be better?* a voice in the back of her head mocked. She shuddered knowing she couldn't hang on to her sanity if Web were jovial and lighthearted about her son's disappearance. It was bad enough that most of the people who had called, including a couple of deputies, were convinced Kobie's disappearance was nothing more than one of Daniel's practical jokes. Only taking Kobie wasn't a joke—there was nothing even slightly funny about it.

Pulling his cap from his head, Web stomped his feet to shake snow from his boots before stepping inside. He stood just inside her front door on a small braided rug, slowly twisting his cap between his fingers, and seemed as much at a loss for words as did she.

"Richards . . . that is, your ex-husband . . . he didn't—doesn't . . ." The deputy was interrupted by a ringing telephone. She glanced toward it, then back at Web, torn between answering it or hearing what he had come to say.

"Go ahead, answer it." He indicated the phone with a nod of his head. "It might be for me. I told dispatch to call me here if anyone needed me."

She reached for the gray and white wall phone with a combination of hope and dread. "Hello," she whispered, then in a forced voice repeated the greeting and identified herself, "This is Shalise Richards."

"Shalise, are you all right?" Her friend Dallas's voice was full of concern. "Has Kobie been found?"

"I—I'm fine, but when I get my hands on Daniel I'm going to . . ." She stopped suddenly, remembering a deputy sheriff stood mere feet away. This was no time for exaggerated threats, even if at the moment she felt angry and scared enough to want to cause bodily harm to the man she'd once loved.

"Look, Dallas, a deputy just arrived to talk to me. I'll call you as soon as I know anything."

"I'm coming out there. You shouldn't be alone," Dallas insisted before Shalise could hang up.

"You don't have to . . ."

"I know I don't have to," Dallas spoke impatiently. "I'll be there in ten minutes."

After hanging up the phone Shalise turned back to Web, who still stood in front of the door frowning. A lock of dark hair fell damply across his forehead, and his brown eyes looked troubled. A small puddle of melted snow ran from beneath the rag rug where he stood.

"Please come in and have a seat." She motioned him toward the chair she'd always considered her grandfather's. She remembered how much Daniel had hated the big old arm chair. He'd wanted her to get rid of all of her grandparents' furniture and replace it with new modern pieces. She had given away most of it, but there had been a few pieces like the armchair she couldn't give up. Somehow it was oddly comforting to see the big deputy settle in the chair. Something about him looked as though he belonged there. She perched on the edge of the sofa across from him for a second or two, then bounced back up.

"Would you like something to drink, Web?" She struggled with the polite conventions, uncertain whether she was stalling out of fear for her son or if the queasiness in her stomach resulted from impatience for the man to tell her all he knew.

"I don't need anything." He took a deep breath and continued. "I came out here to let you know your son isn't with your ex-husband."

"Isn't with . . . ? Then you've found him!"

"Not your little boy. We don't know where he is, but Mr. Richards is in Las Vegas."

"He said he was going to Sun Valley!" She shouldn't have been surprised that Daniel had lied to her again.

"He told the officer who questioned him that he changed his plans after you told him he couldn't take Kobie for Christmas."

"If Kobie isn't with him, where did he leave him?" All the hurt and betrayal accumulated in the ten years of their unhappy marriage, and the painful revelations brought to light through their divorce boiled to the surface. She hated Daniel. It was enough that he'd spent her legacy from her parents, schemed to steal what her grandparents had been able to leave her, and trampled on her pride. But she wouldn't allow him to keep her child from her!

"Where did he leave Kobie?" she screamed at the startled deputy.

"Shalise . . ."

"I want some answers. That idiot has been getting away with murder as long as I've known him. Everyone covers for Danny! If you can't make him give my son back, I'll . . ." She couldn't think of anything terrible enough, but she'd get Kobie back if she had to sell the farm and spend every penny she could get her hands on to pay for private investigators and attorneys. In spite of how hard she'd fought Daniel to keep her house and the farm, she'd sell them or give them away in a second to have Kobie back!

She was right about Daniel being spoiled and protected, but she was missing the point about Daniel not having Kobie with him. Web let his gaze wander around Shalise's house while he tried to think of a way to make the situation more clear to her without scaring her to death. Every available surface was loaded with some kind of holiday knickknack—reindeer, Santas, candy canes, nutcrackers, and colored lights. On a table by the tree sat a carefully painted nativity scene. He shut out memories of another crèche a long time ago, in another place.

The Mary figure kneeling lovingly beside the infant's crib looked much like Shalise. Carols played somewhere in the background, and he wished he didn't have to hurt this woman more than she was already hurting. Especially at Christmas. Web didn't have much firsthand experience with Christmas, but he figured from the way the house looked and smelled, this lady knew a lot about this holiday and what made it something a little boy dreamed about. For just a moment he envied Shalise's little boy.

Stretching out his hand in a conciliatory gesture, he tried to find a way to soften his words. He hadn't handled this well so far. If he were better with words, he'd know what to say. And if he weren't such a clumsy ox around women, he'd not only explain better, but he'd know how to comfort this woman who was so desperately frightened and angry. He didn't want to examine too closely why this particular woman's fear touched him so deeply, or why it had occurred to him to want to comfort her. There wasn't time anyway.

Before he could begin to think of what to say or do, a quick rap on the door sounded and a whirlwind burst into the room without waiting for a response to her knock.

"Shalise!" A tall woman with boyishly cropped red hair flew across the room and engulfed Shalise in a fierce hug. With the back of her hand she brushed away tears from her cheeks and hastily assured the other woman, "Daniel won't get away with this!" Suddenly she whirled around to face Web.

"Why haven't you arrested that irresponsible creep?" she demanded in a no-nonsense tone. She placed both hands on her hips and scowled at him.

It took all the stoic self-control he could muster not to shudder. Shalise's redheaded friend was the kind of woman he feared most. He'd rather bump a few brawling drunks' heads together or shoot it out with bank robbers than face an assertive, smart-mouthed woman like Dallas Delahaney.

"Mr. Richards didn't take his son," he said as rationally and calmly as possible. He didn't want the redhead to yell at him, nor did he want Shalise to suffer. He dreaded the moment when she'd understand that her husband hadn't taken Kobie —someone else had, and that someone intended the boy a great deal more harm than her irresponsible ex-husband would ever be capable of.

"Of course he did!" the redhead refuted his statement, and Web struggled not to flinch. His mother had yelled like that, and when she did, it usually meant something unpleasant was going to happen to him. He'd better explain. He opened his mouth, but once more the ringing telephone prevented him from saying anything further.

"I've got it!" Dallas announced as she scooped up the receiver and held it to her ear. In seconds she was shouting.

"You stupid cretin, you're out of your mind. No, I will not put Shalise on the phone so you can bully her. Get your sorry butt back here and bring Kobie with you!" She paused, then continued to shout.

"What do you mean Kobie isn't with you? Go get him from wherever you parked him and bring him back—or tell me where he is, and I'll go get him!" She listened a few seconds then yelled, "You stupid nincompoop, you'll never convince a judge that Shalise is an unfit mother. Are you so lacking in brains you don't know you're the one in trouble? Kidnapping is a federal offense even when you're the kidnapee's father!" She was quiet, listening for almost a minute, and Web watched as the color drained from the woman's face and her knuckles turned white where she held the phone.

"If you're lying, there's no place you can hide that I won't find you and see you destroyed." Her voice was low and ominous, and suddenly Web decided maybe this bossy woman wasn't so bad. She cared about Shalise and didn't mind telling the jerk on the other end of the line, undoubtedly Daniel Richards, things a deputy would probably lose his job for saying.

When Dallas hung up, she turned slowly to face Shalise, who was staring at her with round, frightened eyes. She took a step forward and once more wrapped her arms around her friend. "I'm sorry," she whispered. "I think he's telling the truth for once in his sorry life. He really doesn't know where Kobie is."

Web felt like he'd taken a blow to the side of his head as he watched the dawning horror on Shalise's face. He braced himself for her scream, but she didn't make a sound. Slowly, silently, she slipped from her friend's arms and slid toward the floor. Lurching forward he caught her just before her head made contact with the stone fireplace.

Effortlessly he lifted her in his arms and turned toward the sofa. When he reached it, he felt a strange reluctance to lay her down. She didn't weigh a whole lot, and though he'd thought her pretty when he'd first seen her, right now she had a waxen beauty that clutched at his heart.

"Put her right here," Dallas ordered as she fluffed a pillow and reached for an afghan thrown over a nearby chair. Reluctantly he did as he was told, and Dallas covered the unconscious woman with the afghan before settling on the floor beside her friend. Slowly she stroked Shalise's face and patted her hands, and Web felt something akin to jealousy flood his heart. For just a moment he wished he were the one touching Shalise and offering her comfort.

"Would you get a damp cloth?" Dallas asked without turning to look at him. "The bathroom's at the end of the hall."

Web raced to do her bidding and stopped, hesitating inside what was obviously the bathroom. She'd decorated this room too. He'd never seen a bathroom covered with Christmas decorations before. Kobie was lucky to have a mother like Shalise Richards. He didn't remember the apartment where he grew up ever smelling like gingerbread and pine trees. There had been no stocking with his name or his brother's hanging on a mantel and no wrapped packages under a tree. And there certainly hadn't been any bright red towels with little shiny, green pine trees on them in the bathroom. He stared like an awestruck kid at poinsettias hanging from the ceiling in baskets, bars of soap shaped like angels, and tiny white lights glittering around the vanity mirror. Good grief! Even the toilet paper had little red Santa Clauses all over it. He wasn't sure the red towels were to use or look at, but he hastily grabbed one and ran it under the faucet to get it wet.

When he returned to the front room, Shalise was struggling to sit up and Dallas was insisting she stay put, someone was hammering on the door, and the phone was ringing. Thrusting the towel in Dallas's hands, he rushed to the door and stared in disbelief. A white-haired couple dressed in red velvet stared up at him expectantly through half-glasses. He felt like the little girl in a storybook one of his foster mothers had read to him years ago who fell down a rabbit hole and her whole world turned topsy-turvy.

"We just got the news." Mrs. Santa charged across the room, her red cape swirling. Mr. Santa smiled apologetically at the big uniformed man, then followed his wife.

"Dora Waverley called to tell us the good news. She's such a dear." She smiled brightly at Shalise. "Danny was ever so naughty to go off to Las Vegas when he told us he'd be in Sun Valley. But everything is fine now. I know tomorrow is Christmas Eve, but we thought it would be fun to surprise Kobie with Santa Claus and Mrs. Claus when he gets here." She patted her red velvet dress and preened, clearly expecting praise for her cleverness.

Web groaned. He'd ordered Mrs. Waverley not to call Shalise, but he hadn't thought to make it clear she shouldn't call anyone else either. Obviously these Santa Claus people were Daniel Richards's parents. He'd have to set them straight. Before he could open his mouth, Dallas turned on them with a snarl, and he wondered if he'd have to protect them from the fierce redhead. But one look at Shalise Richards's face was enough to make him want to close ranks with the Delahaney woman instead.

The telephone was still ringing, and feeling like a coward he turned his back on the commotion behind him to pick up the instrument and growl an impatient hello into it.

Bill Haslam identified himself and asked what he could do to help. Web had been in Orchard Springs long enough to know the man on the other end of the line wasn't just a concerned neighbor. He was also the spiritual leader, or bishop, of one of the two Mormon congregations that met in the old stone church across from the high school. He assumed Shalise belonged to his congregation.

"There's not much anyone can do tonight," Web acknowledged reluctantly. "Mrs. Richards's friend, Dallas Delahaney, is here and I heard her say she plans to stay until the boy's found."

"Tell her I'll be there first thing in the morning, but if she wants me to come sooner I can be there as soon as I get my family back home. I'm calling from the church where I just heard that Daniel had taken Kobie. The ward party was tonight and that's where I heard about this whole ordeal."

"Daniel didn't take the boy," Web spoke bluntly to his friend, then went on to explain. He heard Bill's sharply indrawn breath and knew he understood.

"I'll be right there." Bishop Haslam's voice didn't invite argument, but Web tried to dissuade him anyway. He liked Bill Haslam. The two men had shared a number of deep discussions that had almost persuaded Web to become a Mormon, but he didn't think there was anything Haslam could do for Shalise tonight. Besides, Bill faced some bad roads between Orchard Springs and his place. It would be better if he worried about getting his own family safely home. Putting his hand over the mouthpiece, Web turned toward Shalise. "Bishop Haslam wants to know if you'd like him to come over."

Shalise shook her head slowly. "Tell him I'm sorry Kobie and I weren't there tonight for the pageant . . . and ask him to pray for Kobie."

Web repeated the message and spoke quietly to the bishop for a few more minutes before hanging up. He'd barely replaced the phone in its cradle when it rang again. His voice was gruff when he answered.

"The Salt Lake County Sheriff's Department is on the line," Dora Waverley addressed him in a haughty tone. Clearly she was still in a snit over his earlier reprimand. That was nothing compared to what he'd have to say to her when he got back to the office.

He introduced himself and assured the man who identified himself as Lieutenant Tom Clark that he was the officer in charge of the Orchard Springs missing child case, then listened intently.

"We had a report of an accident in Little Cottonwood Canyon about seven tonight," Clark reported. "When we reached the scene, we found where a vehicle had missed a curve, fishtailed several times, then gone over the side. It took nearly forty-five minutes to get two men down the mountainside to the crash site. It didn't look like anyone could have survived a crash like that. But when the deputies reached the wrecked car, they found blood all over the interior, but there weren't any bodies."

Web's heart lurched. "Why do you think that accident might be connected to our missing boy?"

"We found a backpack in the car. You know the kind little kids haul their stuff to school in. It was light blue with red straps and had the initials K. R. embroidered inside the flap. I didn't think too much about it until I glanced at one of the papers inside. Right at the top in a kid's printed scrawl was the name KOBIE. It's an unusual name, and I knew I'd heard it recently. I was climbing back up to my truck when it hit me. That's the missing kid's name!"

"You searched the area?" Web demanded to know.

"As much as we could," Clark responded with real regret in his voice. "It's snowing heavily here and there's wind. Any tracks the survivors may have made are long gone. We've got a search-and-rescue team mobilizing now, and records is checking the license plate. Our lab people are going over the few items we found in the car."

"Thanks. If I leave right now I should be there in two hours. Give me directions." He picked up a piece of paper and jotted a few notes.

He hung up and noticed for the first time that the room was deathly still. The earlier tumult had ended abruptly. He turned to find Shalise less than a foot away. Her eyes were big and scared, but he sensed she wouldn't faint again.

Forgetting his own awkwardness in dealing with women, he reached for her hand. He drew her back to the sofa where he crouched in front of her with her hand still in his. Carefully he told her all Lieutenant Clark had told him.

"I have to report to Sheriff Howard, then I'll be on my way," he told her. "I promise I won't leave that mountain until your son is found." His thoughts were bleak as he remembered searching the alleys of Detroit for his brother. If he hadn't given up . . . just one more alley and he would have found him, and it might not have been too late. If there was any possibility Kobie was still alive, he vowed he would find him.

"I'm going with you!" The smaller hand in his tightened around his fingers.

"You can't," he spoke gruffly.

"Then I'll follow you." Something in her voice told him she really meant it. He turned helplessly to the other occupants of the room. The older woman was weeping while her husband held her and absently patted her shoulder. Helpless rage played across the older man's face, looking incongruous with his Santa costume.

"Take her with you," Dallas spoke with chilling calmness. "She won't get in your way—she has too much at stake. You can't leave her here to go out of her mind. Kobie is her baby, and she has to be there when you find him. I'll lock up the house for Shalise and see that the Richards get home safely. I'll follow you in a few hours and take her off your hands."

He wanted to argue, but strangely it wasn't the part about Shalise being in his way he wanted to argue; it was the implication that he wanted someone to take her off his hands.

CHAPTER 13

Web drove as fast as he dared, but heavy snow in the canyon made the road treacherous, and he found each delay a frustration. Shalise slept for the nearly two and a half hours it took them to reach Salt Lake. She was out like a light before they reached Logan, curled almost in a ball with her head resting against the folded blanket Dallas had shoved into his truck just as they were leaving. He'd been surprised at first that she'd slept so easily, as worried and scared as she was, but then he remembered the redheaded woman's bossy insistence that Shalise drink a mug of hot chocolate before leaving the house. He suspected the devious woman had made certain her friend got some rest.

The snow had slowed to a few flutters by the time they reached the I-15 construction south of Ogden. If his estimates were right, the creep who snatched Kobie must have hit here about rush hour, and with Christmas shoppers and a Jazz game tonight he'd been forced to a crawl all the way to Salt Lake. Nice to know all this construction served some useful purpose. That had probably delayed him enough to place him in the canyon about the time the storm hit its peak.

Once he reached Salt Lake, Web drove across the valley quickly. As he started up the canyon on the east side, he glanced over at the sleeping woman. He wasn't concerned about her getting in his way. As Sheriff Howard had spelled out so there was no way he could mistake his meaning, the accident site wasn't his jurisdiction. He could assist, but he couldn't interfere with the way his Salt Lake County counterpart conducted the search or handled evidence at the site of the crash. He could live with that. What he suspected he couldn't live with was seeing Shalise Richards fall apart if they didn't find Kobie—or if they were too late to find him alive.

The snow fall became heavier, and the wind howled against the truck as it moved steadily up the mountain road. He approached the mouth of the canyon and slowed at the sight of flashing red lights. A digital sign warned that only vehicles with chains would be permitted beyond that point. Several cars turned around and started back toward him, but he kept going until at last he reached the checkpoint. Rolling down his window, he showed his ID, and the officer allowed him to pass through. His utility was outfitted for deep snow, and the twisting mountain road gave him little trouble.

He slowed, then stopped when he spotted the intermittent flash of red and blue lights again twenty minutes later. A deputy in heavy winter gear stepped to his window. When Web identified himself, he was directed to a wide overlook a quarter of a mile farther up the canyon where search and rescue vehicles and a command unit were already parked, well away from any potential slide areas.

Bringing his truck to a stop a few feet from the big command unit, he switched off the engine. A deafening silence hit his ears. Through the falling snow he could see the dark shapes of pine trees and the skeletal arms of aspens, and he was afraid. Afraid for the woman sleeping beside him. Afraid for a small boy lost on the mountainside. Was Kobie wandering around alone? Was he injured or held prisoner? Did Ferrindale, or someone like him, have Shalise's son?

Ferrindale, again if the kidnapper were Ferrindale, must have been headed for one of the cabins in the canyon. Was it nearby? Had he taken the child there after the accident? The road up Little Cottonwood Canyon wasn't a road anyone took if they were just passing through Salt Lake. It was a destination route—a road that led to ski resorts and cabins. Cabins close to the resorts might be luxurious havens for skiers, but the ones farther away for the most part were summer cabins where work-weary city dwellers escaped for a few weeks each summer and were usually quite basic. If a man like Ferrindale made it to one of those cabins with the boy, it might be better if the kid had died when the car plunged off the cliff.

He let his eyes roam over the woman curled on the seat beside him and felt something tender stir in his heart. He thought he'd learned his lesson years ago, not to care too much, not to want. But suddenly he wanted to see this woman smile. He wanted to see a small dark-haired boy safely held in his mother's arms. This time he wouldn't be too late, he vowed. He swallowed a lump in his throat and reached for the door handle. It was time to check in with Clark and share notes. He glanced once more at Shalise and decided it might be best if she continued to sleep.

* * *

Shalise was conscious of strong arms lifting her from the truck, and she struggled to keep her eyes closed. She didn't want to wake up. She didn't want to face . . . Her eyes snapped open just as Web ducked to carry her through an open doorway.

"Kobie?" she whispered hopefully.

"There's no word yet," a deep voice rumbled in her ear just before she found herself deposited in a chair near a table where several men leaned over a topographical map. The men glanced at her, then turned their pitying eyes back to the map.

Why were they just sitting there? She didn't want their pity; she wanted them to go out there and find her son!

Her mind felt foggy, and she shook her head to clear it. No one spoke to her as she gradually became more aware of her surroundings. She was inside some kind of building—no, it wasn't a building. She was in the back of a truck or trailer loaded with communications equipment, maps, and first-aid supplies. The room wasn't cold, but not exactly warm either. The bitter odor of coffee hung in the air along with an occasional whiff of tobacco smoke. The men around her, dressed in drab brown uniforms, were police officers looking for her son. All the anger and fear came flooding back. Kobie was missing!

Hadn't she and her child faced enough loss and betrayal? She wanted to scream out and demand an answer. Why had God allowed this terrible thing to happen to a child as sweet and innocent as Kobie? Didn't He care that a little boy who tried to be good, and who went to Primary every Sunday, and who said his prayers each night had been wrenched from his mother's arms into unspeakable terror?

No, she wouldn't go that route. She wouldn't blame God. It wasn't God who took her child. Her Heavenly Father had been there for her through the breakup of her marriage, and when floodwaters bore down on her and her son. She would cling to her faith that He was there for them now. It was only weariness and fear causing her to doubt for even a moment. She blinked her eyes and breathed deeply, trying to rouse herself from the despair and lethargy that held her.

She turned her head and her eyes met Web's. He was kneeling beside her chair, a wary, waiting expression on his face. She knew then that her stuporous lethargy was because she'd been drugged, and she knew too that he expected her to blame him. He may have been in collusion with Dallas, but she suspected he'd had no idea what her friend was up to until the deed was done. She didn't even feel any surprise that her friend had arranged for her to sleep the entire trip. Dallas understood her too well. She'd known Shalise needed rest, but would be unable to sleep on her own while her son was in danger. For a moment she wondered why Web assumed she would blame him. She should have been angry, but anger seemed a wasted emotion. All that really mattered was getting Kobie back. She struggled to stand, but a strong arm held her imprisoned in the chair.

"Let me go. I have to find him." She pushed ineffectively against Web's shoulder.

"No, Shalise." Above her fear and anxiety she heard the compassion in his voice. "Trained professionals are scouring the area. You would only distract them and slow their efforts."

"But I can't just sit here waiting. My little boy is out there." She waved vaguely toward the door. "He needs me."

"He does," Web acknowledged. "Little boys shouldn't be separated from their mothers. He should be home in the house you decorated so nice for Christmas. But you can't help him now. You have to be here when he's brought back."

"Ma'am," a voice interrupted. "You shouldn't be here at all. I don't want to spare a man to take you back, but I will if you cause trouble." She looked up at the lean, tough-looking officer she'd failed to notice before. His face appeared to be made of granite, and she recognized the futility of getting in this man's way. However, instead of being frightened, she felt encouraged as she recognized the man's steely determination. Turning back to Web she met the same expression on his face and in his eyes, mixed with some terrible pain. If anyone could find her son and bring him back to her, it was these two men, whom she suspected felt some personal stake in her son's safety.

"All right," she gave in. "I'll stay here. You'll let me know . . ."

"As soon as we know anything," Web promised.

"I'm taking Deputy Bentley to the accident site now," the other man spoke in a no-nonsense voice. "If you need anything—restroom, food, telephone—ask any of the people here." Abruptly he crossed to the door and disappeared into the swirling snow. Web hesitated only briefly at the door, then he too was gone. Before he'd turned to follow the other officer, she'd read the fierce determination in his eyes and felt hope. She didn't know why he cared so much, but she was thankful he did.

A gaping sense of loneliness kept her staring after them long after they disappeared. How had she come to depend on Web Bentley so quickly? Why did she trust him? He was new to Orchard Springs. He'd been in the valley less than two years, and, though she'd seen him a time or two before they were trapped by the flood, she'd never spoken to him until then, and she'd only caught a couple of glimpses of him since then. After all Daniel had put her through, she'd sworn she'd never trust another man her entire life, yet some instinct prompted her to trust this man. Why the taciturn, burly cop inspired confidence in her she couldn't begin to say.

"Mrs. Richards." She became aware one of the deputies was speaking to her, and from the tone of his voice she suspected it wasn't the first time he'd called her name.

"Yes?" She turned slowly toward the three men still seated around the table.

"Clark's a good man." She assumed he meant the militarily stern man who had gone with Web. "He's got three little boys of his own. The youngest is about the same age as your boy. He takes it right personal when somebody messes with a kid."

"Kobie's just a little boy," she whispered, biting back the sting of tears that threatened once more to fall.

"There's a cot in the back," the deputy spoke again. "That deputy that brought you said someone slipped you a sedative before you left Orchard Springs. You ought to lie down for a while, 'til it wears off."

Her first impulse was to refuse his offer, but suddenly she welcomed the opportunity for a few moments of privacy.

"Thank you," she whispered. Rising to her feet she found her legs curiously weak, and she wondered if she could make it to the small alcove separated from the main room by a folding divider. She gritted her teeth and moved her feet, reaching with one hand for the wall to steady herself. By the strength of sheer determination she made her way to the divider, stepped into the small sleeping compartment, and closed the folding partition behind her.

A tiny window high on the wall above the cot let in no light. Snow was plastered to it so thickly, it might as well not have existed. Shalise stared at the small rectangle of snow and shuddered. Could Kobie survive a night like this? She'd dressed him that morning in jeans with a cotton-polyester shirt and a wool sweater. He had on thermal underwear to protect him on the hike from the bus stop to the house, and he'd worn the down snowsuit Daniel had bought him for the ski trip she'd said no to. She'd almost made him take the suit off, fearing he'd be too warm, but when she'd seen the pleading way he'd looked at her, she knew she couldn't. She felt like crying when she remembered the apologetic smile on Kobie's face when he'd donned the bright blue suit. Nine was much too young to be aware that something so small as an article of clothing purchased by his father could be a painful reminder to his mother of all she'd lost.

She shook away thoughts of Daniel and continued her mental inventory of her son's clothing. His mittens clipped to metal loops on his suit, and she hoped he hadn't lost them. He didn't like the metal loops; only babies needed to clip their mittens to their coats, he said. His socks were the heavy athletic type, and his boots were a little too large, a problem his grandfather had solved by stuffing each toe with a handful of wool the two had gathered from the barbed wire separating the orchard from the Andreasens' pasture. The wool, hopefully, would help to keep his feet warm. He had a wool scarf too, which Grammy had knit for him.

She sat down on the edge of the cot as an overwhelming horror swept through her mind. Winter survival was only one part of the nightmare. Kobie might be injured. He'd been in a car that had plunged from a mountain road and been crushed as it rolled and twisted its way down a steep embankment. She'd refused to dwell on that possibility, but now she clutched that terror to ward off the truth that would not be denied. Someone, some stranger, had kidnapped Kobie. She wasn't naive. As a high-school teacher who cared deeply about the social problems that might affect the young people in the classes she taught, she knew more than the average woman of the sick perversions that drove men to steal children and the terrors some children faced at the hands of such evil individuals.

"No, not that," she moaned as she sank to the floor beside the cot, clasping her stomach as though a physical pain were the cause of her agony. Slowly she rocked back and forth crying. Her sobs turned to pleading. "Please, protect Kobie," she prayed over and over. She prayed with all her heart and soul. Burying her face against the scratchy wool blanket covering the cot, she told God of her love for her son and begged Him to keep him safe from fear and pain, to protect him from evil, to give him strength, and to comfort him. She acknowledged her wavering faith and pleaded for strength for herself. At last her words dwindled away, but she continued to kneel, her face pressed against the blanket.

After a few moments she opened her eyes and saw a paper lying on the cot, inches from her hand. She grasped it as though it could somehow dispel her pain. Involuntary reflexes in her hand tightened, scrunching the paper into a ball. Mindlessly she stared at the crumpled paper, then carefully she unfolded and smoothed it, but several minutes passed before her eyes focused on a crudely drawn Christmas tree. It was a child's drawing. Underneath the crooked pine were tiny figures. At first she couldn't make them out, other than the bright red Santa. Then she recognized the tall stick figure as Joseph and the small round one as Mary. A baby with a smile and a halo lay in a lopsided box beside Mary. "Merry Christmas Daddy!" was scrawled in large block letters across the top of the page. It was the kind of picture Kobie might have drawn.

She stared at the crudely drawn nativity for a few long minutes as though it held some hidden message. A momentary flash of understanding humbled her as she remembered that God had seen His son, a helpless baby, thrust into the world where evil men sought to hurt and destroy him. In her heart she knew He understood her terror and shared her sorrow.

One of the men from the rescue team must have dropped the drawing, perhaps even the man who had said she shouldn't be there. One of the other deputies had said he was a father, that he had little boys. She didn't know how many police officers were searching for Kobie, but a sudden picture rose in her mind of the men and women who had left their own warm homes and small children to search for Kobie. Their sacrifice overwhelmed her. She wondered if they'd be home for Christmas Eve with their children tomorrow night. No—tonight—since it was already past midnight.

Once more she closed her eyes and found herself appealing to her Heavenly Father for strength, not only for Kobie and herself, but for all those deputies and volunteers risking their lives and sacrificing holiday time with their families to rescue one small boy—her son.

From the past came her grandmother's words when as an angry, hurt child she'd announced she was too old to believe in Santa Claus and she didn't care about Christmas anymore. "No one is too old to believe in Santa Claus. The jolly gentleman in red, driving flying reindeer across the sky may be fantasy, but the real Santa Claus is the spirit of giving." She heard the gentle reminder in her mind. "Giving is just one part of Christmas," her grandmother had gone on. "Hope is the real reason for Christmas. God sent His son to earth to give all His children hope."

She looked once more at the rough sketch. Fierce determination swept through her. She wasn't strong enough to be certain she could say, "Thy will be done." If Kobie didn't survive this nightmare she didn't know how she could possibly go on living, but she would not allow her faith to fail anymore. She would cling to the hope that in a world filled with evil there was still goodness. The deputies and volunteers out there searching for Kobie were proof goodness still existed. And there was Web. The big deputy had promised he wouldn't leave the mountain until her son was found. Somehow she believed him. He hadn't given up on her when she'd stood frozen on a crumbling ledge, and he wouldn't give up on her son now.

CHAPTER 14

Web straightened, turning his back to the tangled mass of steel that had so recently been a sleek, beautiful Oldsmobile. There was nothing to see inside the wreck. Clark's men had found Kobie's backpack on the floor beneath the spent air bag on the passenger side of the car. They'd also found blood and dog hair on the seat, but until the samples were analyzed, they could only guess whether the blood came from a dog or a human. Far larger quantities of blood were found on the driver's side of the car. Web hoped that meant the boy was in better shape than the man. A tow truck would arrive shortly to haul the car into Salt Lake where a team would go over it more carefully.

The dull gray sky signaled that dawn was close. The storm had passed, and the weather update Clark had been given a short time ago indicated that the next storm front wasn't due for at least twelve hours. On the road above the wreckage, headlights glinted, assuring him that search and rescue was preparing to mount an extensive search as soon as the sky lightened a bit more. With daylight, snowmobiles could be used to cover more territory, but much of the terrain didn't lend itself well to the small machines and would have to be searched by volunteers on skis or snowshoes. Not only was the snow thigh-high, but the searchers would be hampered by the thick growth, steep inclines, and massive boulders in the area.

He was impatient to join the search. He scanned the tree line wondering which way a small boy, one who was possibly injured, might travel seeking help. The snow was too deep to make walking comfortable for a child, but it should make his passage easy to spot—unless the man carried the boy. Clark had already dispatched deputies to follow the frozen stream in both directions. Searchers on snowmobiles were moving toward the cabins in the area.

"Go on back to base," Clark suggested. "The tow truck is here now for the car."

"I'll wait." Web stood his ground. He'd been aware for an hour or more that the lieutenant would prefer he return to base and not assist in the search. He wasn't sure why. It seemed to him Clark should be glad for an additional trained body to aid in the search.

"What is the boy to you?" Clark spoke quietly, but Web detected something suspiciously close to pity in his voice.

"It's my case," he grunted. Even as he said the words, he knew Kobie was more than just a case. A face highlighted by dark brown hair and his mother's shimmering, blue-gray eyes swam before Web's eyes. He had a picture firmly fixed in his mind of Kobie offering Rachel his last stick of licorice, and he recalled the excitement in the boy's eyes when he'd boosted him aboard the chopper that carried them from the flooded canyon. Kobie touched him in a way that went beyond his resemblance to Frankie.

"You involved with the boy's mother?" Clark pursued a line of questioning that was beginning to annoy Web.

Sure, Shalise had been on his mind a lot since he got the call about her missing son. Their ordeal in the mountains at the end of last summer had forged a bond among the twelve people who had been trapped there. Besides, Orchard Springs was a small town, and its residents looked out for each other. Yes, he found her attractive, but he hadn't pursued that attraction. He hadn't even spoken to her for four months until yesterday, and that was only for business reasons.

"No!" He knew his answer was sharper than necessary.

"Hey! I'm not asking for personal details, but I'm not blind. There's something between the two of you." The officer's voice turned stiffly formal. "If you have an interest in the lady, and I think you do, you should be up there with her, not down here, when that car is moved."

It hit him like a blow to the gut, and he sucked in his breath so hard the cold air brought fire to his lungs. Clark expected to find

Kobie beneath the car! The Oldsmobile had rolled on its way down the slope. If Kobie had been thrown from the car and then the car rolled on him there would be no tracks leading from the wreck to the woods. It would explain why the boy didn't respond to the searchers' calls or why there was no sign of his plowing through snow that must be chest-high to the kid.

"I'm staying," he grunted, remembering the fatherly cop who had tried to keep him back to shelter him from seeing his brother's lifeless, broken body. He'd kicked the cop and fled down the alley. He'd seen Frankie and had never regretted kneeling beside him to say good-bye. He'd always believed Frankie hadn't been far away and that it had mattered to him that Web had come. He wouldn't turn away this time either.

He watched a man clad in coveralls over multiple layers of shirts and sweaters slide down the hill with a tow cable. Passively, as though it didn't matter to him, Web folded his arms and kept his eyes on the man as he scrambled for a place to attach the cable. At last he stood and waved his arms. The steel cable tightened so slowly it was like watching an action movie in grotesque slow motion. It took a massive amount of control not to cringe when a harsh, scraping noise grated against his ear. Little by little the Oldsmobile began to move in its slow ascent back up the mountain to the road.

His stomach twisted, and Web wondered if it might lose its contents in a way he hadn't experienced since his early rookie days when he'd been first on a suicide scene. Even so he never blinked. He scarcely breathed as the patch of ground beneath the wrecked car was slowly exposed. He found himself swallowing against a thick lump in his throat, and his legs felt like jelly when Clark stepped to his side and with one hand on his shoulder confirmed what he'd already surmised. The wreckage hid no bodies. This time he didn't argue when the other man suggested he return to the command post for something to eat and an hour or two of rest.

* * *

Web's inner clock woke him minutes before a raised voice had him scrambling to his feet. If that didn't sound like the Delahaney woman! Rubbing sleep from his eyes he stumbled into the main room to find some guy going toe-to-toe with the redheaded spitfire. A couple of deputies were standing around looking helpless, a petite blonde leaned against the door with a concerned expression on her face, and Shalise was tugging at her friend's arm in a half-hearted attempt to intervene in the squabble.

"Enough!" Web roared, and realized it felt good to explode. Every eye turned toward him. The man who had been shouting at Dallas was first to recover.

"I'm Daniel Richards." He spoke as though Web should be impressed. "I want to know what you're doing to find my son."

"What you really want is to intimidate Shalise," Dallas countered.

"This is Shalise's fault. I warned her that living in such an isolated spot was dangerous, and . . ."

"You don't care where I live, you just want the money my property is worth," Shalise accused her former husband.

"If you'd have let Kobie go skiing with Lena and me, this wouldn't have happened." Shalise looked as though she'd been struck, and Web's anger escalated.

"Shalise is not to blame, and what you think is of no consequence to this case," Web stated in a cold, succinct voice. "The only thing that matters is finding that little boy before nightfall sets in again."

"A trained search team led by Bishop Haslam just arrived to supplement the Salt Lake County Search and Rescue team." Shalise turned to face Web, and he detected more than a little defiance behind her words. "He has been teaching winter survival training for ten years, and I took his class last winter, so I'm going with them." She lifted her chin, making it clear she wouldn't be talked out of joining the search.

"Did Lieutenant Clark okay it?" Web asked as amiably as he could. He didn't want to be the one to tell her she couldn't go.

"I didn't ask him because I intend to go whether he likes it or not." Her eyes spit sparks.

"You have to have a partner. No one's allowed out there alone. You going with her?" he turned to Daniel and had to restrain a chuckle as the man's face turned white.

"That's not my job. You're the one who is being paid to protect people from things like this." Daniel drew himself up stiffly.

"Okay, I'll be her partner." He didn't know what made him say he'd accompany Shalise—or allow her to accompany him. He didn't think she had any business being anywhere near the search scene—it was too dangerous. But perhaps it had something to do with the memory of a young boy shut out of the search for his brother, or maybe it was Richards's cocky attitude that had goaded him into saying it. In his mind there was no question which parent was more fit to raise a kid. Daniel turned pale at the mere suggestion of joining the search for his son while there appeared to be no way to hold back the determined Shalise.

"You got gear?" he asked Shalise.

"Yes, Dallas brought it."

He turned a belligerent eye toward Shalise's friend, who merely shrugged her shoulders.

"You coming too?" he asked, hoping the woman would say no.

"Of course," she answered smoothly with what Web could only classify as a smirk.

"Dallas has a partner," Shalise explained. "She's part of the team."

"Is there anything I can do?" the petite blonde spoke up for the first time.

"You know you can't expose your vocal cords to the cold," Daniel scolded. "You can't go out there."

Web looked at the woman and realized she was sincere. She really did want to help. His brief assessment of the woman who was now married to Shalise's ex-husband told him that though she was tiny and appeared fragile, she possessed more guts and determination than her husband knew.

"I'm sorry, but without training you'd only hamper the search . . ." He attempted to soften his refusal.

"It's okay." Lena smiled, though there was a hint of tears in her eyes. "I'll see what I can do around here." She began gathering up Styrofoam cups.

Web ushered Shalise and Dallas out the door ahead of him and looked around for Clark.

They passed a couple of deputies who looked cold and exhausted and who informed them the new searchers were at the wreck site, getting their instructions and assignments from Clark. In minutes they joined the group, most of whom had already disappeared into the trees. Dallas's partner waved impatiently for her. Giving Shalise a quick hug, she hurried to join him, leaving Shalise and Web with Clark.

Before Clark could say anything to them his radio buzzed, and he snapped the speaker on. A man's excited voice cut through the static. "We've found something. A summer cabin due south of base, approximately three miles, has been broken into. The cabin is empty, but the chimney is still warm. Winds are high here, and we haven't spotted any tracks."

Shalise gasped and Web, reacting on instinct, slid an arm around her waist, offering support. She sagged against him for the briefest of seconds, then straightened and took a step forward.

Clark snapped orders into his radio to the unseen caller, ordering him to scrutinize the perimeter further for tracks or any sign of whether the occupant of the cabin had been an adult or a child—or both. "If you find any lead, follow it," he ordered. "I'll move searchers in that direction and call in a chopper." He hung up and turned toward Web and Shalise.

"You heard that." His voice was flat. "It wouldn't do any good to tell you not to go up there, so you might as well accompany me. The chopper will pick us up in twenty minutes."

The short wait for the helicopter seemed like an eternity to Shalise, yet it seemed only minutes from the time she boarded the helicopter until it set down again in a whirling flurry of snow. Web took her hand and growled at her to duck as they charged into the snow. As soon as they were beyond the propeller-generated storm, she saw the cabin. It was small and perched near the peak of a ridge. Snow filled the narrow gap between the cabin and the top of the ridge, making it appear that the back wall of the cabin blended into the mountain. Large pines kept the front relatively sheltered. Sunlight peeked through a smattering of clouds and glinted off two small windows, one on either side of a wooden door. A gust of wind swept across the ridge, sending eddies of snow rippling across the clearing.

A deputy emerged from the side of the cabin and led them to where a side window had been broken to permit entry. Both Web and Clark examined the broken glass and splinters of wood with care before returning to the front of the cabin where the lieutenant used a small tool to open the door. Armed with hasty telephone permission from an absent owner, they entered the cabin.

The summer home was small and rustic. It consisted of one room with a fireplace at one end. Shalise could see the remnants of a recent fire. Tiny flickers of red told her the coals still retained a spark of life. She wondered if her son had sheltered there, safe from the cold. A sofa had been pulled up in front of the fire. A deputy pointed to a faint smear of what was likely blood on the sofa cushion, and Shalise's heart clenched in fright.

Web glanced toward her. His nervous gesture told her he was reluctant to discuss anything or make conjectures in front of her. His voice was low when he spoke to Lieutenant Clark, and she had to strain to hear. "It was likely an adult who broke in here. A kid wouldn't have been strong enough to remove the window boards. There are marks on the floor near the cupboard," he nodded toward the other side of the room, "that might be tracks from a large size boot."

As the men discussed plans for channeling the search from the cabin, Shalise wandered around. There was a built-in bunk, but without blankets it was impossible to tell if anyone had rested there. She opened cupboard doors finding a few cans of beans and fruit. A small frozen puddle on the countertop drew her attention. Drawing off her gloves she raked a fingernail through the frozen spot, then popped her finger into her mouth. Peach juice!

Tears welled in her eyes. With a variety of canned fruits to choose from, Kobie wouldn't have chosen peaches. Kobie wasn't the one who had sheltered in the warm, dry cabin.

"Hey, look at this," a voice came from near the fireplace. She lifted her head to see a young deputy holding a blackened can aloft with the tip of a poker. From across the room she could see it had been hacked open with a knife. A shiver went down her spine, and she turned to a frantic search of the cupboard drawers. She found no knife and no can opener.

"Web," she whispered, and he was instantly beside her. "He has a knife."

"I know," he spoke solemnly, and she knew he'd come to the same conclusion she had. He probably even knew what size the knife was. She told him about the peach juice and saw the misery in his eyes matched the fear in her heart. The man who had kidnapped her child had found shelter and food. Had Kobie been with him or . . . ? She couldn't even put silent words to her fear that her son might be dead, buried somewhere beneath the snow.

Slowly she sank onto one of the two chairs in the kitchen area. Some part of her woman's mind questioned why one chair sat in the middle of the room while the other was neatly tucked beneath the small pine table. As she sat struggling to deal with the jumble of fear coursing through her mind she became aware moisture was seeping through her thick wool pants. Rising to her feet she glanced at the chair, then at its partner neatly positioned by the table. Her eyes rose to the ceiling.

"Up there!" She grasped Web's arm and pointed. "There's an attic. Someone stood on this chair to open that trapdoor."

Web studied the ceiling, then looked at the round wet spot on the seat of her pants. If the situation weren't so serious, she would have sworn he blushed.

"Clark!" he whispered hoarsely to get the officer's attention. He pointed at the chair, then at the ceiling. Nothing further had to be said. Clark didn't make a sound as he approached the chair.

"I'm taller," Web whispered, stepping in front of Clark, who frowned as Web stepped onto the chair. Both men drew their weapons, and the young deputy carefully nudged Shalise back toward the cupboard. He stood in front of her as Web took a deep breath before pushing on the small square of plywood that covered the narrow opening to the attic. The young man in front of her wasn't as tall as Web, but he was built like a football player and was hard to see around.

The simple square of wood popped upward, and Web paused with his gun drawn. After several long seconds he cautiously eased his head into the opening, and Shalise thought her heart would stop beating. She couldn't bear it if some unknown assassin fired at Web's unprotected head.

After a few minutes Web turned to report to Clark that the shadowy interior appeared empty. He struggled to pull himself up through the opening, but there was no way his shoulders and upper arms could find the leverage in such tight quarters to allow him to pull himself through. After several repeated attempts to squeeze through the opening, he withdrew his head from the opening and glanced down at Clark.

"I'm too big," he grumbled. "I doubt you or the deputy can get through here either."

"I can do it, if you give me a boost." Shalise stepped forward, turning her face up toward Web.

"No way," he objected. "I can't see into all the corners. There could be someone hiding up there."

Turning to Clark, she pleaded with her eyes. He granted permission. "We have to know." He spoke without emotion.

Web argued for another couple of minutes, then insisted he be the one to boost her through the small opening and keep an eye on her while she moved about. He stepped down from the chair, and she hurried toward him.

Clamping her lips together in a firm line, Shalise struggled to conceal her fear and hoped Web couldn't hear her pounding heart. If he even suspected how frightened she was, he might persuade Lieutenant Clark to withdraw his permission for her to aid in the search. Strangely all fear for her own safety fled the moment Web picked her up in his powerful arms. She knew he wouldn't drop her and that somehow he'd protect her if anyone threatened her. Her only fear was for her son. She sensed without being told that the three men in the room shared her fear. How could she go on if she found her son's small frozen body in that dingy attic?

CHAPTER 15

With a final push from Web she managed to wiggle her way through the narrow opening, landing flat on her face on the bare floorboards. Fearfully she raised her head and looked around. In the gloom she could see very little.

"Take this." She turned to see Web's hand poking through the trapdoor. In it was a heavy-duty flashlight. With trembling fingers she reached for it and flicked it on. At once she could see there was scarcely room to stand in the center of the attic. On either side, the steeply sloped roof slanted sharply toward the floor. The floor wasn't smooth, but simply a row of rough boards placed side by side over the evenly spaced ceiling joists of the room below, which extended the length of the small attic.

She sucked in her breath, turned the heavy flashlight beam toward one corner, then slowly rotated her body until she'd checked each corner. All were empty. With a rush that sounded suspiciously close to a sob, she released the breath she hadn't been aware she was holding. Only then did she begin to move with careful steps across the rough planks that teetered with each step she took.

She played the beam of light across the boards before her until a glint of silver caught her eye. She knelt to study it closer, hoping it would magically provide some clue to her son's whereabouts, but it was only a sharp, round can lid. Disappointed, she started to stand, then some instinct had her reaching for it. It was new and shiny. It hadn't been in the attic long.

"Web!" Her voice came out in a shaky croak.

"What is it? Are you hurt?" There was no mistaking his alarm and the frustration he felt in not being able to rush to her assistance.

"I'm all right, but I found this." She retraced her steps to hand him the piece of metal. "I don't think it has been here long," she whispered. She watched him turn the lid over several times, then sniff it.

"Tuna fish! Look at this!" She heard suppressed excitement in his voice as he passed the lid on to Lieutenant Clark.

"Looks like some kind of hair or fur caught on it," a muffled voice said from below. Shalise shuddered, envisioning rats or mice in the attic. She glanced around uneasily.

"Shalise." She turned back toward Web in response to her softly spoken name. "Look around a little more. See if you can find the can this lid came from."

"All right," she responded as evenly as she could, trying not to reveal her fear that if she found the can, she might also find a rat. She'd promised Web she'd help in the search and that she wouldn't get in his way. She wouldn't allow her squeamishness concerning rodents to hamper the search for Kobie. If Web and Lieutenant Clark thought a tuna fish can was some kind of clue, she'd find that can if it were anywhere in this attic. She worked her way back across the rough planks. With each step the planks rocked. Since the boards were merely thrown across the studs and were not nailed in place, each step that wasn't near the center of the board caused the opposite end to rise. As she reached the back of the cabin her foot slipped, sending her tumbling into the narrow space between two joists.

Throwing her hands forward to break her fall, her flashlight fell from her grasp and rolled out of sight. She clamped her lips together to keep from screaming as the light disappeared beneath thick boards. Fear that she might fall through the floor to the room below kept her clawing for something to hold onto. Her hands slapped against stones. The fireplace chimney! With all her strength she gripped the jagged rocks.

Her heartbeat slowed, and she took a cautious step to a plank that felt solid. She eased her weight onto it. Through her gloves she felt something unexpected. Heat! The stones she clung to were warm! Heated stones told their own story. If the chimney was still warm, then it hadn't been long since the person who sheltered there had left the cabin. She closed her thoughts against speculating about the man who had ripped the shutters from the downstairs window and built a fire in the fireplace.

"Are you okay?" Web's worried voice reached her ears, and she assumed he'd heard her fall and had seen the light she carried disappear.

"Yes, I'm fine, but I dropped the flashlight." She winced as she turned back toward where the light had slipped from her grasp and rolled beneath the plank flooring. A twinge of pain told her she may have slightly sprained her ankle. Experimentally she shifted her weight to that foot and back several times before heaving a sigh of relief. It wasn't sprained. The slight tenderness went away as she moved her foot.

"Come on back, but be careful," Web called to her. He held another flashlight which he played awkwardly across the floor to guide her way.

"No, it's all right. It's lighter back here by the chimney. There are a couple of small windows. One is broken and it lets in a little light, so I think I can find the flashlight I dropped."

"I don't want you taking any chances." The concern in Web's voice warmed Shalise as she knelt on a wobbling plank and contemplated sliding her hand into the dark space under the board to search for the flashlight. A sudden fear that she might find something more than the light made her hand tremble. With quiet determination she closed her eyes and pleaded to her Heavenly Father for the courage to reach into the gap in the boards where she'd fallen.

Tentatively her fingers probed the narrow space. Almost immediately she felt a smooth round cylinder. Closing her hand around it, she grasped it tightly and pulled it toward herself. Before it was close enough to see, she knew it wasn't the flashlight. It was lighter and tangled with rope. Even in the dim light she recognized it was a rope ladder with wooden rungs, probably meant to provide access from the room below. Briefly she wondered why it had been thrust into the narrow space beneath a floor plank.

Setting the rope ladder aside, she reached back into the hole. This time her fingers encountered the smooth grip of the flashlight. The light clanked against metal as she pulled it out. She hesitated only a second before placing her hand back into the hole. In minutes two cans, a can opener, a spoon, and a pile of rags lay beside her.

"Shalise, come on back," Web's voice called to her. "The flashlight isn't important."

"Just a minute. I—I found some things." Her voice quavered as she contemplated the implications of her find. She reached for the flashlight and gave it a shake. To her surprise, it flickered a couple of times before going out again.

"I think the light is okay," she called over her shoulder. "The bulb probably got knocked loose when I dropped it." Her guess proved correct and in less than a minute a strong beam of light spread over her small trove of treasures. Her heart accelerated when she spotted the label with a big shiny apple on the taller can. Running a finger around the inside of the can she collected a dollop of applesauce. Applesauce was one of the few canned fruits Kobie would eat. The smaller tuna can was as clean and shiny as though it had been washed.

Gathering up the cans, she reached for the pile of rags, only to draw back in horror. Streaks of blood were unmistakable on what appeared to be a ragged towel. Was the blood her son's? Had his kidnapper hurt him or was he injured in the car crash? Or maybe . . . ? Her eyes drifted to the broken window.

Forgetting her fear of the tottering floor, spiderwebs, and dark corners, she rushed to the broken window. When she reached it, she found herself staring at a narrow saddle of drifted snow linking the cabin to the cliff behind it. Ten to fifteen feet of snow filled the space. She didn't know whether or not it was solid enough to support one small boy, but a mother's intuition told her that her son had been inside the attic, and the only way he could have gotten there, outside of being carried there by an adult, was through the broken window.

Excitement began to mount as she swept the beam of light across the fragments of glass littering the floor. If he'd cut himself breaking the window or crawling through it, surely there would be signs of the injury on the glass or window ledge. But to her relief she found no traces of blood.

Between the shards of glass she saw something else. Her eyes widened at the sight of child-size boot prints in the dust that had accumulated months ago beneath the window.

"Web! Kobie was here. I know he was!" She scanned the floor for more boot prints. Near the chimney the tracks were joined by what looked like some kind of animal paw prints. There too, she discovered a blanket wedged between the floor studs. With shaking fingers she reached for it.

The blanket proved to be an old tattered quilt. Gray bits of fur clung to the fabric along with what looked like small dots of dried blood. Hastily she piled the other objects she'd found on it, bundled them up, and headed for the trapdoor.

"What did you find?" Web reached for the bundle she shoved toward the opening in the floor.

"He was here," she choked out as Web passed the bundle on to Lieutenant Clark. "I think some kind of animal is following him! We've got to find him before . . ."

"It's all right," Web attempted to calm her fear as his big hands settled around her waist and he swung her to the floor. "We think he has a dog with him."

"A dog? But he doesn't have a dog."

"He would if you weren't so childishly paranoid about allowing me to give him one," a cold voice snarled. "But, no. You aren't about to allow him any reminders of his father, even a dog that would have saved him from being snatched by some sicko. I hope you're happy now." She whirled around to face her ex-husband.

"What are you doing here?" she gasped.

"Kobie is my son too. I have a right to be here."

"I didn't say . . ."

Web felt like throttling Daniel Richards. Instinctively he shifted his weight forward placing several inches of his bulk between Shalise and her former husband. He didn't even question the protective instinct that had him placing his body between Shalise and any potential danger from the man who seemed intent on provoking a confrontation with her.

"Mrs. Richards is in no way responsible for your son's predicament, and this is no time to badger her." Web's voice dropped to a menacing growl. "If you can't keep your mouth shut, then head back to base camp."

"I don't take orders from you," Daniel snapped back. "If you held any degree of competency, my son would have been found by now."

"Mr. Richards," Clark's authoritative voice brooked no nonsense. "I'm in charge of this investigation and what I say goes. Right now I need to speak with Mrs. Richards. I don't need you, so you either sit down and shut your mouth, or I'll have a deputy escort you back to Salt Lake in cuffs."

Web did his best to smother the smile that threatened to escape as Daniel Richards abruptly sat down on one of the wooden kitchen chairs. Over the years he'd come in contact with a lot of hard-nosed cops, and he'd been accused himself of having an intimidating manner, but he'd never seen anyone quite like Lieutenant Clark. He suspected that even he would sit down and shut his mouth if Clark told him to.

"All right, Mrs. Richards, explain why you think your son was in the attic." Clark folded his arms across his chest in a waiting attitude, though Web suspected he wouldn't patiently wait long.

In a tumble of words Shalise explained where she'd found the items now sitting on the small table. It was her belief that Kobie had crossed the gap between the cabin and the cliff it abutted, had crawled through the window, then used the rope ladder to search the main room below for food and a blanket. Then for some reason, perhaps he'd heard the man who had kidnapped him breaking into the cabin, he climbed back up the ladder and pulled it up after him.

"When Ferrindale ripped the boards off the window, there would have been sufficient warning," the young deputy speculated, excitement growing in his voice.

"Who is Ferrindale?" Daniel was back on his feet glaring at Shalise. "Some idiot boyfriend, I suppose."

"I don't have a boyfriend," Shalise snapped back. "I'm not the one who . . ." Web touched her arm, and she stopped midsentence.

One sharp look from Clark, and Daniel sat back down.

"But who is he?" Shalise turned beseeching eyes toward Web and he swallowed a silent groan. He hadn't wanted to tell Shalise about Ferrindale.

"We don't know that Ferrindale took your son." He began giving as simple an explanation as possible. He didn't want to frighten Shalise, but it wasn't fair to withhold information at this point either. "Ferrindale is a suspect in the disappearance of several young boys in the western states. His description matches that of the man who rented the wrecked Oldsmobile your son is believed to have been a passenger in."

"Why do you suspect him?" Shalise's eyes looked like bottomless pools as she searched his face, and he felt an entirely unfamiliar urge to wrap his arms around her stiff shoulders and draw her head against his chest to offer whatever meager comfort he could.

"He's been known to lure his young victims with an injured puppy," Clark spoke bluntly. Web was glad he stopped there. Nothing useful would come of telling Shalise about the fish line. "Now can we get on with describing what you found in the attic?"

Web felt an unexpected swell of pride as he listened to Shalise. Her observations were sound. He could tell Clark thought so too. Somehow the boy had reached the cabin first and whether he'd retreated to the attic and fell asleep before his kidnapper arrived or whether he'd fled there to escape pursuit, as the deputy had speculated, didn't matter. What appeared significant was that the child had the presence of mind to pull the ladder up after himself and drop the trapdoor into place, putting himself beyond the reach of the kidnapper.

Two other facts emerged as Web and the police lieutenant discussed what had been discovered in the wrecked car and in the cabin. Kobie had reached the cabin alive last night, separate from the man who had abducted him. But for some reason he left before the rescue party discovered the cabin. The chair beneath the trapdoor indicated the man had stood on it in an attempt to access the attic. What was uncertain was whether or not he knew Kobie was hiding in the attic space. It was assumed that the adult failed to gain entry to the attic either because he was too large to squeeze through the opening or because his injuries incapacitated him. There was also the matter of the dog. Indications were the pup was still with the kid.

"Your boy seems to be handling himself well in the snow." Clark's brow furrowed in a deep groove as though he were weighing the odds that a child might survive alone on the mountain. "Does he know this canyon?"

"No," Shalise answered, "but his grandfather has taken him winter camping several times." She glanced apologetically toward Daniel then back to Clark. "He has always loved the stories Gramps told him about mountain men and early Mormon pioneers struggling to survive winters in Cache and Rich Counties." Web surmised Daniel had little patience with his father's stories.

"I don't see how he got this far," a woman's quiet voice broke into the conversation. "I can hardly move through this deep snow without skis, and Kobie isn't very big. In some places the snow must be over his head." Web was as surprised as Shalise by Lena's interruption. She must have arrived with her husband while he was totally engrossed with following Shalise's movements through the attic. For the first time he noticed skis and poles leaning against the wall near the door. That explained how the pair had gotten there.

The woman rose from the sofa beside the fireplace and walked toward them. She stopped behind Daniel and rested one hand on his shoulder as she turned her questioning gaze toward Lieutenant Clark.

Clark ignored her question, turning his attention to the radio he wore strapped to his shoulder so he could communicate while leaving his hands free. He turned his back to the group and listened intently.

"The accident happened before most of the new snow fell." Deputy Mason tried to answer Lena's question. He practically stammered as he spoke to the beautiful blonde. "It wasn't this deep when the kid started out, plus it was a lot colder up here earlier in the week before this storm front moved in. The snow froze pretty solid, and the boy, being so small, likely walked right over spots where an adult would sink up to his teeth."

"Roger. We'll move out immediately." Clark turned back to the group. "Mason and I will search the ridge behind the cabin. We could use your help," he spoke to Web, "but you better stay here and try to keep the Richards from killing each other." The look of disgust that crossed Clark's face would have amused Web any other time. He had no idea what more the man might have said had Clark's radio not suddenly burst forth with a spate of static followed by the helicopter pilot's voice.

". . . glimpse of something blue moving through the trees near side canyon. Circling now for better view . . . lost sight . . ."

"Pick us up on the ridge above the cabin," Clark ordered into his speaker. He was moving toward the door before he finished speaking.

"I'm going with you." Shalise lifted her chin to a stubborn angle and began pulling her gloves back on her hands.

"We're coming too." Daniel gave his ex-wife a dirty look and stood.

"You had any winter survival training?" Clark turned a challenging look Daniel's way. Daniel and Lena both shook their heads.

"We both ski," Daniel spoke defensively.

"You'd only slow us down. Stay here in this cabin, haul some wood in, and see if you can get the place warmed up. It's a lot closer than the command trailer if some of our people need to rest." In two strides he was out the door with Web and Shalise struggling to catch up. Deputy Mason brought up the rear.

Shalise wasn't certain Clark meant for her to follow him or stay behind with Daniel, but she had no intention of waiting around for clarification. All three men were big, and she had to take two steps for each one they took, but she didn't complain. She'd take ten steps to their one, if that was what was needed to get aboard that helicopter.

CHAPTER 16

With her nose pressed against the glass, Shalise stared at the snow-shrouded trees and rocks below. Nothing moved, and she wondered if Kobie could have traveled this far from the cabin. Clark had said a half-dozen snowmobiles were headed for the area, but she hadn't seen them yet.

The helicopter lurched, and far below she saw snow eddy and drift, creating a curtain of swirling white between them and the ground. She didn't have to hear the quiet conversation between Lieutenant Clark and the pilot to know the wind was not only making the search more difficult, but dangerous as well. They'd been flying a crisscross pattern for close to twenty minutes in the area where the pilot had seen a moving speck of blue less than a half hour earlier. The tiny bit of bright blue might not be Kobie's new snowsuit, but in her heart she believed it was. With the escalating wind and no new sighting, Shalise worried that Clark might call off the search.

Please help us find him. Please keep him safe, she pleaded with God silently over and over.

Web sat beside her, and she found his warm bulk comforting as he leaned toward the window and his shoulder brushed against hers. In some indefinable way he reminded her of her grandfather—quiet, solid, and dependable. Suddenly he leaned forward and shouted, "There!"

She jumped, then followed his pointing finger with her eyes to a spot below. She strained to see what had captured his attention. At first she saw nothing but a yawning gorge, its steep walls appearing intermittently through a shifting curtain of white.

". . . going down for a closer look." She heard the pilot explain as the helicopter began to descend, then Clark urging caution. She remembered reading somewhere about unpredictable winds and downdrafts causing planes and helicopters to crash over mountain canyons, but she brushed the thought aside and continued to strain to see whatever Web had spotted.

Web continued to point, and at last she spotted a dark speck moving across the snow along the canyon rim. It moved in an upright position, ruling out the possibility of it being an animal. Excitement and hope sent adrenaline pumping through her body, and as the helicopter's descent became more rapid, she struggled for a better view. In minutes the figure disappeared in a thick copse of pines, and Shalise's shoulders slumped as her mind assimilated the fact that the figure wasn't wearing the bright blue of Kobie's snowsuit. Her hand tightened on Web's, and she became aware for the first time that her hand was firmly locked in his. It never occurred to her to pull her hand free.

"Is that . . . the man . . . who took Kobie?"

"Probably," Web growled, never taking his eyes from the thick shrubbery.

Shalise closed her eyes, feeling excruciating pain. The figure spotted from the air was not her son. The man down there was alone.

Web felt the bite of Shalise's fingernails digging into his hand, but he made no effort to loosen her grip. She was afraid, and if clutching his hand was any kind of solace, he didn't care how hard her nails pressed into his flesh.

"Kobie's down there somewhere, and he's still alive," Web attempted to comfort her.

"How can you be sure? What if that man hurt him and he's buried under the snow back there?" She waved vaguely toward the vast mountain of rocks and trees behind them. She bit down on her bottom lip and widened her eyes in a feeble attempt to fight off the tears threatening to fall.

"The man we saw—he's tracking something, probably your boy," the lieutenant cut in. "That means he's alive, and so far has been able to elude recapture."

"Tracking? But how . . . ?"

"See that line," Web said, pointing to a faint line or indentation beside the man's still visible tracks. "It's downhill almost all of the way from the cabin to here. I think Kobie has improvised a sled of some kind and he's using it to stay ahead of the man."

"The suspect is injured," Clark called from his position beside the pilot. "He's favoring his right leg. Mason, get ready to go down."

"I'll go too," Web volunteered.

"No," Clark countered. "The snowmobiles can't get across the canyon and are taking the long way around. I may need you later."

Web watched the young deputy don a light pack and ski mask. Mason checked the straps and buckles with an easy, relaxed air that spoke of practice as the chopper made a slow descent toward a windswept, rocky outcropping near where the suspect had disappeared into the woods.

Clark left his seat to slide open the side door, then as Mason reached for a cable attached to a winch near the door, he flattened himself against the floor with a rifle tucked against his shoulder. Shalise recognized the significance of the lieutenant's action. The man on the ground could be armed and waiting to pick off anyone who attempted to intervene between him and his intended victim.

Loosening Shalise's grip, Web pulled a ski mask over his face and joined Clark on the floor, his own rifle in his hands. Carefully he surveyed the ragged perimeter of pine trees through the scope. The thick trees would make good cover for the suspect. He tensed, listening for a shot as Mason dangled below the helicopter. Wind buffeted the small chopper, sending the man dangling beneath it swaying. The descent seemed to take an eternity, though Web knew it was only minutes until Mason reached the snow-covered slope and released himself from the line.

When Mason reached the shelter of the rocks, Web breathed a sigh of relief and felt a measure of hope. The odds had just improved that the kidnapper might not be carrying a gun, or that if he did have one, he lacked a ready supply of ammunition. Never easing up on his scrutiny of the wooded area, he continued to watch for movement as Mason moved back out into the open. Not until the deputy disappeared into the trees did he even glance toward Clark.

Clark eased his way backward, then stood. He nodded to Web, indicating he should stay where he was as the chopper rose higher and began a steady sweep of the stand of trees. Web flexed his fingers at frequent intervals to keep them ready for action, but he never took his eyes from the vista of snow and trees below. From the front of the chopper he caught the murmur of Clark's voice and knew he was in communication with Deputy Mason. He wished he could hear Clark's end of the conversation, but between the whistle of wind sliding past the open door and the thrum of rotors, it was impossible.

As he searched for movement or a color out of place, he thought of Frankie. A memory surfaced out of nowhere, and he remembered holding Frankie's hand as they walked ten frigid blocks to an old cathedral that had always fascinated his brother. In their thin coats and ragged mittens they'd pressed their faces against the wrought-iron fence that separated them from the nativity scene the priest had set up on the portico. As he stood there shivering in the cold, he examined each figure critically and admired their warm clothes, especially the robes the statues wearing crowns and riding camels had worn. Their cloaks looked warm enough to keep out the worst winter cold. Then his eyes had fallen to the baby lying in a box of hay, and he felt a surge of anger. The baby didn't have any clothes, just a rag he supposed was some kind of diaper. Little kids shouldn't be cold or hungry—or scared, he remembered thinking.

"Look at 'er," Frankie had whispered. "I wish our ma was like that."

Web shifted his eyes from the baby to the mother. In her hands was a square of cloth, and she looked as if she were about to place it over the baby.

"It's about time," he'd muttered under his breath.

"Ain't she beautiful?" Frankie had sighed.

Web recalled glancing down at his brother, then back at the lady. Her face had seemed to glow, and there was something in her gentle eyes that touched his soul. When he looked again at the baby, he forgot the cold. The baby looked back at his mother with tenderness and trust. He stared raptly for a long time until a twinge of envy stirred in his heart. His mother never looked at him like that, and she'd never put a blanket over him or Frankie. He was big, almost eleven years old, so he could take care of himself—but Frankie was little, just six. When he finally looked back at his brother, he was startled to see Frankie watching him with the same gentle trust the artist had sculpted on the baby's face. It made him feel good then, but added to his guilt later.

Frankie's trust had been misplaced; his big brother hadn't watched him closely enough. He'd let Frankie down and Frankie had died.

"He's forgiven you. He knows you were a boy yourself and did your best." He heard Gage's voice in his mind, overriding his guilt and strengthening his resolve. He'd been a boy then—now he was a man who had glimpsed that same look of trust in Shalise's eyes more than once since Kobie had disappeared.

Please, God, he found himself silently praying to the god Bishop Haslam and Gage insisted was real. *Don't let me disappoint Shalise Richards. Please keep Kobie safe until I get there.*

Shalise watched Web scan the terrain below. He never once looked away from the scope of the rifle he held. He was a big man, and flattened on the floor wearing a bulky parka, he appeared even bigger. If his size didn't intimidate criminals, surely the grim look she'd seen on his face before he donned the ski mask would. He didn't know Kobie well—he barely even knew her—yet she sensed something deeply personal in his search for her son and the man who had stolen him from her.

The helicopter banked sharply, and she raised questioning eyes toward the pilot. Clark was pointing toward something. She sensed excitement in his action. Anxiously she turned to the window, flattening her face against the glass. At first she saw nothing, then a tiny speck of blue caught her attention. Kobie! It had to be Kobie.

A few seconds later she caught another glimpse of blue in the swirling snow and beyond the blue, a deep chasm. Her heart lurched, and she stuffed her fist in her mouth to keep from screaming. Her son was far too close to that steep drop-off. Even though she reminded herself that her angle of perspective distorted distance and depth, she still feared he would slip on the snow and plunge into the canyon.

The intermittent glimpses she caught of the small figure below convinced her it was her son. He moved slowly, obviously wading through deep snow. The gentle slope he'd followed from the cabin was gone, and he was now struggling to move uphill, following the rim of a deep canyon. A large brown object clung to his back, and she had no idea what it might be.

She wished he'd look up and see how close help was, but he seemed oblivious to the helicopter's presence. Her heart ached for her child. He was so close, but still beyond her reach. He had to be exhausted and terrified. If he were unaware of the chopper, he was possibly unaware also of how close he was to the edge of the canyon. To a worried mother, it seemed the helicopter was moving away from her son instead of drawing closer.

The small air vehicle banked away, and this time she knew she wasn't mistaken. She returned her attention to the interior of the chopper with an impatient frown. Web was buckling himself into the harness Mason had used to reach the ground. Mason! How long had it been since the deputy last reported in? Had something happened to the young man? She turned fearful eyes to Web, and, without even voicing the question, she knew it was the same one running through his mind. Web's eyes met hers, and he shouted, "I'm going down. The wind's too strong to get any closer. Each time the pilot tries to get closer to Kobie, the draft from the canyon whips the tail, threatening to send us all to the bottom."

"Be careful," she whispered back. He couldn't have heard her, but he smiled, indicating he understood the message anyway.

Once more Clark assumed the position on the floor, rifle ready, as Web pushed off. She wanted to do something, to help, but there was nothing to do except watch Web's slow descent. The wind was even more fierce close to the canyon rim than where Mason had gone down, and she gripped her hands into fists until her knuckles turned white as she watched Web sway and rock far more than Mason had. Several times the helicopter bucked in the gale-force wind, and once she thought she heard a popping sound similar to gun shots. But when the noise didn't come again and Web continued his descent, she decided she must have imagined it.

She looked toward the spot where she'd last seen Kobie and saw nothing but roiling, blowing snow in the ground-level whiteout. Her face and hands pressed into the glass as she willed the snow to part, allowing her a glimpse of her child.

The whirling snow did part, permitting a glimpse of the snow-covered ground. But it was a man, not Kobie, she saw. Instantly she knew the man following Kobie wasn't Deputy Mason. As quickly as the man was revealed to her, he was once more swallowed up in the blowing snow.

Flinging off her seatbelt, she crawled toward Lieutenant Clark. The chopper tilted, and she hastily scrambled for a handhold. Grasping a seat support she inched closer to the man sprawled on the floor.

"I saw the kidnapper. He's following Kobie and he's close!" she shouted, hoping to make herself heard over the dual roar of the wind and the chopper. Clark nodded his head almost imperceptibly and pointed to something behind her. She glanced around with a sense of desperation and didn't understand at first what Clark was telling her. Then she noticed a tangle of straps and understood he wanted her to buckle herself to the safety line Web had used earlier.

She finished fastening the belt around her waist in time to see Web disappear into the whiteout below. She didn't see him release himself, but she knew he was no longer attached to the cable because she could see it slowly retracting to prevent it from tangling in the trees.

She saw Clark stiffen. Frantically she peered through the open hatch, searching for whatever had caught his attention. Further to the left than she had expected to see him, Kobie's form appeared, crawling up a steep jumble of boulders. They stood like a small island above the churning mass of white.

Clark signaled for the pilot to move closer, but as the chopper edged toward the canyon, a fierce wind threatened to suck them over the edge where they would smash against the narrow walls before plunging to the boulder-strewn canyon floor. Feeling herself sliding toward the open door, Shalise scrambled against the floor in panic until her hand caught hold of the seat support again. At the same time, she felt Clark's hand grasp her shoulder. Taking deep gulps of breath, she steadied herself as the helicopter backed away from the canyon. She breathed a silent thank you for the sturdy safety line and for Lieutenant Clark's insistence that she use it. At the same time she felt frustrated that they weren't able to get closer to Kobie.

She didn't notice when Clark removed his steadying hand, but she was aware when he returned to his prone position and that he wasn't just using his scope to scan the area, but was focusing steadily on something he could see below them. His face looked grim and angry, giving rise to a sickening fear inside her. Edging back toward the doorway, she peered in the direction his rifle pointed. A second figure emerged from the swirling ground storm, mere feet behind the smaller blue form.

Once more she used a bunched fist to stifle the scream rising in her throat, watching as the stranger laboriously pulled himself up the rocks. Kobie turned his head, then resumed climbing, seeming to move faster than before.

"Go, Kobie," she found herself whispering in encouragement. Perhaps she only imagined it, but she could feel his fear. She could also feel the waves of anger emanating from his pursuer. Beside her, Clark tensed as he trained his rifle on the man.

The helicopter bucked in the wind and rolled toward the mound of rocks, changing the angle of vision. Instinctively Shalise searched with hands and feet for a better hold. As her foot wrapped around the closest seat support, she noticed the field glasses Mason had left in the jump seat. Grasping them, she fitted them to her eyes.

At first she saw only a smear of foggy white, but as she adjusted the lens, the rocks came into view, then Kobie. Tears stung her eyes, and she swallowed hard to keep back the choking sob that threatened to strangle her. The blue clad figure was definitely Kobie! She recognized his snowsuit and the scarf wrapped around his face. Her son was alive, though still in danger. How she ached to reach for him, assure him of her love, and let him know she was there for him.

She moved the glasses slightly and noted the dark object on his back appeared to be a backpack. She wondered where he'd gotten it since his own pack had been found at the accident site. Peering fearfully over the top was a small gray head. A puppy! Web had been right—her son had a puppy with him!

Kobie staggered and began to slide backward.

"No!" Shalise gasped, and her hands tightened on the field glasses. The helicopter rocked, and she saw Kobie wasn't sliding backward on his own. The man who had been following him clasped one of his legs.

She could clearly see the man's face, and she nearly dropped the glasses in horror when she caught sight of the vicious rage showing there.

Kobie squirmed and kicked, struggling against his captor. He gained a moment's freedom, but the man grabbed for him again, pulling the pack from the boy's shoulders. Angrily he thrust it aside and lunged toward Kobie again, who was madly scrambling up the rocks.

"Oh, Father, please help him," Shalise prayed.

Kobie reached the top and stood on a small plateau. He glanced behind him, and Shalise knew he was torn between trying to escape and going back for the puppy. Her heart ached for his dilemma even as she silently urged him to go on, to escape the madman pursuing him. The man crawled over the top and surged toward the small boy.

"Shoot him!" she screamed at Clark.

"Can't!" Clark shouted back. "Too unstable . . . wind . . . might hit the boy . . . or Bentley."

The stranger was on Kobie before the child could react. Once more Kobie struggled to free himself, but the man clasped his arms around the boy, pinning his arms to his sides as he swung the small body off the ground. With legs flailing, Kobie continued to battle. A solid blow to his assailant's knee cap sent them both to the ground.

The large, heavy man emerged on top, straddling the child. With one hand on the child's throat, he fumbled in his pocket. Shalise began to scream when he raised his hand revealing a knife. In some distant part of her mind, she felt the increased rocking and bumping of the chopper and knew the pilot was trying to get close enough to give Lieutenant Clark a clear shot.

The man paused and glanced up, as if noticing for the first time that the helicopter hovered near where he struggled with the child. His face tightened in a grotesque caricature of a smile, and he raised the knife higher in a dramatic gesture. Then suddenly he pitched forward.

A high, wailing scream rose over the powerful thrum of the chopper and the howling wind. Shalise was only vaguely aware the scream was coming from her own throat. Too frightened to release her grip on the field glasses, she watched in horror as the man swung one arm in an arc as though searching for something, then he rose to his feet with Kobie in his arms. Kobie lay limp, no longer struggling to free himself. The man staggered toward the sheer drop, stumbled to his knees, then rose again, never releasing his grip on her child. Then he fell again, and as he fell, he flung his burden toward the whiteness shrouding the sheer drop to the canyon below. The small blue bundle slid toward the precipice, then slowly slipped over the side.

CHAPTER 17

Web flung aside his rifle and threw himself toward the cliff edge, his hands grappling for the slick nylon fabric. But he was too late. Kobie's small body disappeared beyond his reach.

"Kobie!" he screamed, but heard no answering shout. He scanned the steep mountainside searching for a way down, but only jagged rocks poking through blowing snow met his eyes. It was at least three hundred feet to the canyon floor. No one could survive a fall like that, and Kobie may have already been dead before he'd been flung from the cliff. He had to face reality. The boy was dead. Fierce pain stabbed his chest as he remembered he'd also been too late to save Frankie.

Turning with the pent-up fury of twenty-five years, he reached for the man slumped on the ground. Grasping him with one fist clenched in the thick fabric at the man's throat, Web jerked him to his feet. The man's head lolled to one side, and a dark stain dripped to the snow at their feet. Web barely restrained himself from pounding his other fist into the unconscious man's face. One look at that face confirmed his suspicions—the perpetrator was Lester Ferrindale. Sick disgust had him thrusting the man away to collapse softly back into the snow. Taking no chance that Ferrindale might regain consciousness and put up a fight, he cuffed him before unfastening the man's coat to check the extent of his wound. Though it filled him with disgust to try to save Ferrindale's life, he pulled his ski mask from his face and used it as a pressure bandage against the gaping bullet hole in the man's abdomen. While holding the pad in place with one hand, he methodically searched the downed man with the other. In the deep right-hand pocket he found Mason's police issue .45. It had been fired twice. He remembered the shots he'd heard as he swung beneath the helicopter.

Knotting the man's own shirt around the bandage to hold it in place, Web stepped back.

He couldn't look at Ferrindale. He feared if he even touched the man, he would kill him. He was a peace officer dedicated to saving lives, but at the moment he wished the single shot he'd been able to get off had killed the man. Beyond being responsible for molesting and murdering any number of little boys, it appeared he'd ambushed Mason, and he'd left Shalise with a pain that would never go away. Slowly Web raised Mason's gun. *Ferrindale should die for what he's done to all the little boys like Frankie, for what he did to Kobie.*

"Bentley, put the gun down." Clark's voice was understanding rather than condemning. Nevertheless, it was a voice Web instinctively obeyed. As he lowered his arm, he was shocked to see it shook. Had he really contemplated shooting an unconscious suspect? A shudder swept through him, and he knew Gage was right. It was time to let the past go before the memories destroyed him.

Shock riveted Shalise to the seat Clark strapped her into until she learned Lester Ferrindale would be loaded on the helicopter for the short trip to the University of Utah Medical Center. Revulsion twisted her stomach—there was no way she would stay aboard with that man. The pilot took pity on her and walked her through the necessary steps to secure herself to the cable, then eased her to the ground.

Lieutenant Clark freed her from the cable and grumbled something about civilians having no business getting in the way of an official investigation, but his heart didn't seem to be in it. Later she would remember the compassion in his eyes.

Standing on trembling legs, she attempted to walk and stepped right into Web's arms. He held her crushed to him, his cheek against hers. At first he said nothing, only rocked her gently back and forth until she became aware his tears melded with hers, forming a joint river of sorrow.

"I'm sorry," he whispered huskily into her ear. In spite of her pain, she sensed his sincerity. He hurt deeply for her and her child.

"You tried," she murmured back. "You did all you could."

"It wasn't enough." He took the blame. With one gloved finger, she brushed his cheek.

"Don't blame yourself." She felt an urgency to make him understand. "There's a numbness inside me that is all that is keeping me from shattering in rage. I think it's God's way of keeping me sane as my mind tries to accept what I saw with my own eyes. Sorrow will come later—now all I feel is anger. But I don't blame you, nor do I blame God. That evil man is solely to blame for what happened to Kobie."

He shook his head and walked away. He stopped briefly to speak with Clark, then moved toward the thick grove of trees where Mason had disappeared earlier. She would have followed him, but Clark's voice stopped her.

"Mrs. Richards," he told her. "I've been in touch with your son's father. He took the news pretty hard. He's still at the cabin, and some of the search party is there with him including your bishop. Haslam and one of his people, along with two of our search and rescue people with snowmobiles, will head up the canyon immediately to recover the body, but I suggested that your ex-husband wait at the cabin for you. I'll send the chopper back for both of you as soon as possible."

"What about Web?"

"He'll wait here with you. I'll leave emergency supplies for the two of you so you can get out of the storm and have something to eat. Bentley wants to search for Mason. I told him ten minutes is all I dare wait. Fuel is running low, and Ferrindale is in pretty bad shape."

In less than the allotted ten minutes, Web emerged from the trees half-carrying, half-dragging Mason.

"He needs a doctor. Fast!" Web shouted as he plunged through the drifting snow toward the helicopter. In spite of the blackness of her own sorrow, she felt a measure of joy that the young deputy was still alive.

Clark hurried to meet them and lost no time getting the seriously wounded young man aboard the helicopter.

"Jumped me in the trees. Left me for dead," Mason gasped as he was being strapped to the cable, in spite of several chest wounds and a sickening gash across his throat. Then the cable began to draw him upward.

"That kid has what it takes. I think he'll make it," Web spoke as he stood beside Shalise watching the chopper bank and turn away. "He's lost a lot of blood, but he kept fighting. He was ambushed on the other side of the grove of trees, but I found him less than fifty feet from this side. He crawled all the way."

Shalise glanced down at the snow eddying around her knees and shivered. Adrenaline had kept her oblivious to the cold until now. She gazed longingly toward the place where her son had slipped over the edge. How she wished she could go to him, hold him just one more time.

She felt Web's arm settle over her shoulders, and she leaned into him. They stood that way for several minutes.

"I need to get closer," she spoke brokenly.

"I'm not sure that's a good idea," Web hesitated.

"I have to go over there," she insisted.

"All right," he conceded. "Clark tossed a survival kit out over that way, so we might as well go pick it up." He didn't move his arm from her shoulder as they walked.

When they reached the edge of the cliff, they stood silently and Web tightened his grip. She bowed her head and prayed, asking God to watch over her small son. Suddenly memory of that day he'd thrust his way into life, ready to meet each challenge that came his way, flashed into her mind. He'd been a beautiful baby, and her heart had melted at the first sight of him. They'd been happy then, the three of them. She didn't know then that Daniel felt confined or that he hated the old house she loved.

There had been good times as Kobie grew. Birthdays and Christmases were precious memories. He'd been an adorable, mischievous two-year-old, a solemn kindergartner, a teasing second-grader. She recalled something her grandmother once said about how everyone expects to someday have to bury their parents, but no one expects to outlive their children. Gran had lost her son when Shalise lost her father, and Shalise knew the loss had been as hard for her grandparents as it had been for her. Was Kobie with them now, safe with her parents and Gran and Grandpa?

"Is there any chance he could still be alive and suffering down there?" she whispered the dreadful fear that had crept over her as she stared at the shifting white void.

"I don't think so." Web's answer wasn't entirely satisfactory, and she sensed he shared her uneasiness.

A sound caught her ear, and she jerked her head to the side where it seemed to come from. It was an eerie wail, an almost human cry. She glanced hurriedly at the canyon, but she knew the sound didn't come from there. Was it the wind?

"The puppy!" Web exploded into action. "I forgot all about the dog." Guiltily she realized she had too. She'd find it and keep it, she vowed. It apparently had afforded Kobie some kind of comfort during his ordeal, and for his sake she would care for it.

They both turned toward the backpack lying a few feet away on the snow. The wind had erased any tracks the little dog may have left, but the puppy's mournful cry led them back to the jumble of rocks Kobie had laboriously climbed in his last, futile attempt to escape.

"Wait here," Web spoke to her before beginning the climb.

"No, I'm coming too." She followed him, taking care to stay back from the edge. At the top she paused to catch her breath, and her eyes went to the spot where she'd last seen Kobie. She choked back a sob and struggled to control her emotions. She blinked several times before beginning a visual search for the dog. Web was already two-thirds of the way across the small plateau when he stopped, picked something up, and thrust it into his pocket. She hurried after him.

The little dog crouched on a windswept boulder with his shaggy, gray head resting on his front paws as he stared into the abyss below. At almost even intervals he raised his head to release a mournful cry, then settled back to his vigilant position.

They took turns trying to coax the puppy to come to them, but the animal steadfastly refused their overtures.

"I'll have to go get him," Web shouted over the roar of the wind and suited action to words. Nervously she watched him clamber over the slippery rocks and held her breath when he got close enough to reach for the puppy. The puppy sidled a few inches closer to the edge of the cliff.

Using slow, deliberate steps, Web worked his way closer to the dog, and she heard the soft murmur of his voice, though the wind blew away the words. He took a circuitous route to place himself between the dog and the drop-off, so that if the puppy backed away from him it wouldn't tumble over the edge of the cliff.

Shalise held her breath as Web once more extended his hand. The dog stood, arching his back like a cat. It looked first at the precipice, then at Web, then back to the cliff as though he meant to jump. An unexpected surge of emotion had her praying for the dog's safe rescue.

"No," Shalise moaned and closed her eyes. "Don't jump, puppy. Please let us save you." When she opened her eyes, she saw Web waving frantically for her to come to him. The puppy hadn't gone over the edge, but was now jumping around making a shrill yipping sound. She understood that due to his ordeal, the puppy might be frightened of men. He might respond better to a woman. She glanced dubiously toward the chasm, then began working her way over the rocks. For Kobie's sake she'd do whatever was needed to save the dog.

When she reached Web, he clasped her shoulders and pointed toward the chasm. She saw something in his eyes that made her shiver. She wasn't certain whether it was hope or dread that had her following his directions as she flattened herself to the ground and he grasped her ankles. Cautiously she inched forward until her head and shoulders hung in open space. Acrophobia tied a knot in her stomach. Then she saw what Web had only caught a glimpse of—a bright blue shape wedged tightly in a small crevice behind a gnarled tree growing out of the cliff wall, almost fifteen feet below them.

"Kobie!" she screamed, but the blue figure never moved, and no response drifted to her ears. "Kobie," she called again and again without any response. Crying and shaking, she scooted backward until she could sit up. "It's him. I know it's Kobie," she whimpered as Web pulled her into his arms. "We have to get him out of there."

"I know," he whispered and tightened his hold on her. "We will. But you have to understand, the odds he's still alive are pretty slim. I found Ferrindale's knife and . . . it doesn't look good. When I shot Ferrindale and he fell forward, he may have fallen on his knife himself, but he also might have stabbed Kobie before he threw him over the cliff. Fifteen feet is a pretty long drop."

"But the blood on the knife might be Mason's."

"Yes, that's possible too."

"And it's possible Kobie is still alive." She lifted her chin defiantly. "Web, I have to . . ."

"Yes, as long as there's a chance he's alive, we have to find a way to reach him. Wait right here." He removed his arm from her shoulder and urged her to lean against a large rock. "I'll get the emergency pack. There's usually a rope in law enforcement survival kits."

When he returned with the kit, he set it down and began digging through it. He noticed that Shalise had moved closer to the mongrel pup and that it was allowing her to stroke her gloved fingers absently along its shaggy back. Both stared down at the snowy abyss before them, heedless of Web's actions.

He ignored most of the contents of the pack, but he noticed a small wireless phone beside the neat coil of rope. Hurriedly he pulled out the length of nylon rope, hesitated, then reached for the phone.

"Here." He handed the phone to Shalise. "See if you can contact anyone and let them know what we're doing."

He turned away, searching for a sturdy anchor for the rope. He selected the largest tree in a small clump of aspen. It would have to do. He secured the rope around it and tested his weight against it, then looped the rope around a smaller tree as well, for good measure, before looping the remainder of the rope around himself. He wished he had a little more rope, but he was grateful he had any at all. He squared his shoulders and stepped toward the cliff.

He stopped beside Shalise, and she rose to her feet.

"Did you get through to anyone?" he asked with a nod toward the cell phone in her hand.

"No, there's no response to the emergency number listed, and I only get the out-of-range message when I call Dallas."

"Keep trying."

"I will." He started to move, and she reached out a hand to touch his sleeve. He looked at her questioningly, and she swallowed before speaking.

"I don't know if you believe in God or if you belong to any church, but I want you to know I'll be praying—not just for my son, but for you too. God loves you. I know that deep in my heart. I can never thank Him enough for sending you to be here for me and for Kobie." Her words shocked and humbled him. He didn't know what to say. Never had he given much thought to whether God loved him. He'd heard men, including Bishop Haslam and

Gage, express a love for God, but he'd never considered that God might actually love anyone back.

Awkwardly he touched her cheek with his gloved fingertips. He wished he could put his thoughts into words. He'd like to tell her about Frankie, and how Frankie loved the baby Jesus and His mother in the Christmas crèche so long ago, and how Frankie was the only person who had ever loved him. He wondered if it were possible that God might love him too. The thought brought a warm comfort he couldn't explain or reason away.

Shalise watched Web lower himself over the canyon rim and disappear from sight. She longed to peer over the edge and keep him in sight, but he'd made her promise to stay back from the slippery edge. She prayed harder than she'd ever prayed before in her life, and she held the puppy and whispered all the words she longed to say to her son. Seconds seemed like hours and minutes stretched to infinity while she waited. She picked up the phone and again punched in every number she'd ever memorized. On the chance Daniel had his cell phone with him, she called him as well, but it was useless. The signal couldn't penetrate the rugged mountains.

A wet speck of cold touched her cheek, and she lifted her face to the sky and shivered. Thick, snow-laden clouds obscured the late afternoon sun and promised a stormy night. The wind whipped nearby trees to a frenzy, tapered to a gentle breeze, then lashed in fury once more. Flecks of snow were carried on the wind, but soon the sky would open to dump a deluge on the hapless humans below. The predicted snowstorm wouldn't wait until Christmas morning, she speculated.

"Kobie!" Once more she called her son's name.

The dog's ears perked up, then Shalise heard the sound too. Web was calling her name!

Grasping the rope with one hand as he had instructed her, she leaned forward to shout an acknowledgment that she had heard him.

"He heard you!" came Web's jubilant shout back to her. "He's alive, but hurt!"

"Thank you, God." She dropped to her knees, lifted her eyes toward the sky, and breathed her gratitude—heedless of the tears running down her face, tears that mingled with the first snowflakes of the pending storm.

"Kobie! Mommy's here. I love you," she shouted. "You're safe now."

"Shalise, he's unconscious again. We have to move quickly. The tree I'm standing on is unstable, and it could break any minute. If it does, we'll both go. Empty the emergency pack, buckle . . . to rope . . . send . . ." The wind blew away the rest of his words, but Shalise scrambled to dump the sleeping bag and remaining emergency supplies from the pack. Her hands shook, and she had to bite off one of her gloves before she could fasten the buckle around the rope and send the heavy canvas bag down to Web. She had a sudden vision of the puppy peeking from the leather pouch on her son's back and knew what Web planned to do. Her heart thudded in hope and fear.

The leather backpack lay beside the items she'd dumped into the snow. She guessed it had belonged to the evil man who had stolen her son and that he'd brought it to carry the puppy he'd used to ensnare Kobie. Guessing the puppy wasn't all the pack had contained, she searched through it until she found the roll of nylon fish line she'd heard the men mention when they thought she was out of hearing. After dropping the line inside the canvas duffle bag, she pushed the bag over the side and watched as it slithered down the rope.

Straining to hear, she flattened herself against the ground and gripped the rope, pulling herself as close to the edge as she dared go. The gray mongrel paced beside her, his head cocked as though listening. Once he leaned forward and growled into the canyon. Edging forward, she peered below and gasped. The tree was gone, and Web dangled from the end of the rope, the bulging canvas bag strapped to his back.

"Web! Kobie!" she screamed.

Web lifted his head as though searching for her, and she saw a slash of red across his face. "Arm . . . can't feel . . . behind tree . . . pull."

Stumbling backward, she raced to the trees where the rope was anchored. Bracing her feet against a rock, she pulled as hard as she could. The rope never moved. Web was too heavy—she couldn't budge his dangling weight. Biting back a sob, she flipped back the lock of hair that had come loose from her hood, tightened her grip, and pulled harder. She wasn't sure, but the rope may have moved a little.

"Please God," she prayed, as she strained to use the smaller tree as a fulcrum to help her lift Web and her precious son.

"Shalise!" A shout came from nearby. Startled she nearly released her hold on the rope.

"Over here," she gasped, hoping she wasn't imagining things. She lifted her eyes to see two figures moving toward her through a curtain of snow. Lieutenant Clark must have returned in spite of the storm!

"Hurry! Help me!" she screamed. "Kobie is alive, but he and Web are hurt. I can't pull them . . ."

"Kobie is alive?" A hand settled on the rope, and she looked into a face wild with grief and shock. Daniel, not Lieutenant Clark, stood before her, and in his eyes she could see anger warring with hope.

CHAPTER 18

"Help me. Help Kobie," she pleaded, her voice coming in breathless gasps. Why couldn't the man before her be Lieutenant Clark? Clark would know what to do. She could count on him. "Kobie didn't fall all of the way. Web went down to get him, but the tree broke. Now he's hurt, so he can't climb back up. They're both dangling from the end of this rope." Once more she tried the hand-over-hand pull she'd learned in survival class.

Daniel opened his mouth as if to question her further, then snapped it shut and turned to yell, "Lena, leave your skis here, then get as close to the canyon edge as you can. Hold onto the rope, and let me know what's happening." He released his own skis as he spoke. Grasping the rope with both hands, he continued to shout, this time at Shalise. "On the count of three. One . . . two . . . three!"

Shalise let him synchronize their rhythm. It was working. She could feel the rope slowly carrying its load toward the surface. With each pull of the rope she implored deity to grant her strength. Her arms and shoulders throbbed with pain, and her breath came in painful sobs. She could hear Daniel's labored breathing and added an appeal to her prayers for God to bless Daniel with endurance.

"There's a dog over here," Lena called. Daniel's head swiveled to look at Shalise, and she nodded an acknowledgment.

"That puppy led us to Kobie."

"I can see Kobie, just the top of his head, but I can see him!" Lena's excited shout drifted back to them lending them both renewed strength. "The deputy said to keep the rope taut so he can use his legs to help."

Shalise's eyes smarted, not just from exertion and cold, but because of her concern for Web. She didn't know how she'd come to care so much about him in such a short time, but Lena's words told her why. Even when injured, exhausted, hungry, and cold, he thought of others, tried to ease their burden.

"Shalise, tie the rope slack off. I don't want to risk their slipping back," Daniel panted. "I'll hold them, you help them over the ledge. Lena can't do it alone. She's too small."

Daniel was right. She'd have to move forward to help Web. Injured, he wouldn't be able to pull himself over the edge to level ground. She hesitated only a moment, wondering if she could depend on Daniel to hold the rope and keep them from falling back into the canyon. Experience had taught her he frequently overestimated his true capabilities. But she had no choice. In spite of her vow to never trust Daniel again, she had to believe their son's life mattered as much to him as to her. Without loosening her grip on the rope, she tied the excess rope off and hurried forward.

When she reached the rocky ledge from where the rope dangled, she threw herself to the ground and wormed her way to the edge to lie beside Lena and the whimpering puppy. A dusting of snow covered Lena's chic snowsuit, and her hair stuck out at wild angles beneath her cap, but she seemed oblivious to her appearance or the increasing accumulation of snow around her. Her attention was focused on the events below.

"Lena," Shalise spoke softly, not sure how to speak to the other woman. Their relationship over the previous months had been anything but cordial, but now she needed Lena's help. "Do you think you could hold my legs so I won't slip when I help them over the edge?"

"Yes," Lena responded without hesitation and began to slide backward. When she was in position with her body wedged securely behind a boulder, Shalise wrapped one leg around the rope and scooted forward again with Lena's hands firmly clenching her legs just above her boots.

When she peered over the edge, she found Web closer than she had expected. His head was only half a foot below the rim. His face was turned up toward hers, and a kind of glaze covered his eyes. He blinked, then attempted a crooked smile when he recognized her. She put out her hand and touched his shoulder, feeling the dozen or so strands of fish line he'd wrapped around himself and the pack on his back in an attempt to secure her son. Over the top of Web's head she could see Kobie's blue hood, but she couldn't see his face, and he made no movement. Beside her the puppy gave several excited barks.

With his good arm Web clasped the rope, and with his legs he attempted to climb while keeping his torso away from the cliff wall enough to protect Kobie from being slammed against the hard rock surface. The wind blew snow across the ledge, and it clung to the stubble of beard on Web's face and whitened his eyebrows, giving him a ghostly appearance.

Shalise tugged at Web's coat, urging him upward. Finally she grasped the rope, once more matching Daniel's rhythm as he began to pull again. A few more inches and again she reached for his shoulders to pull and tug as Web laboriously struggled to pull himself over the rocky ledge. At last his upper body settled on the snow-slickened rock, and she grasped for his legs to help him pull them up. With relief she felt herself sliding backward as Daniel and Lena pulled them both back from the edge.

She disentangled herself from the rope and lunged toward the place where Web lay face down in the snow. The puppy was leaping frantically at the canvas mound on Web's back. She snatched at the pack and struggled to free her son. Daniel was beside her in seconds.

"Knife . . . pocket," Web groaned, and Shalise remembered him picking up an object from the snow earlier. She plunged her hand into his pocket and in seconds cut the line securing the man and boy together. With trembling fingers she pulled back the top of the canvas pack. Daniel's hands joined hers to tug the small body free.

Kobie's eyes were closed, and he was as limp as a rag doll. She pulled him against her and with her lips brushed his eyebrow where it showed between his scarf and hood. His skin felt so cold, and his breath was coming in slow irregular puffs.

"How much longer until the helicopter . . . ?" Shalise turned anguished eyes toward the sky where thick clouds obscured the mountain and a steady barrage of snow descended toward them. Wind tugged at her clothes, and a new fear stole her breath.

"That's why we came," Daniel shouted. "To let you know storm conditions are too severe for the helicopter to return before morning. Clark called on the radio to the rescue workers at the cabin to tell us. He said you'd be okay until morning because you had supplies and you were both experienced winter survivalists, but we decided to ski out here and let you know—besides . . ."

"Daniel had to see for himself where Kobie went over the cliff," Lena added quietly and Shalise understood.

"He needs a doctor! I'll ski out with him." Daniel's voice revealed real terror now.

"No," Web's voice was little more than a groan as he struggled to sit up. Lena rushed to help him. "Not enough time. The storm will get worse. Take him . . . under the trees where I can check for injuries. We need . . . to warm him."

Shalise rose to her feet with Kobie in her arms. She looked down at Web and was torn, knowing he needed help too. His injuries needed tending, and he suffered from exposure. The time he'd spent dangling from the rope over the side of the mountain had cost him body heat. Her heart swelled with tenderness for the big, unselfish deputy who had risked his life to save her son. She looked down at the unconscious, though breathing, boy in her arms, then once more at Web.

"Here," she said and turned to Daniel, gently passing the small, blue-clad bundle to him. He smiled gratefully as he hugged Kobie to his chest. "We'll meet you under the trees," Shalise added.

Turning swiftly away, she knelt beside Web. Tenderly she brushed the snow from his face. "Can you stand?" she asked, and with her help he struggled to his feet. He swayed a moment before steadying himself with one hand on her shoulder.

"Sleeping bag . . . other supplies," he spoke through clenched teeth.

"I think I've got most of it," Lena said. Shalise hadn't even been aware of the other woman scurrying around to collect the supplies scattered on the ground. The leather backpack, bulging with the items Lena had gathered, hung from her shoulder. One arm held the sleeping bag and the other, the small gray puppy. Skis and poles trailed in the snow from their precarious positions under her arms. Lena turned to follow Daniel, and Shalise felt an odd sensation just under her breastbone as the pair disappeared with her son into the falling snow. It was hard to believe she'd voluntarily handed Kobie over to Daniel's care, but she knew deep in her soul it had been the right thing to do.

When she and Web caught up to Daniel and Lena, they were huddled beneath a thick spruce that provided some relief from the falling snow.

"A little further . . . where I found Mason . . . there's better shelter," Web spoke in abbreviated snatches. "Need to go on."

Shalise breathed a sigh of relief when Daniel didn't dispute Web's authority. Keeping an arm about Web's waist, she trudged on. Every maternal instinct demanded that she turn to keep an eye on Kobie, but reason told her she had to continue to trust Daniel with the child while she lent her meager strength to Web. As they walked, he gradually leaned more on her, and his breath came in increasingly painful gasps.

When at last he stopped, she knew he'd chosen well. A narrow pocket or fissure between two rock walls provided respite from the wind and snow, and thickly bunched pines added to an oasis of calm in the storm. She urged Web to rest against the rocks and instructed Lena to roll out the sleeping bag beside him while she delved into the supplies in the pack.

Daniel carried Kobie to the sleeping bag and Lena unzipped it. As Daniel began to lower the child, Web spoke. "Get him out of those clothes."

"He's already freezing," Daniel protested.

"Daniel, he's right," Shalise hurried to his side. "We have to check for injuries—hypothermia victims warm faster if their wet clothing is removed."

"His suit is waterproof," he shot back, as though defying her to dispute his claim.

"The suit probably saved his life," Web intervened. "Its thick layers likely protected him from serious injury in the accident and kept him from freezing last night. But he's been in it for nearly thirty hours, and he's been pushing hard. He may have been perspiring until he was pushed over the cliff, and . . . well, little boys sometimes have accidents. Under similar circumstances, adults have accidents too. Especially if they're scared."

"All right," Daniel agreed as he gently placed the boy on top of the bag.

Shalise began undressing Kobie, probing each bone for injury as she uncovered it. Web knelt beside her and followed her movements with his eyes. She encountered bruises on her son's chest and legs, but no broken bones. Several deep scratches on his scalp and on his face had bled, and the dried blood had left stains on his hood and scarf. That he had sustained no grievous injury seemed a miracle.

With both Daniel and Web's help she placed his small body into the sleeping bag, then gently cupped his face with her bare hands, willing some warmth into his pale cheeks. "He's too cold to generate any body heat," she whispered and reached for the zipper of her snowsuit. "I'll get in with him, and he can draw on my warmth."

"Wait." Daniel stilled her hand. "You need to look at Bentley's shoulder and that cut across his cheek. I'd do it, but you know I'm no good at that sort of thing. Since he'll have to take off his coat and shirt anyway, he might as well get in that sleeping bag with Kobie. The guy's beat, and he's going to need some rest before we can go on to the cabin."

"I'm all right," Web protested.

"No, you're not." Shalise turned to him. As difficult as it was to admit it, Daniel's suggestion made sense. She reached for the first button on Web's bulky coat. As she did, she spoke over her shoulder to Lena. "Snuggle up as close as possible to Kobie and hold your hands to his face until I have Web ready. Daniel will have to help me get him out of his shirt and coat."

She knew they hurt him as they pulled his shirt down his arm, but he didn't say anything. His shoulder and a large portion of his upper back appeared red and swollen. She suspected the redness would change to dark bruises before morning. His arm didn't feel broken, though it might be cracked. She wished she'd had more than rudimentary first-aid training. She couldn't be certain, but she strongly suspected his collarbone was broken. She expressed her fears aloud to Daniel.

"I don't know any way to set a clavicle. Don't doctors put some kind of shoulder harness on their patients that holds the shoulders straight for six weeks or so?" Daniel mused, as Shalise draped Web's coat back around his shoulders.

"I suggest we get him in the sleeping bag," Lena spoke up. "There's nothing we can do about the shoulder other than keep him from moving around."

Web shook off Daniel's and Shalise's help. "Don't waste time worrying about me. I'll be fine as soon as I catch my breath." As he spoke, Web reached for the lacings on his boots. He frowned, but didn't resist when Shalise knelt to help him. In seconds he was gingerly crawling into the sleeping bag. With his good arm he pulled Kobie close to his bare chest.

Web was aware of the other three adults hovering around him, and it was tempting to just drift asleep. But the child in his arms moaned, and he snapped to full consciousness. Body heat wasn't enough to save the boy's life. They had to get him warm. The others were tired and cold too, and he doubted they would all make it through the night without a fire or shelter, especially if the storm turned as bitter as Clark's forecast had predicted. Somehow they had to get back to the cabin. That was the closest real shelter.

"I can ski back to the cabin. Some of the snowmobilers might still be there." Lena's statement forced an awareness of the argument going on over his head in whispered tones, and he knew the others were aware of the danger. He shuddered at the prospect of tiny Lena making her way back alone. If she were to lose her skis, she would struggle as hard as Kobie had to navigate the deep snow.

"No," Daniel spoke with more resolution than Web had expected from the man. "You can't go alone."

"We all need to go," Shalise put in softly, and he became aware that her hand was inside the sleeping bag stroking her child's face and at frequent intervals brushing his own. He felt a warmth grow inside his chest threatening to thaw a piece of him that froze a long time ago, long before he ever saw this mountain.

"I could ski out with Kobie on my back," Daniel pointed out, "but he'd get cold again, and we can't take the sleeping bag from Bentley."

"I'll be just fine. Take care of the kid," Web inserted into the argument.

"I have an idea." Shalise's voice held a note of hope. "Kobie traveled most of five miles using a backpack for a toboggan. Couldn't we use Daniel's skis for runners and turn the sleeping bag into a sled?"

"It's uphill all of the way," Daniel spoke hesitantly, as though he were mulling over the idea. "We've got rope, and if the two of us pulled together . . ."

"What about me?" Lena's voice was indignant. "I can help pull."

"Someone will have to carry the pack and Bentley's rifle." Daniel attempted to mollify his wife. "And don't forget the puppy. He'd never make it alone."

"The puppy can ride with Kobie," Lena insisted. "It might help keep him warm." Adding action to words she carried the dog to the sleeping bag and thrust it inside where it immediately curled up against Kobie's chest. Its fur tickled Web's nose, but he didn't mind. One of the first things he planned to do when they got back to Orchard Springs was to buy the little mutt the biggest steak he could find.

"Being on skis, you'll be able to pick out the best route for us to follow," Shalise added, as another point to the argument.

"I'm not helpless," Web suddenly roared. "The plan's a good one, except one of the women needs to be in this bag with Kobie. Women generate more heat than men anyway. I can help Richards."

"We'll start out with Bentley in the bag." Daniel suddenly took over the plan as though it were his own. "Give you a chance to rest a little longer," he spoke directly to Web. "When we reach deeper snow, we'll need your larger body to get through, so rest as much as you can now."

Web didn't like it. He felt like a chicken trussed for the oven when Shalise got through tying the sleeping bag, complete with occupants, to Daniel's skis. Begrudgingly he admitted she was thorough and she knew how to tie the right knots, but he still thought that he should be the one taking charge, tying the knots, and getting this bunch of civilians back to the cabin.

The kid moaned again as they began to move, and Web wished he'd wake up. The boy had still been semiconscious when he'd first found him in that cleft in the rock, conscious enough to explain how he'd fallen on the tree but had been afraid he'd fall out of it, so he'd wedged himself into the cleft the tree grew out of. He'd lapsed into unconsciousness soon after, but had roused when Shalise called his name. He'd tried to answer and had croaked "Mommy" several times before drifting into unconsciousness again. With his big hands Web held first Kobie's hands, then his small feet, willing heat into the child.

Progress was slow, and he continued to chafe at everyone's insistence that he stay in the bag. He kept his head mostly inside the thick cocoon, but he could tell the snow was falling steadily, and as they moved back away from the canyon rim the wind made walking more difficult. Richards's long legs were doing fine, but Shalise was only average height for a woman, and she was having a greater struggle. Web wanted to be the one to help her, not the other way around.

"Mommy!" A faint cry reached his ear, and a small hand pushed against his chest.

"It's all right," he attempted to assure the child that he was safe, while his own heart felt near to bursting. He fought an urge to hug the child tighter for all the times he hadn't been able to comfort Frankie. For the first time in his life he wanted to thank God for something. "Your mom is here. She wants you to get warm."

"Mommy . . . Mom . . ." The child's feeble cries tore at his heart. Web had had enough! The kid had been through major trauma, and he ought to be with his mother!

Thrusting his head out of the narrow opening Shalise had left in the top of the bag, he roared, "Stop under the first tree you come to. Kobie wants his mother!"

CHAPTER 19

"Kobie! Oh, baby, Mommy's right here." Shalise dropped to her knees and reached for her child as soon as they halted. Two massive fir trees provided a semblance of shelter, though there wasn't nearly enough protection from the wind-driven snow that was falling faster now.

"Mommy," Kobie whispered, and a fat tear slid down his face. She brushed it away with the tip of her gloved hand and resisted the urge to pull him into her arms.

"Slide down in the bag with your puppy, and we'll get you to a cabin where we'll warm and dry you as quickly as we can."

"Mom . . ."

"Shhh, don't talk. We have to hurry."

"Daddy's here too." Daniel crouched beside her. "Mommy is going to get into that sleeping bag with you, and Deputy Bentley is going to help me pull you and Mommy to the cabin. Deputy Bentley said you should try to stay awake and talk to Mommy as much as you can."

Taking care to keep Kobie covered by the down bag, Shalise unzipped it far enough for Web to ease his way out. When he stood on his feet she rose too and called for Lena to bring the supplies. Working as quickly as she could, she immobilized Web's right arm with the tape and elastic bandage from the first-aid kit. Emotion choked her throat as she fought a desire to throw herself into his arms and lean against his broad chest. She needed to both give and receive comfort—to share her joy and fear. Some instinct told her that he, and only he, would understand. Why she felt this intense pull toward Webster Bentley at this time she couldn't explain, but it was something she knew she'd think long and hard about as soon as he and Kobie were out of danger.

A gust of wind screamed through the tree tops reminding her there was no time for examining feelings, and it lent her a sense of urgency. They had to get moving again. They were all tired and cold with hypothermia lingering just one misstep away. With as much care as she could manage, she eased Web's heavy coat back over him and fastened it to keep him from struggling at the task with one hand.

"You're hurt—you shouldn't have to do this," she whispered as she rose up on her toes to brush his cheek with her lips before wrapping her own scarf around his face. Taking a quick step toward her son, she stopped abruptly when she felt Web's hand on her sleeve. A fierce light burned in his eyes, filling her heart with soothing warmth.

"We'll make it . . . all of us. I promise you'll have Kobie home for Christmas." He spoke through the thick folds of her scarf, but she understood every word and she believed him. If anyone could get them to safety, it was Web. Her heart told her she could trust him to keep his promise.

Settling into the sleeping bag with Kobie snuggled in her arms, she remembered tonight was Christmas Eve. She'd prayed for a Christmas miracle, and surely finding Kobie alive was an answer to her prayers—but maybe, saving Kobie wasn't the only miracle taking place. She brushed the thought aside. Later, when she and Kobie were back in their own home, she'd think about it.

Less than a mile from the cabin, Daniel relented in his determination to keep Lena with them and allowed her to go on ahead. Five minutes later the tempo of the storm built to blizzard proportions, and both men stumbled repeatedly as they struggled up the last long incline. Black specks danced before Web's eyes as he struggled against dizziness and overwhelming fatigue. Snow covered the precious bundle they dragged behind them and coated both him and Daniel.

Grateful he'd been blessed with a strong sense of direction and the ability to accurately recall his recent aerial view of their route, he knew they had to keep moving uphill, keeping the canyon on their left. Their laborious movements were all that stood between them and certain death.

His shoulder ached and his arm felt numb. With only one functioning arm he lacked a hand to clear the snow that persistently caught against his eyelashes and built up at the top of Shalise's scarf.

Each time he shook his head to clear his vision, sharp pain lanced through his shoulder. Once he might have quit, given in to the pain and fatigue. He'd heard that freezing to death wasn't particularly painful. A person only needed to stop to rest, then drift into endless sleep. But his fate wasn't the only one at stake. He'd promised Shalise he'd get her and her son to safety. He'd crawl through the snow if necessary to keep that promise.

A thought occurred to him, something he'd never once considered before. Jesus suffered pain beyond human comprehension. Might He have quit if only His own future had been all that was at stake? Was it the love He bore for His smaller, weaker brothers and sisters that made His heroic sacrifice possible?

He shook his head, wondering if he was becoming delusional. Hypothermia, cold, and fatigue were known to invite hallucinations. Surely he wasn't comparing himself to the Savior, nor did he love Shalise and her son. But he felt something for them. He remembered the quick kiss she'd given him and acknowledged he was attracted to her, but that wasn't the same as loving her, was it? And the boy? He cared about the welfare of all children, and somehow Kobie was all mixed up with Frankie in his mind, but that wasn't the same as really loving him.

Daniel suddenly lurched forward, falling to his knees. Automatically Web extended his hand to help him regain his feet. As he did so he saw his own emotions mirrored in the other man's eyes. Daniel was scared, cold, and numb with fatigue—but he would fight on. Not only were his son and the child's mother at risk, but a new fear for Lena, who was alone somewhere ahead of them, drove the man on. He was a man who had always quit when the going got tough, a man who looked for the easy way, who dreamed of wealth and position. But he harbored deep inside himself a better, finer man, a man who had just learned he loved someone else more than all his petty dreams. Web knew with searing certainty that Daniel wouldn't quit this time, and he suspected that when Daniel left this mountain, it would be with a finer sense of self-worth and greater purpose. With steely determination, they staggered on together.

A dark shape loomed before them, and Web caught a whiff of smoke in the air. Incredible! They had made it! Web suddenly found the strength to increase his stride, and Daniel surged forward too with the added burst of adrenaline that came with knowing their journey was almost at an end. They topped the ridge and moved quickly toward the small structure barely visible through the snow. The door of the cabin opened, and there stood Lena framed in the doorway with the soft glow of a lantern behind her. Two men bundled in massive parkas towered on either side of her, ready to brave the storm in search of them. Daniel moved more quickly. Web watched him free one hand to briefly hug Lena before stepping inside the cabin. Both of the would-be rescuers and Lena practically tripped over each other in their hurry to free Shalise and Kobie from their cocoon.

Web experienced a rush similar to what he'd seen minutes ago in Daniel's eyes when Shalise's head popped through the top of the sleeping bag and her eyes met his. He felt a silly grin spread across his face, and he didn't care if it made him look foolish. He only saw Shalise and the beautiful smile that lit her face as she cradled her son in her arms and then made visual contact with him above the boy's head.

As the cabin warmed, all four adults gradually shed their heavy outerwear. Shalise wrapped Kobie in the quilt she'd found earlier and took turns with Daniel holding their son. Lena heated soup and insisted they eat while Web fiddled with the radio. Over static and skips he explained their situation to an anonymous voice somewhere in the valley and requested an evacuation helicopter as soon as the storm eased. He asked about the search party and learned that all of the searchers had made their way safely back to the command unit.

Gradually Kobie shook off the lethargy that held him, and he became more alert, though he began to complain of pain in his fingers and toes. Shalise searched out a tin bowl and filled it with tepid water to bathe his hands and feet. Web knelt beside her and examined him critically for frostbite. "There are a few spots on his toes that look questionable, but they're small," he finally concluded. "A couple of spots on his upper cheeks bear watching too." She could feel his eyes on her as she gently bathed Kobie.

"Pat, don't rub," he cautioned when she reached for a towel to dry Kobie's feet.

"I know," she said with a smile, and he felt foolish for telling her something she had already learned from her winter survival training. When she finished drying Kobie, she patted an ointment she found in the first-aid kit on the spots she suspected were frostbitten, then wrapped him snugly in the quilt again. She kissed his forehead as she laid him down on the sofa. He smiled sleepily and closed his eyes. She wondered if it were safe to let him sleep now.

"He's all right," Web assured her. "But it might be a good idea to wake him several times through the night and give him a little more soup."

Suddenly Kobie's head popped up, and the appalled expression on his face was almost comical. "Did I miss Christmas?"

"No, honey," Shalise attempted to reassure him. "This is Christmas Eve."

"Does Santa Claus know where I am?" he worried.

"Doesn't matter," his father sat on the floor beside him and joined in the discussion. "He knows where you live, and he'll leave more than enough presents under your tree. You'll just be a little late getting there to open them." He turned a knowing look toward Shalise and winked. A picture of all the Christmases when Daniel's parents had ignored her pleas and gone overboard for their only grandchild swam before her eyes, and she found herself grinning back at Daniel. There wouldn't be a toy left in town when Kobie's grandparents learned he was alive and coming home.

Shalise leaned back marveling at the change in Daniel. She hadn't seen his charming side for a long time, but this wasn't only the easy charm of their courtship or of when Daniel wanted something. He seemed happier and more at peace than she'd ever seen him before. Could it be that discovering he loved someone else more than he loved himself had made the difference? There was no doubt in her mind that he truly loved Lena and Kobie and they loved him back. Once that knowledge would have brought her pain. Now it seemed right and good, and she was happy for him.

As she turned back to Kobie, she caught a strange look on Web's face. He'd witnessed the brief exchange between her and her former husband and he didn't like it. Could he possibly be jealous? The thought filled her with a quick surge of pleasure. But no, he couldn't be jealous. They hardly knew each other, yet a voice in the back of her head told her they had gotten to know each other better in two days than she'd ever known Daniel. Besides she had really known him longer than two days. Somewhere deep inside she'd always known him. She'd certainly trusted him since the moment he'd stepped onto that ledge above the flooded canyon months ago.

Web drifted to sleep in a large chair drawn up before the fire. He didn't know how long he slept, possibly a couple of hours. When he awoke he lay still, without opening his eyes. Something had changed while he slept, and for a few disoriented minutes he didn't know what that something was. A peace such as he'd never experienced before filled the room. Then he heard a sound. Music came as though from the throat of an angel, and he listened to the pure, sweet strains of "Silent Night."

Lena sat silhouetted before the fireplace, singing to Kobie. That such glorious music could come from someone as small as Lena seemed unreal. He caught a whiff of pine and opened his eyes. While he'd slept, Daniel had gone back outside to find a tiny, lopsided Christmas tree. A few bits of paper and a couple of soup can lids mingled with a pinecone or two for decorations. He suspected that was Shalise's doing. He felt a pang of something akin to homesickness shiver through him when he thought of the brightly decorated home she and Kobie would return to tomorrow.

Lena and Daniel had spread the sleeping bag on the floor before the fireplace, and they sat there together with the fire serving as a backdrop. Shalise and Kobie snuggled together at one end of the sofa. He watched one of the search and rescue volunteers pass around an odd array of cups that smelled like hot chocolate. Some deep, hidden longing reached down into his heart, and he knew he'd never outgrown his desire for a real Christmas. Peace and love were so near, they might have been tangible. A woman he could easily love forever sat only a few feet away with a boy he would joyously claim as a son. A Christmas tree, a fire, and music that touched his soul made the picture complete. This came closer to the Christmas he'd always wanted than any other in his life, but it wasn't enough. He felt greedy; he wanted more.

"Would you like some hot chocolate?" Shalise asked in a low voice when Lena's last note faded away. She seemed to be the only one aware he had wakened. "Lena found several packets of mix in the emergency supplies, and she boiled snow to mix it in."

"It's good," Kobie chimed in. "Lena made some for me first." He hefted his cup to show it off.

"Okay, if it's not too much trouble." Web glanced toward Lena who sat cross-legged before the fire.

"I'll get it." Shalise rose to her feet, and he watched her walk across the small room. She was a beautiful woman—perhaps it was desire that brought a rush of warmth to his chest and caused his pulse to accelerate, but he didn't think so. He couldn't deny he felt a powerful physical attraction toward the woman, but there was more than that. Sometimes he thought she was the part of himself he'd been missing all his life.

"Mr. Bentley," a small voice interrupted his thoughts.

"Yes." He turned to the child, who sat at one end of the sofa, snuggled in the blanket his mother had found earlier in the attic. The gray puppy lay in a ball in his lap sporting a new bandage on his injured foot.

"I got a Christmas present." He patted the little dog's shaggy coat. "Mommy said I can keep Shadow. That's what I named him."

"He's a fine dog." Web smiled at the little boy who seemed to have already bounced back from his ordeal with remarkable speed. Then Kobie's smile turned to an angry scowl.

"Did you shoot the bad man?" he asked.

"Yes." Web squirmed uncomfortably, but didn't consider telling the child less than the truth.

"Is he dead?"

"No, but he's in serious condition at a hospital in Salt Lake. When he is strong enough to leave the hospital, he'll go to jail."

Kobie was quiet for several minutes, then he started to cry. "I wish he was dead, 'cause he's a really mean man. He made me fall down, and he cut Shadow's leg and tried to throw him in the river. He . . . he said bad words about me, and he said Mom doesn't w–want me. I think he was going to hurt me really bad."

Some instinct had Web moving from the chair to the sofa to lift Kobie into his arms even before his father could reach him.

"Don't ever doubt that your mom wants you," he whispered in fierce tones. "That man lied to you. Both your mom and dad love you, and they always will, no matter what."

"You're a cop. You said so, and Daddy calls you 'deputy.' You should have shot that man dead, then he couldn't ever take me again!" Web had a sudden understanding of the fear behind Kobie's words and experienced a brief flashback to one of the talks he'd had with Bishop Haslam. *Pray always. If you keep a prayer in your heart, you'll have the inspiration you need to deal with sudden emergencies.* He hadn't stopped praying since the moment he'd gotten the call telling him a child was missing. Something told him this was one of those emergencies, and he hoped the prayer in his heart would be enough to grant him the inspiration to say what Kobie needed to hear.

"Listen, Kobie." He spoke in the gruff, no-nonsense tone he usually used in dealing with speeders and various minor disturbers of the peace. He didn't know how to talk to kids, but most of them he'd come across through the years had responded well enough when he told them the truth and kept it simple. He hoped that would work with this little guy. "That man won't get out of jail until you're grown up and bigger than him, if he ever gets out at all. Anyway, he won't get a chance to bother you again. It's hard to think about now, when you're angry with him for the mean things he did, but sometime you should think about how close you came to being the one to die, and that if you had, you'd be happy up in heaven because you have grandparents there who love you and who would have come running to meet you and take care of you. Maybe it's best that Mr. Ferrindale didn't die because no one would have been happy to see him, and instead of being safe and happy in heaven, he would probably be in some dark, unhappy place. As long as he's alive, he has a chance to repent. When someone dies without repenting that's what's really sad. Your mom told you about repenting, didn't she?"

"She said that's being really sorry for something I did that was bad and never doing it again." Kobie scrunched his face up in serious thought as he struggled to maintain his end of the conversation. "She said if someone does something bad to me, and they're sorry they did it—like when Daddy gave me a broken bike, or when Nathan lost my new football—I have to believe them and go on being just like we were before."

Out of the corner of his eye Web saw Daniel's look of surprise and knew the man wished to defend his gift of an unassembled bicycle, but before he could, Kobie went on. "I don't want to forgive that mean man. Mommy said Daddy didn't know my bike was broken in pieces in the box, and Nathan's my best friend, so it wasn't real hard to forgive them. But that man won't ever be my friend. And I don't want to see him ever again."

"You don't have to see him," Web attempted to comfort the small boy. "Your bishop and I had a long talk once about repenting. He said people who don't repent can't ever go where Jesus is, but if you do what's right you can be with Him. And the only way you might see that man again is if he became good enough to live with Jesus too." He struggled to explain a concept he was only beginning to understand himself. "But your bishop also taught me that repentance has two sides. There's forgiveness too. Bishop Haslam said its like we all carry a bag around on our shoulders, and every time we don't forgive, we stick a big rock in the bag. It gets heavier and heavier until all we can think about is the big heavy load we're carrying around. But if we forgive we can dump the rocks out and start thinking about other, happier things."

"Did Bishop Haslam tell you that because you did something bad?" The innocent question brought a tiny gasp from Shalise and an embarrassed cough from Daniel.

"No, it was the forgiveness part we were talking about." Web smiled faintly. He still held Kobie, but it was Shalise's understanding he sought. "When I was a boy, a few years older than you, my mother had a friend who did bad things. One day he took my little brother away while I was playing with some of my friends. I hunted and hunted for Frankie, and the police helped me look, but Frankie was dead when the police found him. The man who took him hurt him and left him in a garbage dumpster."

Shalise gasped and her eyes filled with tears, but Web went on. "I hated that man, and I swore I would never forgive him. I became a cop so I could punish men like him, but Bishop Haslam told me I had to forgive so I could stop hurting inside. He said it was time to stop reacting to the past and start looking forward. And he was right. I've only just learned that the little Christmas Baby was born to show us how to forgive, and to give us hope for a better life."

"I could do that," Kobie brightened. "I could be a deputy when I get big and catch bad people."

"You can if you want to." Shalise sat down beside them and reached for one of Kobie's small hands. "But I think what Deputy Bentley is trying to tell you is that it's all right to be sad about what happened to you—"

"And Shadow."

"Yes, and Shadow, but if you stay angry or scared all of the time and are always thinking about the bad things that happened to you, you won't have time to play baseball, or ride your bike, or even play with Nathan. You have to make up your mind to let the law and God take care of Mr. Ferrindale while you think about growing up and being the person you want to be. If you give bad feelings a place in your heart, they take all of the room, leaving no space for happiness."

"Like you and Daddy. You're sad 'cause you're still mad at him." Kobie's lip quivered "Sometimes I'm mad at Daddy too."

Web felt Shalise stiffen, then as her shoulders relaxed she pulled Kobie onto her lap. He looked up to see Daniel crossing the room to crouch before Kobie and Shalise. Over their heads, Web's eyes met Lena's, and he knew she too suffered pains and regrets over the past—and perhaps a little fear for the future.

Daniel reached out to touch his son's shoulder, and Shalise placed her hand, still twined with Kobie's, on top of his. "I'm not angry with your father anymore," she spoke quietly. "I think we can be friends again. And I know he'll always be a good Daddy to you."

"Son, I'm sorry." Daniel's voice was husky. "I never meant to hurt you. Whether she believes me or not, I never really meant to hurt your mother either. I want to be her friend again."

"Does this mean you're going to come back home and live with us?" The hope and excitement in the boy's voice was evident. Daniel looked pained and Shalise squirmed with discomfort. Web felt something painful deep in his own heart and had to admit that he didn't want Shalise to reconcile with her former husband.

"Lena is my wife now," Daniel tried to explain and held out his free hand to Lena, who slowly threaded her fingers through his, a look of sorrow shadowing her beautiful face. "I thought you liked Lena."

"Course I like Lena," Kobie exclaimed. "She could come too. She could have the room next to mine." Web found himself smiling, wondering how Daniel would extricate himself from the verbal minefield he'd walked into.

"Your father and I will never live in the same house again," Shalise clarified, stepping in to rescue her floundering ex-husband. "We're not angry anymore, but we want different things from life now. But your father and Lena will always be welcome to visit our house and spend time with you. I know now that they love you more than their own lives, just as I do, and they'll always have a place in their home for you. Some kids have two homes," Shalise went on to explain. "While you're small, you will live with me most of the time, but your Daddy and Lena's home will be yours too. When you get bigger, you can stay in whichever home you want for as long as you like. It won't be so bad to have two homes and two moms." Lena blinked back tears and flashed a look of gratitude toward Shalise for the brief acknowledgment of her place in the child's life.

A look of mischief suddenly lit Lena's eyes. She spoke to Kobie, but she was watching Web's face. "Someday you might also have two daddies." Web felt his ears turn hot and noted that Daniel first looked as surprised as he, but then his expression turned speculative. He was careful not to look at Shalise.

"Two?" Kobie sounded startled. "Who would be my other daddy?"

"Someone who loves your mom a lot and thinks you're pretty special too," Daniel assured his son with a hint of laughter in his voice. Web wasn't sure whether he wanted to punch Shalise's ex-husband or examine the idea a little closer—maybe even do a bit of dreaming. He and Shalise could provide Kobie with a stable home and maybe a brother or sister or two in time, while Daniel and Lena could give the boy travel and excitement. All four adults in the room had demonstrated their love for the boy in the past twenty-four hours, with the unexpected bonus of granting each of them confidence in the others' commitment to the child.

Who was he kidding? A woman like Shalise would never want to get serious with him. Unable to resist any longer, he let his eyes drop to Shalise's face. Either she was windburned or she was blushing, but something in her eyes told him more than he'd allowed himself to see in the past. Perhaps his chances of a future with her weren't as impossible as he'd thought.

CHAPTER 20

Wade watched the two young men stride across the parking lot toward his car. Bryan had caught up to Trent in height, but reaching six feet wasn't the only way Bryan had grown. Wade felt a surge of pride in his son. He no longer wore earrings or strange hairstyles, but the outward signs of change paled beside the inner ones, and today he particularly glowed with happiness. Trent had flown to Chicago after his school term ended to baptize Bryan just four days after Bryan's eighteenth birthday. His son hadn't been asked to wait—both he and Chelsea had given their son permission to be baptized months ago—but Bryan had elected to wait until Trent could come to Chicago to do the honors.

"They're coming!" Rachel tugged at Wade's hand, urging him toward the curb where Bryan had pulled up the car. Looking over her head at his wife, he caught Chelsea's eye and smiled. He noticed her eyes were red and knew she shared the emotion that had nearly brought tears to his own eyes when Trent brought Bryan up out of the water in the baptismal font. There had definitely been a few tears on his cheeks when Trent, the missionaries, and Bryan's new bishop gave him a blessing following the baptism. "Confirmation" was the term Bryan had used.

"Hurry, Daddy!" Rachel dropped his hand to dash toward the waiting car.

"Would you like to ride with us?" A rental car pulled up behind their own, and Emily stuck her head out of the window. Rachel looked torn as she looked toward one car then the other. She had been as excited as Bryan to see Trent, but she'd been delirious with excitement when Emily and Diane had walked into the room minutes before the baptismal service began.

"May I ride with Emily and Diane?" she turned to ask her father, and when he nodded his head, she practically danced her way to the car where they waited.

Wade turned back toward the church, searching for Chelsea, and found her shaking hands with the bishop's wife before hurrying toward him. She made a lovely picture in her bright red coat with the wind ruffling her curls. She was thinner now than she'd been last summer, but it wasn't just her slender form that made her so striking. She moved with an air of confidence that turned heads. Surviving the flood, seeing him through his angina attack, spending time at the gym, and returning to school had all played a part in transforming Chelsea physically and mentally into the woman who walked toward him, confident of her worth.

He supposed he'd changed too. He didn't feel so driven to succeed financially as he used to, nor as quick to blame others when mistakes happened. And he certainly valued life and his family more than he had before he'd almost lost them. If he ever thought of Amanda at all, it was with a sense of having managed a narrow escape. When he'd returned to work after his recovery, she was gone. She requested a transfer to the New York office the day Chelsea had called to inform his company of his condition.

He held out his hand to Chelsea to assist her into the car. Bryan gave his mother a nervous look before pulling out into traffic.

"I know I look a mess, Bryan," Chelsea said. She reached forward to pat his shoulder. "I didn't get red eyes because I'm upset over your baptism. I was doing fine until that blessing."

"Confirmation," Bryan corrected.

"Yes, that's right. It was while Elder Braithwaite was confirming you that I got all choked up and started crying. Then I just couldn't seem to stop."

"That was the Holy Ghost letting you know Bryan was doing the right thing," Trent told her.

"It might have been a hint that you should start taking the missionary lessons too, Mom," Bryan added.

Wade noticed Chelsea didn't refute their son's statement. He'd suspected for some time she might be thinking about taking the lessons. He wasn't sure how he felt about that, but he had a pretty good idea what her father would say. Bryan was obviously thinking along the same lines.

"Grandpa Niederhauser will jump me the minute he sees those red eyes." Bryan gave an exaggerated groan.

All four occupants of the car laughed. Wade knew Bryan had invited his grandparents to his baptism. They had declined, though they'd promised to attend a small party in Bryan's honor afterward. They would be waiting at the house.

The number of cars parked around their house surprised Wade. Bryan had mentioned that a few friends planned to drop in after the service, but the noise and laughter that met him as he opened the door appeared to be more than "a few." A flurry of congratulations from Bryan's friends greeted them as they entered the house. Wade's parents and his mother-in-law stepped forward with stiff smiles. He hugged each of them. Grandpa Niederhauser was conspicuously absent.

"Where did all this food come from?" Chelsea spotted rows of plates and covered dishes lining the dining room table.

"I hope you don't mind," an efficient-looking woman said as she came forward to introduce herself as the president of some society. Wade's father-in-law chose that moment to walk in from the kitchen carrying a huge platter of sliced turkey, which he placed beside an equally large platter of ham.

"Bryan's grandfather invited us to wait inside. We brought everything in with us so it would be ready when you got here. He was even kind enough to volunteer to run to the delicatessen for meat platters," the woman explained to Chelsea.

Chelsea was clearly speechless. She hadn't counted on her father even showing up or, if he did, being the least bit supportive. And she'd taken Bryan's announcement that a few people were coming over afterward to mean something far different from what their son considered "a few." Wade looked at the crowd of people gathered in their home and hid a smile, remembering the low-fat ice cream and cookies Chelsea had sent him to the store to buy this morning. She'd be all right. In a few minutes no one would know she hadn't planned the whole thing. He'd learned that about his wife since their trip out west last fall. She was strong and competent—someone he could count on. He wondered if she felt she could count on him. He planned to spend the rest of his life proving that she could.

"Thank you, Brother Niederhauser. That was thoughtful of you." The woman who seemed to have taken charge beamed at Chelsea's father. The moment she turned her back, Grandpa Niederhauser grimaced in Wade's direction, showing his chagrin at being called "brother." Still Wade noticed he seemed rather proud of himself for jumping in with a contribution to the party, until Rachel said, "Wow! Grandpa will you give me a party just like this when I get baptized?" Shaking his head Grandpa Niederhauser went in search of his wife.

* * *

Gage and Cassie held hands as they entered the sealing room where Gage escorted Cassie to one end of the altar then took his own place, kneeling at the other end. Cassie's mother hurried forward to smooth her daughter's skirt. Gage was conscious of the presence of his family in the sealing room, except for his younger sisters, who were outside on the lawn entertaining his nephews and nieces. From the corner of his eye he watched his mother lift a lace handkerchief to her eye and knew that any tears she shed were tears of happiness. She'd fallen for Cassie the moment they'd met last Thanksgiving.

Cassie's parents and grandparents were present too and made no secret of their pleasure in the proceedings. From near the end of the front row, Gage caught a quick grin from his brother. For a moment he again felt regret that in two years when Trent finished school, either he or his brother would have to search for work on another ranch. In spite of that, he knew his marriage to Cassie met with Trent's approval. Trent had gone out of his way to encourage their relationship. He'd even volunteered to take over helping Jena with her chores at Christmas when Gage had gone to Kansas with Cassie to meet her family.

His eyes met Cassie's, and everyone else seemed to fade away. As the words were said uniting them forever, warmth and joy swelled in his heart until he thought he would burst. Never had he known it was possible to be so happy. His lips met hers in the first tender kiss of their marriage, and he rejoiced that Cassie was at last his wife.

Following congratulatory hugs and handshakes from their families, they made their way back to their dressing rooms. Gage found it difficult to release Cassie's hand for even the few minutes it would take them to each change clothes for photos.

Trent joined Gage in the dressing room to help him into his tuxedo.

"I think this thing goes around your waist." Trent held up the cummerbund.

Gage reached for it and, in his hurry to rejoin his bride, dropped it. Trent retrieved the cummerbund and slowly smoothed the pleats before encircling his brother's waist with the piece of cloth.

"Can't you hurry?" Gage grumbled good-naturedly as Trent fumbled with buttons and cuff links. He found his own fingers useless for the detailed task.

At last Gage was dressed. Grinning at his brother, he started for the door.

"Gage." Trent reached out a hand to stop him. As Gage turned questioning eyes toward his brother, Trent mumbled, "Jena asked me to give you this." Trent handed him an envelope. Gage took it and began shoving it into his pocket, but Trent stopped him. "I think you should read it now."

Puzzled by the somber note in his brother's voice, he slid an impatient finger beneath the seal and pulled out a thin sheet of paper. He turned it over and began to read.

> *Dear Gage,*
>
> *I know what I have to say will come as a shock, but I want to ask you a question and give you a wedding present. When first you, then Trent, went away to school, Daddy wouldn't let me go because he believed college would be wasted on a woman, but now I've decided I'm going to do it anyway. Trent is transferring to Utah State in Logan, and I've enrolled for next semester there—to get the education I need and also to be near him. Now that the ranch is mine (thanks to you) I feel a need for learning more about managing a business—and following my heart. Over the past months I've discovered*

the reason I couldn't love you was because I was already in love with your brother, though I didn't realize that fact until recently. Trent and I plan to marry next March, and we'll be away from the Bar C much of the time while we're going to school. Will you be my foreman until Trent and I graduate?

And now for the wedding present. The deed for the valley that joins our two properties is in Trent's pocket. It's yours and Cassie's.

Be happy,

Jena

"Trent?" Gage turned to his brother.

"Yeah, well." Trent rubbed one hand across the back of his neck. "I've always been crazy about Jena, then while you were gone on your mission, I discovered I was in love with her. I didn't figure I had a chance with you around. Besides you were the man Pat wanted for a son-in-law."

"What about the Church? Didn't you mean what you said about not marrying outside the temple?"

"Yes, I meant what I said. That is part of the reason I never pursued my feelings for Jena until you broke up with her and she approached me with some questions about the Church while you were in Kansas last Christmas. She told me that after Pat died she started reading the Book of Mormon you gave her and found comfort in it, but there were parts she didn't understand. She was understandably reluctant to ask you, so she turned to me. She was baptized just before I went to Chicago to baptize Bryan. Two weeks ago we became engaged, but we decided not to make an announcement until after your wedding."

"I don't know what to say." Gage couldn't quite grasp what his brother was telling him.

"Congratulations would be nice." Trent's smile held a rueful edge.

"You're right. Congratulations are certainly in order." He hugged his brother. Feeling a little hesitant he asked, "It doesn't bother you that Jena used to be my girl?" Hurrying on, he added, "You do know, don't you, that as much as I've always admired and cared for Jena, the connection between us was never what I felt from the start with Cassie?"

"Yes, I've always been aware that you didn't love Jena the way I do." His voice was soft, but his eyes met Gage's straight on.

"But what about Emily? I thought you two were dating." Gage suddenly remembered his new sister-in-law.

"Emily is a lot of fun, and we did go out a few times, but we discovered early on that our greatest interest in each other was in finding a way to get you and Cassie together." His brother's admission brought a chuckle to Gage. Then he sobered, remembering Jena's gift.

"I can't accept a gift as valuable as the Bar C's half of that valley from Jena."

"Yes, you can," Trent argued. "Jena knows how much Pat considered you a son and wanted you to have the ranch. She won't ever feel she has a right to it or be comfortable doing what she wants to do, instead of what her father planned, if you don't have the part of the ranch you love most. Besides, think of it as a gift from your brother and future sister-in-law."

"That's a pretty valuable gift." Gage swallowed hard, feeling overwhelmed by Jena's generosity.

"I know how much you always wanted to run the Bar C . . ." Trent looked awkward and a little unsure of himself.

"Cassie is worth a million Bar C's." Gage punched his brother's shoulder. "Besides I rather like the idea of being the Bar C's closest neighbor. And with a smaller spread to run, I can accompany Cassie on some of her engineering trips."

"Cassie still plans to work?"

"For a while, at least until she fulfills her contract with the company where she interned." Gage started walking, then looked over his shoulder at his brother. "Something tells me the next few years are going to be pretty hectic with you and Jena both going to school, Cassie looking for drill sites, and me splitting my time between two ranches."

Trent laughed and pointed to their father striding toward them. "I've a hunch it'll get even more hectic if we don't get out there for pictures on the double."

* * *

"Dad, you'd better come home." Web felt the familiar rush of pleasure when Kobie called him "Dad." Kobie had started calling him Dad the day he'd found out he was going to get a little brother or sister. He'd explained offhandedly that the baby might get mixed up if he went on using Web's name. The word "home" brought its own special thrill.

"You'd better hurry." The worry in the boy's voice over the telephone line put his senses on alert. "It's Mom."

"I'll be right there!" He slammed down the phone, grabbed his parka, and headed for the door. It was too soon. Doc Fielding said the baby wasn't due for three more weeks!

"I'm out for the rest of the night," he yelled at Mrs. Waverley as he flew past the dispatch office and ran down the hall, passing several deputies on his way.

"Need a police escort?" Johnson looked up with a sly grin from where he lounged over the desk of the department's first female officer, who happened to be young, single, and pretty. Web shook his head and rushed on without speaking. He didn't have time for Johnson's teasing. He had to get Shalise to the hospital in Logan. A new storm was forecast, and the canyon road was already slippery.

He took the corner leading from the road to the lane a little too fast, but he scarcely slowed down as he charged up the hill. In spite of his concern he experienced a jolt of pleasure at the sight of the old farmhouse decked out in lights with a huge Christmas tree twinkling in the front window. He never drove up the lane without feeling an intense sense of homecoming, but there was something about Christmas lights that always brought a lump to his throat.

He opened the door to chaos. Shadow ran about the room barking, Gramps was huffing down the stairs with a suitcase, and Grammy was urging Shalise to stay on the couch. Lena's new Christmas album was playing much too loudly on the CD player, and Kobie was shouting into the telephone, telling his father he was going to be a big brother any minute and that he better come get him and his grandparents. The air was filled with the aroma of baking gingerbread, and suddenly Dallas appeared in the kitchen doorway with a spoon and mixing bowl in her hand to inform Kobie his daddy didn't need to come get him—she'd brought his grandparents out to the farm, and she'd take them all back.

Web swept Shalise up in his arms and headed back outside with Gramps trailing in his wake with the suitcase. Shalise's body tightened and she gasped for breath.

"Kobie . . . ?" she asked.

"He'll be fine," Web tried to reassure her, but his voice revealed his own nervousness. "Dallas and his grandparents scarcely let him out of their sight, and you know Daniel and Lena will love spoiling him for Christmas."

"Don't worry, Mom," Kobie rushed to her side. "I'm not a little kid anymore."

She smiled a wry smile, and Web knew she was thinking of that Christmas two years ago when Kobie had been only nine. He knew she didn't want to miss a single Christmas with her son, but it didn't look as though she had much choice in the matter.

"I'll bring him to the hospital to see you and the baby tomorrow," he promised as he slid her onto the seat of his Cherokee. Dallas and Grammy rushed forward to tuck a quilt around her legs.

"Drive carefully!" Dallas ordered, but Web didn't even flinch. He'd discovered he and Dallas saw eye to eye more often than not, especially where Shalise's welfare was concerned.

A faint glimmer of moon showed through the clouds as they started through the canyon, lending the night an element of drama. He drove as fast as safety permitted, but he could tell by Shalise's soft moans as they drew closer to Logan that her contractions were getting closer and harder. The first fat flakes of snow spattered against his windshield as they pulled into the city and were keeping his windshield wipers flapping full speed by the time they reached the hospital.

He hated to leave his wife's side for even the few minutes it took to park his car. When he returned to the maternity ward, the nurses were preparing Shalise for their child's birth. One handed him a hospital gown, which he quickly donned, but his hands shook as he attempted to tie the strings behind his back. After Shalise was given a shot, they found quiet moments interspersed between her contractions. During those intervals they talked softly, reminiscing about the events that brought them together. As the contractions became harder and closer together, the doctors and nurses seemed to increase in number and activity as well.

Web stroked Shalise's hand, and for the first time in a long time he wished again that he knew how to talk to a woman. He'd managed to tell her he loved her three months after their ordeal in the mountains. It was the night he'd been baptized, and also the night he'd been so euphoric he'd managed to ask her to marry him. He'd been lucky because Shalise proved to be a woman who didn't need a lot of words, but right now his heart was so full of sympathy for her pain, and of joy in their marriage, he longed for the words to tell her of his emotions. She squeezed his hand, and he knew she understood. Still she deserved the words.

"I love you," he mumbled, but wasn't certain she heard him because a contraction stronger than any of the previous ones claimed her attention, and he knew she was barely managing not to scream.

The doctor checked her again, then made a soft exclamation and rose to his feet. He grinned as he spoke to them. "It seems you're about to get a little bonus."

"I thought so," Shalise laughed, and Web turned puzzled eyes toward the doctor.

"Your wife's first ultrasound wasn't clear, but even then I suspected she was carrying twins. Several times recently I thought I detected an echo when I listened to the baby's heartbeat. That's why I scheduled another ultrasound for the day after Christmas, but it seems your little ones wanted to stage a surprise."

"Twins!" Web only grasped half of what the doctor had to say after that one word. He was still suffering from shock when the first baby made her noisy arrival, followed three minutes later by a sister who made it clear she wasn't to be outdone in the lung department. He trembled as the nurse placed first one daughter, then the other in his arms. Shalise turned her head to smile tiredly at him and he thought his heart would burst.

"I love you," he mumbled again, then repeated the words louder. He didn't say them often, but he wanted to be sure she heard them this night. Besides, he realized now that he'd really better learn how to talk to females.

"I love you too," Shalise whispered back and reached to touch first one baby, then the other before her hand settled on his cheek.

Shalise drifted to sleep, and daylight was just beginning to creep into her room when she finally opened her eyes. "Merry Christmas, darling," she whispered with a sleepy smile.

"Merry Christmas to you too." He smiled, then hearing a sound at the door looked up to see Kobie standing in the doorway with Gramps and Grammy and Dallas. Two more heads peered around the corner looking sheepish, and Shalise motioned to Daniel and Lena to come in as well. Both Gramps and Kobie were carrying cameras. He thought of the camera in his coat pocket. He'd been so busy worrying about Shalise and trying to grasp the reality of the sudden addition of two more females to his family, he'd forgotten all about taking pictures. He reached for the little Minolta Kobie had given him for Father's Day six months ago.

"Congratulations!" Daniel held out his hand.

With the camera in one hand, he reached for Daniel's hand with the other, graciously accepting the man's hearty congratulations. Daniel's parents had treated him like a second son from the moment he'd arrived at the farmhouse with Shalise and Kobie two years ago. And though he would never quite consider Daniel a replacement for his own younger brother, he knew he would always feel a connection to him through the son they both loved.

"Kobie couldn't wait." Dallas looked apologetic, but not repentant.

"It's okay." Shalise held out her hand, inviting them all to come closer. Kobie rushed to Web's side where he could get a good look at the babies, who were bundled tight in receiving blankets in separate small Isolettes.

"Two! Wow!" Kobie appeared awestruck, then a little doubtful. "They're awful little."

"They'll get bigger," his mother assured him. The telephone at her elbow rang, and Web lifted the receiver and handed it to her.

"Chelsea!" she exclaimed after a moment, and a broad smile covered her tired face. "They're beautiful. I'll send you pictures as soon as one of these men around here gets his film developed." They continued to chat for a few minutes. When she hung up, she smiled at the group gathered in the room.

"Guess who just got a mission call?"

"Bryan!" Kobie shouted, then ducked his head and looked sheepish when one of his new sisters started to cry. His mother beckoned him closer and patted a spot on the bed beside her. When he was seated, she placed the crying baby in his arms. The baby stopped crying and stared at Kobie as though memorizing every detail of her brother, and a suddenly delighted smile spread across Kobie's face. Web snapped a picture, capturing the moment.

"This is the best Christmas I ever had." Kobie beamed at everyone in the room and Web echoed the sentiment in his heart. He'd thought nothing could match the joy he'd felt when Gage baptized him and then joined Bishop Haslam to confirm him a member of the Church of Jesus Christ of Latter-day Saints, or the moment when he and Shalise had knelt across the altar of the Logan Temple and sealed their marriage for all eternity, or even the first Christmas the three of them had spent together as a family at the old farmhouse. But this went even beyond that—and yet included all those things. Peace and stillness filled his being, and understanding filled his heart. Bishop Haslam's words came back to him from that hot August day just before the dam broke and changed his life forever. He'd found his treasure—and where his treasure was, so was his heart.

ABOUT THE AUTHOR

Jennie Hansen graduated from Ricks College in Idaho, and Westminster College in Utah. She has been a newspaper reporter, editor, and for the past twenty years has been a librarian for the Salt Lake City library system.

Her Church service has included teaching in all auxiliaries and serving in stake and ward Primary presidencies. She has also served as a den mother, stake public affairs coordinator, ward chorister, education counselor in her ward Relief Society, and teacher improvement coordinator.

Jennie and her husband, Boyd, live in Salt Lake County. Their five children are all married and have so far provided them with six grandchildren.

Abandoned is Jennie's eleventh book for the LDS market.

Jennie enjoys hearing from her readers, who can write to her in care of Covenant Communications, P.O. Box 416, American Fork, UT 84003-0416.

EXCERPT FROM LACK OF EVIDENCE

Reggie Mandel couldn't believe her eyes as she pulled the Firebird into her regular parking spot outside the Banister Detective Agency. She did a double take and still couldn't believe what she was seeing.

"It's Derrick's Corvette," she muttered to herself. "I'd know that car anyplace. But why is it parked here in his old spot?"

Reggie hadn't seen the car since the day Derrick had quit his job and gone traipsing off to the Hawaiian Islands more than four years ago. She'd just assumed he had taken the car with him, since it was the thing he loved the most in the whole world. She killed the engine and stepped out of her car, figuring today was a good day to enter the office through the back door so as not to walk into any unwanted surprises.

Finding the back entrance unlocked, she pushed open the door and peered inside. From the angle she was at, she could barely see Derrick's old desk, but it was enough for her to see him seated at it. Jerking back, she closed the door and stood there, trying to catch her breath. After a moment, she cracked the door an inch and peered inside again to verify her imagination wasn't working overtime and that it really was Derrick. But what was he doing unpacking a cardboard box at his old desk?

"Oh!" she gasped as the reality suddenly struck her. "He's moving back in! How can this be?"

Reggie hadn't heard one word from Derrick in more than four years, and all at once here he was, moving back in. Her heart beat so frantically it was nearly a full minute before she could compose herself enough to ease through the door and make a mad dash for

Clint's office. Thankfully, Derrick didn't seem to notice. She didn't bother to knock at Clint's office, but barged right in, hurriedly pulling the door closed behind her.

"What is Derrick Beatty doing here?" she whispered loud enough for Clint to hear but not loud enough for her voice to carry past the closed door. Clint's mouth curled up into a grin that Reggie had learned always preceded an unexpected bombshell. "Oh, no!" she gasped. "You've talked him into taking his old job back!"

Clint stood and rounded his desk. "I would have mentioned it sooner, but . . ."

"You'd have mentioned it sooner?" she shot back. "Well you know, that might have been nice! It would at least have given me the chance to prepare myself. I have half a mind to take a week off starting this very minute! You have a mile-wide cruel streak, you know that, Clint Banister!"

Clint held out a hand. "Now, now, now, Regg, take a deep breath and just relax. When the shock passes, you're going to thank me for hiring Derrick back. It's not like I'm blind to your real feelings for the guy."

Reggie hated Clint's ability to read her like a book. "I do not have feelings for him!" she fumed, knowing full well her lie was falling on deaf ears. "Derrick is an insensitive man who cares for nothing but his job, airplanes, and that stupid Corvette parked out there in the lot." She bit her lip and tried to force herself from saying the rest of what was pressing on her mind. She wanted to say something about Derrick probably being married by now, but somehow she managed to hold back. She knew that the Derrick and Brandilynne thing had never meshed. Brandilynne herself had made that plain when she and Albert Hainsley had linked up. But it had been over four years, and Reggie knew Derrick might have met and married someone else. Clint's next statement made her wonder if he knew for sure that Derrick was still single or if he was just guessing.

"Not true, Regina. The guy's nuts about you. If you'd give him the slightest hint you might care for him too, he'd fall all over himself proving it."

Reggie shook her head in disgust and crossed the room to face Clint. "Let's get one thing straight," she staunchly insisted. "Derrick works with Earl. I'm perfectly happy with Chandra as my partner, and I don't want any ripples on the water."

Clint slid an arm around Reggie's shoulder and gave it a squeeze. "You know I always tag up a guy with a gal, Regg. Putting you with Chandra was temporary until I could fill the vacant spot."

"Fine! Then pair me up with Earl and put Derrick with Chandra!"

"Nope! You and Derrick were the best team I ever had working for me. I always say not to mess with perfection."

Reggie pulled back a step and glared at Clint, regretting that her hair had chosen today of all days to turn stubborn. And why had she worn these old Dockers and this ugly yellow top? "You had this planned all along, didn't you?" she fumed. "You figured some way to get Derrick back, and you knew from the first you'd put us back together!"

"Am I interrupting something? Should I come back later?"

The sound of Derrick's voice sent an icy chill running down her spine as Reggie whirled to see the door cracked open and his head peeking around it. How much of her conversation with Clint had he heard? One thing she knew for sure—the look on his face revealed he was obviously no more thrilled about this reunion than she was. "Nope, you're not interrupting a thing," she heard Clint respond. "Bring it in, pal, and let's get down to the nitty-gritty."

Reggie felt her heart pound as Derrick eased the door open and stepped into the room. For a long moment he paused, just looking at her. The years had been good to him, and if anything, he was better looking than ever. His hair was black, almost as black as her own, only his had a streak of silver over his left eye that had always intrigued her. His eyes were deep blue, and they had an almost hypnotic effect when he turned on his charm. Right now, it wasn't charm she saw in his eyes—it was something else. Anxiety? Concern? She wasn't quite sure. But it was obvious he was as ill at ease over this meeting as she was. Pulling back his shoulders, he walked over to face her. "Hi, Regg. You're looking good."

Reggie was a woman who didn't know the meaning of the word *fear*. She had looked down the business end of more than one loaded gun barrel and had confronted scoundrels of every sort and character.

But at this moment, she wished she could turn and run as fast and as far as her legs would carry her. "Hi to you too," she heard herself say. "Or should that be *aloha?*"

He tried to laugh, but it sounded hollow. "I think I've had enough alohas for a while. It's sort of nice being on the mainland again."

"Okay," Clint broke in. "Enough of this chitchat. Let's cut to the chase. I've spoken to Regina about partnering the two of you up again, and she's pleased with the idea. How do you feel about the deal, Derrick?"

Reggie's mouth dropped as her eyes shot open. How could Clint say such a thing? He almost made it sound like pairing her and Derrick up had been *her* idea. She glanced to see that same indiscernible look still on Derrick's face. His answer came with apparent difficulty. "You're the boss, Clint. If the lady has no objection, then neither do I."

Clint put one arm around Reggie's shoulder and the other around Derrick. "Okay, then it's settled. Regina here isn't aware of the deal we worked out, Derrick, so I'll lay it out for her. Derrick took his old job back on one condition, Regg. He wants the chance to do some checking on his dad's disappearance. I agreed and figured out a way to juggle our workload enough to give the two of you a couple of weeks' time to spend almost exclusively on Samuel's case."

This new revelation caught Reggie's interest. She personally had never spent any time on the mystery of Samuel's disappearance, but just about every other investigator in every capacity in these parts had scrutinized the case from the inside out. It wasn't that she didn't welcome the chance to add her talent to the search for the missing legend, but it was just that the effort seemed so futile. After all, every rock that could be turned had already been turned multiple times with no success. The mystery of Samuel's disappearance was no closer to being solved today than it was the day almost five years ago when he fell off the edge of the world.

It made perfect sense, though, that this was what brought Derrick home. Wanting to take one last shot at learning his father's fate was only natural. Reggie knew she would be lying to herself if she denied wishing she might have had some small part in his decision to come home, but she might as well face the truth that it was Samuel and Samuel alone who drew Derrick home.

"What about Melvin Phillips?" she asked Clint. "His court case comes up a week from tomorrow, and I have tons of work to do before completing the case the defense has asked for."

"Get me the file, Regina. I'll handle Melvin personally. His is a big-dollar case, and I want it done right."

There was no doubt in Reggie's mind that Clint had thought this all out way in advance. She fully realized the futility in arguing with the man once he had his mind made up. And whether or not she wanted to admit it to herself, Clint was right. In spite of her masquerade, she really was glad Derrick had come home—she just wasn't ready to show it yet. "All right," she agreed. "I'll turn Melvin over to you, Clint. But you'd better not blow it after all the time and energy I've put into proving the guy innocent."

"You don't know for sure he's innocent, Regg—not until we get the results back on the blood samples you sent to the lab. When are those results due, by the way?"

"They're due tomorrow, but don't tell me I'm not sure of my findings. The DNA won't match Melvin's. Take my word for it."

"Hey, I'm not doubting your word. If you tell me you're that sure, then so be it. And you can put your mind at ease. I won't drop the ball." Clint lowered his arms and turned to Derrick. "So, where do you want to start, pal? Got anything in mind?"

"I do if the agency's Cessna is available. I'd like to look over a couple of things."

Reggie grinned to herself at this request. Clint's detective agency may have been small, but since he refused to forgo the fun of owning his own plane, why shouldn't he list it as an agency resource? It made good sense when tax time rolled around. Derrick was the only other pilot who could use it. "The plane is yours," Clint responded. "As long as your license is up-to-date."

This brought a laugh. "Come on, Clint. Do you really believe I'd stay out of a cockpit for any length of time? What do you think I spent my Saturdays doing on Oahu?"

"I should have known." Clint grew strangely quiet, something out of the ordinary for him. When he spoke, it was with clear-cut difficulty. "Go ahead and get things squared away at your desk, Derrick. I'd like just a minute with Regina, if that's okay."

Reggie raised her brow, considering what this might be about. Derrick took the hint and headed for the door. If Clint's suggestion bothered him in the least, it didn't show. As the door closed, Reggie looked at Clint. "I want you to know what getting Derrick back means to me—to the agency, Regg. You know you've always been my number-one investigator. And you know you and Derrick made the number-one all-time team when he was here before."

"If you're trying to apologize to me for the way you handled this, don't bother, Clint. You couldn't have handled it worse if you'd called a staff meeting to brainstorm the ways. I'll work with Derrick, and I'm sure we'll get along just fine. Probably just about like we did before." Reggie laughed to herself. What more could she hope for than getting along with Derrick just about like before? Derrick was afraid of relationships then, and she was certain he was still afraid of relationships now.

"There's one more thing, Regina. You know I've been promising you a raise. Well, I'd say the time has come for me to keep my word. How does fifteen percent sound to you?"

Suddenly a light came on. "You had to give Derrick a big raise to get him back, didn't you?" she laughingly guessed.

"Well, I . . ."

"You were afraid I'd find out and let you have it right between the eyes!"

"Hey, that's not fair. I've promised you a raise for weeks now. Long before I got Derrick back onboard."

"But not before you knew you were going to try to get him back on board. Fifteen percent, you say? How much did you give Derrick?"

Clint's lip turned down as he shrugged. "A little more than that— maybe."

Reggie laughed and headed for the door. "Whatever you gave Derrick will do just fine for me," she said on the way out. Pausing at the door, she turned and gave him a wink. "And don't think I won't find out what that is. As you say, I'm the best investigator on the staff."